# DEBRA WEBB

# THE DARKNESS WE HIDE

mira

mira™

Recycling programs
for this product may
not exist in your area.

ISBN-13: 978-0-7783-0947-5

The Darkness We Hide

Mira
22 Adelaide St. West, 40th Floor
Toronto, Ontario M5H 4E3, Canada
www.Harlequin.com

Printed in U.S.A.

# Praise for the novels of Debra Webb

"The twists and turns in this dark, taut drama make it both creepy and compelling, multiplying the enjoyment. It's hard-edged and emotional, ensnaring the reader in a world perfectly imagined. I bid a grand welcome to a new voice in the thriller world."
—*New York Times* bestselling author Steve Berry
on *The Longest Silence*

"Webb weaves incredible twists and turns and a mind-blowing conclusion with multiple villainous perpetrators."
—*RT Book Reviews* on *The Longest Silence*

"This psychological thriller is rife with tension that begins on page one and doesn't let up. It's a race against the clock that had me whispering to the pair of flawed, desperate protagonists, 'Hurry, hurry.' A gripping read."
—#1 *New York Times* bestselling author Sandra Brown
on *The Longest Silence*

"A dark, twisted game of cat and mouse! Debra Webb mines our innermost fears as a police detective takes on a serial killer with help from an unexpected ally—or is he the bigger threat? You will fly through the pages of this action-packed thriller!"
—*New York Times* bestselling author Lisa Gardner
on *No Darker Place*

"A well-crafted and engrossing thriller. Debra Webb has crafted a fine, twisting thriller to be savored and enjoyed."
—*New York Times* bestselling author Heather Graham
on *Traceless*

"Interspersed with fine-tuned suspense...the cliffhanger conclusion will leave readers eagerly anticipating future installments."
—*Publishers Weekly* on *Obsession*

### Also by Debra Webb

## SHADES OF DEATH

*The Blackest Crimson* (prequel)
*No Darker Place*
*A Deeper Grave*
*The Coldest Fear*
*The Longest Silence*

## THE UNDERTAKER'S DAUGHTER

"The Undertaker's Daughter" (novella)
*The Secrets We Bury*
*The Lies We Tell*

Look for Debra Webb's next novel,
available soon from MIRA.

For additional books by
*USA TODAY* bestselling author Debra Webb,
visit her website at www.debrawebb.com.

This book is dedicated to Denise Zaza! A great editor and friend who has always believed in me.

# THE
# DARKNESS
# WE
# HIDE

# RIP

Burton Johnston
May 5, 1940–March 9, 2020

Burton Johnston was born in Winchester, Tennessee, on May 5, 1940. He was a loving husband and a respected public servant. His work with the healing of animals made him one of the most beloved citizens in all of Franklin County. He served as county coroner for four decades. Despite being nearly eighty years old, Burt worked every day. He loved his work and loved his hometown. He will be greatly missed. Burt was predeceased by his beloved wife, Mildred. He is survived by a sister, Sally Jernigan, of Tullahoma.

The family will receive friends on Thursday, March 12, 6:00 to 8:00 p.m., at the DuPont Funeral Home. The family has requested donations to the Franklin County Animal Shelter in lieu of flowers.

# *One*

*Winchester, Tennessee*
*Monday, March 9, 7:35 a.m.*

Rowan DuPont parked on the southeast side of the downtown square. The county courthouse sat smack in the middle of Winchester with streets forming a grid around it. Shops, including a vintage movie theater, revitalized over the past few years by local artisans lined the sidewalks. Something Rowan loved most about her hometown were the beautiful old trees that still stood above all else. So often the trees were the first things to go when towns received a face-lift. Not in Winchester. The entire square had been refreshed and the majestic old trees still stood.

This morning the promise of spring was impossible to miss. Blooms and leaves sprouted from every bare limb. This was her favorite time of year. A new beginning. Anything could happen.

Rowan sighed. Funny how being back in Winchester had come to mean so much to her these past several months. As a teenager she couldn't wait to get away from home. Growing up in a funeral home had made her different from the other kids. She was the daughter of the undertaker, a curiosity. At twelve tragedy had struck and she'd lost her twin sister and her mother within months of each other. The painful events had driven her to the very edge. By the time she finished high school, she was beyond ready for a change of scenery. Despite having spent more than twenty years living in the big city hiding from the memories of home and a dozen of those two decades working with Nashville's Metro Police Department—in Homicide, no less—she had been forced to see that there was no running away. No hiding from the secrets of her past.

There were too many secrets, too many lies, to be ignored.

Yet, despite all that had happened the first eighteen years of her life, she was immensely glad to be back home.

If only the most painful part of her time in Nashville— serial killer Julian Addington—hadn't followed her home and wreaked havoc those first months after her return.

Rowan took a breath and emerged from her SUV. The morning air was brisk and fresh. More glimpses of spring's impending arrival showed in pots overflowing with tulips, daffodils and crocuses. Those same early bloomers dotted the landscape beds all around the square. It was a new year and she was very grateful to have the previous year behind her.

She might not be able to change the past, but she could forge a different future and she intended to do exactly that.

Closing the door, she smiled as she thought of the

way Billy had winked at her as he'd left this morning. He'd settled that cowboy hat onto his handsome head, flashed that sexy smile and winked, leaving her heart fluttering. Four months ago he'd moved into the funeral home with her. The one-hundred-fifty-year-old three-story house didn't feel nearly so lonely now. She and Billy had been friends most of their lives and, in truth, she had been attracted to him since she was thirteen or fourteen. But she'd never expected a romantic relationship to evolve. Billy Brannigan was a hometown hero. The chief of police and probably the most eligible bachelor in all of Franklin County. He could have his pick of any of the single women around town. Rowan hadn't expected to be his choice.

She had always been too work-oriented to bother with long-term relationships. Too busy for dating on a regular basis.

Billy had made her want long-term. He made her believe anything was possible, even moving beyond her tragic past.

The whole town was speculating on when the wedding invitations would go out. Rowan hadn't even considered the possibility. This place where she and Billy were was comfortable. It felt good. Particularly since fate had given them a break the past four months. No trouble beyond the regular, everyday sort. No calls or notes from Julian. No unexplained bodies turning up. And no serial killers had appeared looking for Rowan.

Life was strangely calm and oddly normal.

She would never say as much to Billy, but it was just a little terrifying. The worry that any day, any moment, the next bad thing would happen stalked her every waking moment. Somehow she managed to keep that worry on the back burner. But it was there, waiting for an opportunity to seep into her present.

"Not today," she said aloud.

Today was important. She and Burt Johnston, the county coroner, had breakfast on Monday mornings. She locked her vehicle and started for the sidewalk. The Corner Diner was a lunch staple in Winchester. Had been since the end of the Great Depression. Attorneys and judges who had court often frequented the place for lunch. Most anyone who was someone in the area could be found at the diner. More deals and gossip happened here than in the mayor's office.

But breakfast with the coroner wasn't the only event that made this day so important.

Today she intended to offer her assistant, Charlotte Kinsley, a promotion and a part-ownership in the funeral home. Since there were no more DuPonts—Rowan had no children and couldn't say if that would ever happen—she needed to bring someone into the family business. Someone younger who could carry on the DuPont legacy.

Rowan paused outside the diner. The iron bench that sat beneath the plate glass window was empty. Surprise furrowed her brow. Burt usually waited there for her. She surveyed the cars lining the sidewalks as far as the eye could see. No sign of Burt's. He was never late but there was always a first time. After all, he wasn't exactly a young man anymore.

She sank down onto the bench, dug her cell phone from her bag and sent him a text. She was the one who generally kept him waiting and he never once complained. She certainly wasn't going to do so. His car was a little on the vintage side as well. Maybe he had car trouble this morning. Worry gnawed at her. A dead battery or a flat tire. Surely he would have called her.

"Morning, Rowan."

She glanced up, smiling automatically. Lance Kirby, one of the attorneys who was not fortunate enough to have an office on the square. The ones who had been around a lifetime held on to that highly sought-after real estate. The others, like Kirby, waited patiently for someone to retire or to die. Meanwhile they showed up for coffee in this highly visible location bright and early every morning.

"Good morning, Lance."

Kirby was a couple of years older than her. He'd lived in Winchester his entire life other than the years he spent at college and law school. He was divorced and had three kids. He'd asked Rowan out to dinner on several occasions. She hoped he didn't ask again this morning. Coming up with an excuse to turn him down was becoming tedious. Surely he was aware that she and Billy were a couple now.

The idea startled her a little. This was the first time in her life that she was half of a couple in the truest sense of the word.

"If you're waiting for Burt, he's parked around back. Every spot around the square was taken before seven this morning." Kirby reached for the door. "People have come early hoping for a chance to get into the Winters trial. Everyone wants to hear the story on that family."

Rowan had been reading about the trial for weeks in the *Winchester Gazette*. "That explains why I had to circle around for a while before I found a spot." She'd forgotten about the small parking area in the back alley behind the diner. "Thanks for telling me. I was worried he'd stood me up."

Kirby laughed. "I don't think any man still breathing would stand you up, Rowan."

She glanced at her cell phone as if it had vibrated. "Oops. I have to take this."

The instant she set the phone to her ear, Kirby went on inside the diner, the bell over the door jingling to announce his entrance.

Thank goodness.

For appearances' sake she kept the phone to her ear a half a minute, then put it away. To pass the time she counted the yellow daffodils brimming in the rock planter built around the tree at the edge of the sidewalk. Those lovely yellow flowers were coming up all around the funeral home, too. Her mother had loved gardening. Early-spring blooms were already bursting all over the yard. Maybe her mother had hoped to chase away some of the gloom associated with living in a funeral home.

Since her father's death, Rowan had hired a gardener. Somehow her father had managed to keep her mother's extensive gardens alive and thriving for all those years. Rowan did not have a green thumb at all. She had killed every plant she'd ever tried to nurture. She was not going to be the one who dropped the ball on the family garden.

She glanced up then down the sidewalk. Still no sign of Burt. With a sigh, she pushed to her feet. Maybe he was on the phone, which would explain why he hadn't answered her text. Rather than keep waiting, she cut through the narrow side alley to the small rear parking lot. With his taillights facing the back of the diner,

Burt's white sedan was nosed up to the bank that faced North Jefferson Street.

Rowan quickened her pace and walked up to the driver's side of his car. Burt sat behind the steering wheel, staring out the windshield.

For a moment Rowan waited for him to glance over and see her but he didn't move. Whether it was the lax expression on his face or some deep-rooted instinct, she abruptly understood that he was dead.

She tugged at the door handle. Thankfully it opened. Her heart pounding, she bent down. No matter that her brain was telling her he was already gone, she asked, "Burt, you okay?"

Her fingers went instantly to his carotid artery.

Nothing.

Rowan snatched her cell from her bag and called 911. She requested an ambulance and the chief of police, then she laid the phone on the ground and reached into the car and pulled Burt from his seat. She grunted with the effort of stretching him out on the pavement. On her knees next to him, she pressed her ear to his chest. No heartbeat. She held her cheek close to his lips. No breath.

Rowan started CPR.

The voice from the speaker of her cell phone confirmed that the ambulance was en route. She informed the dispatcher that she'd started CPR.

Rowan continued the compressions, her eyes burning with emotion. Burt was her friend. She had been gone from Winchester for a very long time and he had made her feel as if she'd never left. She did not want him to die. Other than Billy, he was the person she felt closest to.

The voice of logic reminded her that Burt was just two months shy of his eightieth birthday.

She ignored the voice and focused on the chest compressions. "Come on, Burt. Don't you die on me."

Facial color was still good. Skin was still warm. He couldn't have been in this condition for long. Hope attempted to make an appearance. But it was short-lived. Even a few minutes could be too many.

Damn it!

The approaching sirens drove home the realization that this was all too real.

The paramedics hurried across the parking lot and took over her frantic efforts. Rowan pushed to her feet and backed away, her muscles feeling suddenly weak.

"Hey."

She looked up and Billy's arms were suddenly around her. She leaned against his shoulder and fought the urge to weep.

Burt didn't respond to the efforts of the paramedics. Dr. Harold Schneider, a local physician who had attended the university with Burt, came to the scene and pronounced his old friend dead.

By the time the ambulance and Schneider were gone, Rowan felt drained. This was not the way she had expected this day to go. This was supposed to be a good day.

"I'll have one of my officers take Burt's car home," Billy said. He reached into the driver's side floorboard and retrieved Burt's cell phone. As he did, the screen lit. "Looks like he was typing a text for you." Billy glanced at Rowan.

She moved in next to him and looked at the screen. At the top was the text she had sent to him. He hadn't opened it. Behind that was the text box into which he had been typing. She read the words.

I found something you need to see.

Rowan frowned. "Why didn't he just call or…?"

Her words trailed off. Because he had died before he had the chance to finish.

"Maybe he planned on talking to you over breakfast," Billy offered. "He may have recognized that he was having a heart attack and tried to send you a message."

Rowan shook her head. "If you think you're having a heart attack, why not call 911? Why waste precious seconds sending a text about something unrelated to your potentially impending demise?"

It didn't make sense. Burt dealt with death all the time. He was too smart to do something so foolish.

"Can I keep his phone for a while?" She looked to Billy. "I'd like to go through his calls and messages just to be sure there isn't something else in there I need to know about. I'll be sure to get it to his sister when I'm finished."

Billy shrugged and passed her the phone. "We have no reason to believe foul play was involved. Since I'm certain he wouldn't mind, I don't see why not."

"Thanks." The phone felt like a brick in her hand. As little as half an hour ago Burt may have been holding it, typing those words to her. Her stomach twisted. What had he wanted to show her? Was it so important that he would put telling her above his own safety? If he hadn't been aware he was dying, why try to send a text when they were about to have breakfast together? He was already at the diner, only steps from her.

This was the downside to having friends. Growing up in a funeral home one would think she would have gotten used to death. But it was different when it was someone close. This was the part that you never got used to.

"I have to get back to the office," Billy said, regret in his voice. "I can take you home first if you'd like."

She shook her head. "I'll be okay." Breakfast was out of the question. She couldn't eat if her life depended upon it. After his wife passed, Burt had told Rowan many times that he wanted her to take care of his final arrangements when the time came. She would need to go back to the funeral home and pick up the hearse so that she could go to the hospital and take charge of his body. "I have to pick up Burt and take care of him. That's what he wanted."

Billy grimaced. "I figured. You're sure you don't need me to help?"

"Charlotte is working today. She'll want to help." Rowan managed a smile. "Thanks anyway."

She watched Billy drive away before she headed back through the narrow alley and to the front side of the diner where she'd parked her SUV. It had taken two months for Billy to stop being so overprotective. After what happened just before Halloween with Wanda Henegar and Sue Ellen Thackerson, he'd been determined to keep her under constant surveillance. Finally, she'd convinced him that she was okay to drive around town and to be at the funeral home alone. She was armed, her handgun was in her bag and she was vigilant about paying attention to her surroundings.

Rowan settled into the driver's seat of her SUV and started the engine. After her father's murder last year,

she had expected to put helping to solve homicides behind her. She had come home to take over the funeral
home. Preparing and burying the dead was the only
relationship she had expected to have with death. But
her father's murderer, Julian Addington, had had other
plans. He had haunted her life, even daring to show
up in person. Rowan had shot him. Unfortunately he'd
survived.

No. She was glad he had survived. She needed Julian
alive. There were answers she still needed. Perhaps that
was why her shot had been so far off that day. As much
as she wanted him to pay for all that he had done, she
also wanted the whole truth. She was sick to death of the
bits and pieces of her mother's history. A million little
pieces that Rowan couldn't seem to cobble together in
a way that made any kind of sense.

She stared at Burt's cell phone, wishing it held the
answers she needed, but of course it did not. Admittedly, she had learned a good deal since returning to
Winchester. Her mother had been involved with Julian
Addington, currently one of the most prolific serial killers in documented history. The depth of her involvement
was unknown. If Anna Addington, Julian's ex-wife, was
to be believed, Julian had been obsessed with Norah,
Rowan's mother. After her death, he had become obsessed with Rowan—all that was left of her since his
own daughter had murdered Rowan's twin sister, Raven.

If all that wasn't complicated enough, Norah DuPont
appeared to have had many friends besides Julian who
were killers. Like the one who had curated the faces
and skin of his victims—all of whom turned out to be
serial killers who were never caught. The FBI had had

them labeled as inactive. Finding those faces had solved hundreds of cases.

There was even some circumstantial evidence that Rowan's father, Edward, was involved on some level. Julian would have Rowan believe that Edward had killed Julian's daughter, Alisha, after she murdered Raven. But Rowan refused to believe such nonsense. Her father had not been capable of murder. She would never believe otherwise.

But finding the truth she sought was not easy. Her parents were dead. Herman Carter, her father's lifelong friend and assistant at the funeral home, was dead. Herman had taken his own life after Rowan discovered his treachery—the black marketing of stolen body parts. It seemed the harder she searched for accurate information, the taller the brick walls and the murkier the pictures she discovered.

Her mother had been a loner—at least, that was what everyone had always thought. She'd traveled frequently doing research for her writing. Norah DuPont had been a self-proclaimed writer. She'd had no friends—at least, no real ones that Rowan had found. Her father's one good friend was dead.

Rowan certainly couldn't trust anything Julian told her.

As grateful as she was for the past few months of peace and quiet, the uneventful period also worried her. What was Julian up to? It was possible he was dead, she supposed. The consensus of most involved with the investigation was that she had only winged him. But he had not been spotted since she shot him in May of last year. She had heard from him a couple of times but nothing since last fall.

If he was alive, he was no doubt readying for some sort of strike. Lining up all his ducks, as they say. But last October another facet had been added to this strange situation. A man whose name she did not know had appeared to help her out of a deadly situation. He had claimed her mother sent him to protect her.

But her mother was dead. Had been for almost twenty-eight years.

Rowan shook her head. Just when she thought she had cleared up one aspect of this insanity, two more things cropped up adding additional questions and leading her in a whole new and bizarre direction.

She stared at Burt's phone. Touched the home key to awaken the screen. Luckily he had no passcode. She checked his text messages and his call log. She even reviewed his emails. Nothing except veterinary and coroner talk. Conferences. New cutting-edge drug therapies.

Nothing about her or her family or Julian.

"What in the world did you need to show me, Burt?"

A sharp rap on her window made her practically jump out of her skin. Her heart in her throat, she lifted her gaze to the figure hovering only inches from the glass.

*Lance Kirby.*

She dragged in a breath as she powered down her window. Somehow she produced a smile for the persistent man. "Sorry. I was a thousand miles away."

Actually, she'd only been a few but he had no need to know that.

"I didn't mean to startle you." He reached through the window, squeezed her shoulder, his fingers lingering a little longer than necessary. "I just wanted to say how sorry I am. I heard about Burt." He jerked his head toward the diner. "It's a shame. A real shame."

Rowan nodded. "It is. He'll be missed."

Kirby launched into a list of all the ways he would be happy to help in whatever way she needed. Rowan finally found an opening in his monologue and explained that she had to go pick up Burt.

Kirby managed a strained smile and said he understood. He stepped back and stood on the sidewalk watching as she drove away.

She probably should feel badly for blowing him off, but she didn't.

The only thing on her mind right now was taking care of Burt.

# *Two*

Burt had been a tall man. A little better than six feet. Like many, he had put on some extra weight as he grew older; his thicker abdomen warned of how much he had loved sweets. Charlotte had helped Rowan handle moving the body. Now Burt was undressed and positioned on the mortuary table, his head stationed on the head block.

His longtime friend and personal physician, Harold Schneider, had come by and examined the body. With Burt's recently diagnosed heart condition, a sudden heart attack was common. Dr. Schneider took care of the necessary paperwork for the death certificate. Since there was no indication of foul play and in light of Burt's advanced age and recent medical history there was no need for an autopsy.

His body had been washed, disinfected and moisturized. Rigor mortis had invaded his limbs. Rowan had massaged them to help loosen up the muscles. Lividity had set along the backs of his arms and his torso but more prominently in his buttocks and the backs of the thighs since he had been in a seated position when his heart first stopped beating. Moving him so quickly after death had shifted the lividity to some degree but the darker discoloration remained in the initially affected areas.

No matter that both rigor and lividity were present, Rowan checked his corneas, finding them cloudy, and then his carotid pulse, which was no longer present. This final examination before beginning the no-turning-back steps was a part of the process she never ignored. Her father had told her a few startling stories passed down from his father and grandfather about undertakers making incisions for the pump lines only to discover the heart was still beating, sending blood spewing. Better to take every precaution first.

After making the necessary incisions in the preferred arteries, she inserted the tubes for draining the body fluids and replacing them with the preserving chemicals used in the embalming process. The process required approximately forty-five minutes.

The sound of the pump churning filled the room. The sound was as familiar as her own heartbeat. This moment was certainly the end of an era. First, her father had died, then Herman and now Burt. The three had been in the business of taking care of the dead in this town for half a century or more.

With a sigh, Rowan removed her gloves, mask and apron. She sat them aside for when she returned and went upstairs to find Charlotte. There hadn't been time to talk after she arrived back at the funeral home with Burt. As sad as this morning had started, Rowan wanted to move forward with her plan.

She found Charlotte in her office already laying out

the design for Burt's memorial pamphlet. Rowan paused behind her chair and studied the image on the screen.

"That's a great photo of Burt." He looked like the jolly man everyone had known him to be. "The layout is nice. Burt would be honored."

"Thank you. I wanted to do this in a way that I knew he would like. I found the photo in all those pics we took at the dinner you hosted at Christmas."

Rowan smiled at the memory. Burt's wife had died only a month before and his sister was on a holiday cruise that had been planned for nearly a year. Rowan had insisted Burt come to her dinner. She had invited her staff, including the cleaning team. By the time the day of the party had arrived it had turned into such a large gathering she'd held it in the lobby instead of in her kitchen in the living quarters.

"That was a great party," Rowan said, mostly to herself.

"It sure was," Charlotte agreed. She glanced over her shoulder. "You know you'll have to do that every year from now on."

Not in a million years would she have ever thought she would be hosting parties in this funeral home. But Charlotte was right. It needed to become a tradition. Their work was so somber, infusing happiness wherever possible was important. Rowan took a breath. It was time she started a number of new traditions. This was her home, her business, now. She was no longer just the undertaker's daughter; she was the undertaker. There were many things she could do.

Rowan pulled up a chair. "Do you have a few minutes to talk?"

Charlotte spun her chair to face Rowan. Worry darkened her expression. "Of course. Is everything okay?"

Rowan nodded. "Other than Burt's sudden death, yes, everything is great."

That voice, the one that whispered to her far too frequently, reminding her that the other shoe could drop at any moment, nagged at her but Rowan ignored it.

"I'm the last DuPont," Rowan announced. "There's no one else."

Charlotte gave her a look over the top of her computer glasses. "You and Billy are getting married and having babies. There will be plenty of DuPont-Brannigans."

Rowan laughed. She couldn't help herself. "I appreciate your optimism, Charlotte, but I hit the big 4-0 recently. I'm not holding my breath. Besides, there has been no proposal from the other half of your equation." She cocked her head and studied her assistant. "Unless you know something I don't."

Frankly, Rowan wasn't sure she was ready for that step for numerous reasons. She and Billy had been best friends for so long the idea of doing anything that might damage that relationship was terrifying. She'd struggled with that fear when they decided to take their relationship to the next level. The idea of getting married—a lifetime commitment—was truly frightening. What kind of wife would she be? Good grief, what kind of mother would she be when she had only Norah for an example?

Charlotte held up her hands. "I do not know anything. I'm just saying."

Rowan waved her off. "Anyway, I'm having my attorney draw up a contract."

A frown marred the other woman's face.

"I'm giving you a promotion along with a substantial raise." She named the figure and Charlotte's jaw dropped. Before she could voice a protest, Rowan went on. "I'm also going to add a bonus of five percent interest in the funeral home starting this year and one percent each year of service moving forward—as long as the profit margins remain stable or rising."

"Oh no. You can't do that! The very idea is far too generous, Rowan. The salary increase alone is more than enough."

"Trust me," Rowan argued, "this is a better deal for me than for you."

The younger woman pressed a hand to her chest. "I'm so flattered and grateful. I don't know what to say." She blinked against the emotion shining in her eyes. "I can't tell you how much this means to me. I love working with you and I love the job." She laughed. "I know it sounds strange, but I enjoy working with the dead and their families. I feel like it's very important work."

Rowan smiled. "This is why you're a perfect partner."

Charlotte swiped at her eyes, her lips trembling with the effort of holding a smile in place. "Thank you."

"When the attorney has the agreement drafted we'll have him bring it here for signature and then we'll have another party." Rowan stood. "I should go check on Burt."

Charlotte thanked her again before she could get out the door. The reaction was what Rowan had hoped for and certainly bolstered her low mood. She headed back along the hall and down the stairs to the basement and on to the mortuary room. There was an elevator for transporting gurneys and coffins from floor to floor but she only used it when she was moving a client.

Freud, her German shepherd, was stretched out on the floor in the corridor just outside the mortuary room door. He lifted his head from his paws as she approached. The mortuary room was off-limits to Freud but she had a feeling he understood that their friend Burt was in there.

"Hey, boy." She scratched the top of his head. "You missing our buddy, too?"

Freud and Rowan had much in common; they both had painful pasts. The first three years of his life had been spent being kicked around and neglected by his drug trafficking owner. Rowan had found him when she and her team from the Nashville Metro Police Department were investigating a man who had murdered at least four people. As soon as the scumbag was arrested, Rowan went back for Freud. Of course, she hadn't known his name. The dog hadn't been registered. He hadn't ever been to a vet. She made sure he had everything he needed, including a complete checkup, and he was answering to the name Freud in no time.

They had been good for each other. They had both survived their broken pasts and learned to trust again.

"Come on, boy. We'll make an exception today. You can join me in the mortuary room."

Freud followed her to the stainless steel table where Burt waited. Freud stretched out on the cool tile floor. Rowan checked the pump's progress. Another five minutes and the task would be complete. She donned her apron, mask and gloves once more. After she removed the tubes and pushed the pump aside, she closed the incisions she had made.

A few more minutes were required to check the rest of her work. His face was set. Jaw wired shut. Lips and eyes sealed. The nose and other orifices had been cleaned and packed to ensure no leakages. Since his wake and funeral wouldn't be for a few days, she would wait about adding any topical cosmetics.

She rolled the gurney next to the mortuary table, applied the brakes and transferred Burt onto it. She adjusted the sheet covering his private areas and added another larger sheet that would cover him fully. For now, she would park him in refrigeration until time for his service. His sister was trying to get an earlier flight from Cozumel. She hadn't planned to return until this weekend. Under the circumstances she hoped to be back by Wednesday. Burt's viewing, wake or visitation as many called it was tentatively scheduled for Wednesday. All Rowan needed at this point was some direction on the clothing his sister wanted her to use. She was supposed to call with an update.

"See you tomorrow, Burt."

Rowan exited the refrigeration unit and locked the door. Since a body had been stolen last October she had started locking the unit door. That likely wouldn't stop anyone determined enough to force his way into the funeral home but with the security system it made getting in and then out far more difficult to accomplish in the scarce few minutes between the alarm going off and the police arriving.

Her stomach rumbled and she reminded herself that she hadn't eaten today. Breakfast had been long forgotten and then she'd needed to take care of Burt. It was almost noon and this was the first time she'd thought of food.

Freud followed her into the lobby. The front entry to the funeral home was fairly grand. Folks expected it to be. The lobby was spacious with clusters of seating areas. Charlotte ensured the many plants adorning the spacious area were watered and pruned as necessary. Lots of windows allowed the light to pour in during the day. At night the blinds behind the heavy drapes provided privacy and a sense of coziness. The shiny floors were blanketed with muted Persian rugs that were nearly as old as the funeral home itself. If she were to continue beyond the lobby there was a corridor that led to a refreshment lounge, her office and the public rest-rooms. In the other direction were the viewing parlors and the chapel. Directly across from the main entrance and set back to ensure it was visible as a backdrop to all else stood the grand staircase that ascended up to the second floor.

Rowan stood at the newel post, looking upward as she often did. The wide stairs were lined with a Persian runner. The stairs rose up and spilled onto the landing. The ornate railing stood beneath the massive chande-lier that lit not only the lower but also the upper level as well. Beyond the chandelier was the towering stained glass window depicting angels ascending to heaven. When Rowan was a child, her mother had painstak-ingly restored the beautiful stained glass.

But that had been before.

Before she tied a rope to that ornate banister and hung herself. Just in time for her only surviving daugh-ter to walk through the front entrance and find her. The police had come, and when they had finished document-ing the scene, her father had been allowed to pull her mother over that railing and cut her loose. He had held her in his arms and cried like a baby.

Rowan couldn't climb these stairs without thinking of how her own mother had betrayed her, which was why she more often than not used the back staircase. But sometimes these stairs were just handier. Besides, if she faced that hurtful part of her past often enough, perhaps she would grow immune to the pain.

Next to her Freud whimpered.

"Come on, boy." Rowan started the climb and Freud followed.

Before everything happened—before her closest friend and mentor, Julian Addington, had been revealed as a serial killer—Rowan had come to terms to some degree with what her mother had done. Since she had hung herself only months after Raven drowned, Rowan had always assumed that her mother had loved her dead daughter too much to go on without her. Too much to grin and bear life for her remaining daughter.

During the past year Rowan had discovered many secrets about her mother. Not the least of which was that she had likely blamed herself for Raven's death, which might explain why she couldn't live with what happened.

Still, she had left Rowan as a twelve-year-old child to grow up believing her mother hadn't loved her enough to stay. But Rowan had had her father. He had always been the perfect parent. Loving, patient, kind.

Sadly, he had been keeping secrets, too.

So very many secrets had been buried and so many lies had been told. So much darkness to find her way through.

It was difficult to distinguish what was fact from what was fiction.

At the top of the stairs, she made the right into the corridor that led to the living quarters. The second floor and the smaller third floor had served as the family home for several generations of DuPonts. When the funeral home was built a century and a half ago, that had been the plan. All these years later, that reality had not changed.

Rowan unlocked the door that separated her private space from the public funeral home space. This was new as well. Billy had insisted she have as many security barriers as possible between her and any trouble that found her.

She smiled as she opened the door. Now she had Billy, too.

On Halloween night last fall she had invited him to stay with her. It was the first time they were together in that way. She closed the door behind Freud and moved on to the kitchen. She opened the fridge door and scanned the contents.

Being with Billy was exactly as she had imagined. Amazing. Beautiful. Perfect.

At first she had been terrified. What if things went wrong and she and Billy's friendship was damaged by the falling apart of their physical entanglement?

So far that had not happened. Shortly after that first time together, he had moved in. They shared the same room she had slept in her whole life before going off to college. They had talked about cleaning out the larger bedroom that had belonged to her parents but until all these mysteries were solved she just didn't want to tackle the job. It felt as if she needed everything to stay just as it had always been.

Besides, for now they were taking things one step at a time. No rushing. No stress. Just enjoying this new aspect of their relationship.

She grabbed the bologna and mustard. One of Billy's go-to snacks. And made a sandwich. When she'd filled a glass with water, she gave Freud a snack and went to the table. As she ate she thought about dinner at Billy's parents' house yesterday. Dottie, his mother, had hinted repeatedly at the idea of a wedding. She wanted grandchildren. But first and foremost she wanted her son happy. Dottie understood that Billy wanted to be with Rowan. Dottie was a wonderful mother. She was kind and generous to Rowan and she would be an amazing grandmother.

But what if things didn't work out?

She was so worried that her relationship with Billy would be over completely if this new, closer, more intimate relationship fell apart.

Rowan looked down at Freud, who watched her every move in hopes of getting a bite of her lunch. "It's complicated, boy. It's not easy being human."

She laughed. "It's not easy being a dog either, huh?" Freud had definitely survived a few complications of his own.

Rowan finished off her sandwich and cleaned up the crumbs. She pushed in her chair and walked to the window that overlooked the backyard. Was she ready for the next steps? Marriage? Children?

She shook her head, reminding herself she hadn't been asked. Dottie and Charlotte were putting foolish ideas in her head.

Her arms went around her waist as another cold, harsh reality invaded her thoughts. There was the ever-present concern about Julian. She couldn't pretend he was gone forever. She could hope, but there was no way to be certain. He would destroy Billy just to get at her. The serial killer Angel Petrov, who had showed up at the funeral home with a body in her suitcase, had warned Rowan that Billy might not be long for this world.

*He has a very large target on his back.*

Whatever else she did, Rowan had to be sure there was no threat to Billy. Just because there had been no contact from Julian and no other killers had shown up with messages or bodies didn't mean the nightmare was over.

Rowan exhaled a big breath. It might never be truly over.

# *Three*

Rowan stared at the expanse of wall next to her mother's desk. The desk sat in front of a window that overlooked the backyard, but on either side of the window was wall space. Rowan had removed the family photos from this right side. The framed photographs still lay on the nightstand where she'd placed them almost five months ago.

She had made a case board on the six-foot width of wall. At the top of her case board, probably six and a half feet or so off the floor since she would need a ladder to go higher, were photos of her parents. Edward and Norah DuPont. Norah was in her midthirties in the photo since it was one of the last ones taken of her before she died. The photo of her father had been taken Christmas before last, just before his seventieth birthday.

Her father had been a handsome man, her mother a beautiful woman. Their many photographs together throughout well over a decade and a half of marriage showed a happy couple. But something had been wrong even in the photos from back then. Rowan could see it now when she studied the family albums. An ever-so-slight distance. A disconnect. It was more noticeable in the eyes or perhaps in the way they no longer looked at each other during their final years together. The photos from the early days of their marriage showed the two looking longingly at each other or touching in some way but not in the later photos, the ones that came after Rowan and Raven were born.

What happened between her parents?

The next photo on the board was of Julian Addington. Handsome, charming, intelligent. His blond-gray hair and blue eyes made Rowan turn away for a moment. He had come into her parents' lives somehow and changed the definition of their relationship and the very journey upon which their lives were set. Turned everything upside down.

Was Julian Rowan's biological father? Was it an affair that came between Norah and Edward?

Rowan forced herself to look at Julian again. There were far too many similarities to ignore. The line of her nose…the almost nonexistent dimple in her chin.

*Don't obsess.*

She moved on to the next photo. In this one, her mother and father stood with Herman Carter, his wife, Estell, and the man they knew to be Antonio Santos. Santos, who had operated in Winchester under the alias Carlos Sanchez, had, it seemed, murdered at least twenty-six people. He'd kept their faces and skin from other parts of their bodies and made books. The Bureau called them the books of the dead. His victims, at least the ones they knew about, didn't fit the typical profile of a victim. Each of the identified remains belonged to a serial killer. All had been in the Bureau's database.

The bones from the more than two dozen victims had been discovered in a cave right here in Franklin County.

This photo with Santos showed another man whose identity remained a mystery.

Rowan assumed this unidentified man wasn't from the area since no one seemed to know him. Special Agent Josh Dressler, the head of the task force working on the Julian Addington investigation, had not been able to ID him either.

Then came the pieces of evidence Rowan and Billy had discovered. The cocktail napkin she had found in a pair of her father's trousers. There was nothing written on the napkin, only the imprint of the Night Owl, a local bar. According to the owner of the bar, Rowan's father had met there with a man matching Julian's description January before last. The two had a brief exchange and her father left.

The silver necklace with the sun and moon charms was the first conclusive piece of evidence found that linked the DuPonts with the Addingtons. The necklace was uncovered with the remains of Alisha Addington, the daughter Julian had with his former wife, Anna. The daughter and wife he had kept secret from Rowan. Apparently, the daughter had learned about her father's affair/fascination with Norah and she had come to Winchester to *kill* the competition. She had succeeded in murdering Raven but she had ended up dead before she could kill Rowan or Norah.

Julian would have Rowan believe that her father had killed Alisha after learning she had drowned Raven, but Rowan didn't believe him. No matter that she understood now that there were many secrets and lies in her parents' history, she could not help the need to protect her father.

Beyond the videos the Bureau had discovered that proved Julian had been watching Rowan since she was a child, there was little other proof of a connection between her parents and the man. Her mother's stories—the copious pages of notes—pointed to numerous killers. One would think Norah DuPont had fancied herself a suspense writer, but Rowan wasn't so sure her notes and stories were fiction. Santos had been one of the characters she had described and he definitely had not been an imaginary character.

The Bureau—Dressler, in particular—had kept Rowan out of the loop in regards to the identity of the killers who, apparently, had been murdered by Santos. Without that information she couldn't determine if any of the other characters in her mother's writing had been real. She couldn't deny the certainty that her mother had, it seemed, drawn killers.

The big question was why?

And did Rowan suffer that same curse?

Rather than tackle that question, she went through the files and notes she had made over the past year. The trouble was, none of it pieced together the way she needed it to in order to make any accurate conclusions.

Like too many afternoons, the hours slipped away with her in the past. She stilled and listened for the shower upstairs. Billy had come home fifteen or so minutes ago, given her a kiss on the cheek and headed for the shower. He'd alerted Rowan that his mother was bringing by a casserole.

Rowan wondered if Dottie Brannigan worried that her son would starve living with Rowan. Admittedly, she was no gourmet chef. She wasn't even a decent cook. Billy made dinner or lunch as often or more than she did. She had lived alone for most of her adult life. In Nashville she'd had dinner delivered more often than not.

No matter that Billy reminded her that his mother had always brought food to his house, Rowan still didn't feel any better about her bringing it here.

Dottie had always been so good to Rowan. Maybe she had liked Rowan better as a friend to Billy.

Rowan dismissed the worry and scanned the rest of the photos on her makeshift case board. The victims Julian had taken in Winchester had been to accomplish some goal—to gain access to the funeral home or to hurt Rowan. The same could be said for the final ones he had taken in Nashville.

Finally, there was the bizarre message from that bald biker guy with the mustache and long beard. Rowan called him a biker guy when she hadn't actually seen him speed away on a motorcycle but she'd heard the engine in the darkness beyond that shack in the middle of nowhere.

He had insisted that Rowan's mother had sent him to help.

Obviously that was impossible.

Her mother had been dead for almost twenty-eight years. What possible motive could the man have had for bringing her mother into this?

Rowan stared at the drawing of the bald man. The forensic artist from Nashville had generously offered to create the drawing for Rowan. They had worked together for years when Rowan was with Metro. She was genuinely grateful for the contacts and friends she had made during her career there. Detective April Jones, the lead detective in the unit in which Rowan had been assigned, briefed Rowan on many of the things Dressler often left out of what he shared with Billy or with Rowan.

Rowan suspected the agent still wasn't entirely convinced that she was not somehow feeding information to Julian. He refused to see that she wanted nothing to do with Julian. She wanted him found and prosecuted to the fullest extent of the law. Actually, she would love to watch him die but that would be too easy for the bastard. He needed to pay dearly for his crimes.

The most important reason for wanting him alive was that *she* needed answers. Answers that she felt reasonably confident only he could give.

Assuming she could trust anything he told her. So far, she wasn't so sure about the veracity of his statements.

The cell phone in her pocket vibrated and Rowan startled. She exhaled a breath and dragged the device from her pocket. She smiled when she saw April's number on the screen.

"You must have known I was thinking about you," Rowan said instead of hello.

"That's good to hear," April said.

The tone of her voice told Rowan that something was wrong. "What's happened?"

There was a span of silence, only four or five seconds but enough for Rowan's stomach to tie in knots.

"This news isn't being released, Rowan, but you'll be receiving an official call in the next hour or so."

Anticipation spread through her like fire through dry leaves. "Has Julian been caught?" Better yet, maybe he was dead. She closed her eyes. She had waited for this moment for almost a year now. The man had murdered her father and countless others. He was pure evil.

But if he was dead she might never know the truth.

"Dressler is missing."

Rowan's eyes flew open at the same time that the air exited her lungs. When she could speak, she asked, "When did this happen?"

As frustrating as the man had been since the murder of Rowan's father—as many times as she had wanted to punch him—no one deserved to have this kind of horror taking over his life.

"He didn't show up at his office this morning. No one got excited at first. His colleagues assumed he'd had an appointment that he forgot to mention or that whomever he had mentioned it to had forgotten. It happens. An unexpected call can distract even the best. But by four this afternoon, it was obvious he was MIA. We haven't been able to track his cell. We think someone disabled it."

"Of course they did. Anyone smart enough to kidnap a federal agent would know about the GPS capabilities of cell phones." Her chest hurt with the need to breathe. "No one in his family has heard from him?"

Foolish question. April wouldn't have called if all those options hadn't been exhausted already.

"We've spoken to everyone close to him. He's gone. Vanished. We found his car at the coffee shop he stops at every morning. No one saw him get out of the car and none of the baristas remember him coming in."

Rowan ran the fingers of her free hand through her hair. "Tell me what I can do to help."

Another of those pauses warned that her old friend

and former colleague's request wouldn't be one Rowan liked.

"If you hear from Julian," she said, her voice stiff, "let us know. If you have any potential way of getting a message to him, do what you can."

Rowan felt as if the other woman had slapped her, but she had known and respected April Jones too long to say any of the things burning on her tongue just now. "You can rest assured that I will do all I can. Please keep us posted on the situation."

"Of course." Another strained pause. "We'll talk again soon, Rowan."

The call ended and Rowan was left with the feeling that too much had gone unsaid. There had to be more that April hadn't been able to say to her. Had someone been listening to their conversation?

Rowan shook her head as she shoved her phone back into her pocket. There was only one answer: she was a suspect. For whatever reason the Bureau and Metro believed that she was aware of some aspect of Special Agent Josh Dressler's disappearance.

This was insane.

The doorbell rang and Rowan forced herself to shake off the ridiculous idea. She walked out of her parents' room and to the door where Freud already waited. The double chime of the bell told Rowan the visitor was at the front entrance of the funeral home. She peeked out the living room window that overlooked the front parking area. Billy's mother. Her truck was parked at the main entrance.

Rowan unlocked the door and headed along the corridor, Freud on her heels. At the top of the stairs her hand rested on the banister and she started downward, her mind ever aware that only a few feet away her mother had swung from that railing.

She shivered and quickened her pace.

At the door, she hesitated. "Sit," she said to Freud.

The Brannigans had an old bluetick hound who was so sweet and not nearly as nosy as Freud. And though Dottie adored Freud, Rowan preferred he be on his best behavior whenever guests visited.

Freud dropped to the sitting position and Rowan reached to unlock the door. Considering the call she had just received, she checked to ensure it was indeed Dottie and that she was alone, then she unlocked the door.

Rowan pushed aside the worrisome call she had received and produced a smile for the lady. "Hey. Billy said you were coming by." She opened the door wide for Dottie to enter and then closed and locked the door behind her.

Dottie grinned. "You know I can't help myself."

The older woman looked wonderful as always. Her dark hair was pulled back into a bun, emphasizing the gray steaks at her temples. But Dottie wore her gray streaks like a badge of honor. She stayed fit and looked like a woman half her age in her jeans and pullover sweater.

For the first time ever, Rowan hoped she could usher Dottie away in a bit of a hurry. Though she cherished his mother, she needed to talk to Billy privately.

Rowan accepted the covered casserole dish. "It smells divine." The aromas wafting up had her stomach rumbling. This would no doubt be far better than a bologna sandwich.

As they climbed the stairs, Dottie chattered on about the new yoga class being taught at a local gym. She urged Rowan to join for a way to destress. Rowan promised to consider the idea but deep down she recognized that she would never take the time to do so.

Freud traipsed along beside them hopeful that all those good smells wouldn't be wasted on Rowan and Billy alone.

When they reached the kitchen, Dottie asked, "Do you have green beans or sweet peas? Either would be really good with this chicken and rice casserole."

Rowan sat the casserole on the counter. "As a matter of fact, I believe I do."

She kept a number of frozen and canned green vegetables handy. Over the past few months she had learned that whenever Dottie brought over a casserole or other entrée, which was at least three times each week, Rowan needed to produce a proper pairing. Dottie Brannigan firmly believed that every meal must include a green vegetable. No exceptions.

Rowan searched the cupboards until she found a can of sweet peas. "I'll pop them in the microwave for a quick warm-up."

While Rowan opened the can and dumped the contents into a microwave-safe bowl, Dottie passed along the news about the bake sale the ladies at church were organizing for a fundraiser. Billy's parents were heavily involved in their church. For such a small town, Winchester had quite a number of churches. Rowan hadn't been to church since she was a child.

Dottie suddenly stopped midsentence and said, "That reminds me, Billy's father and I are sincerely hoping the two of you will join us for the Easter service."

*Easter.* That was next month, wasn't it?

"I'll talk to Billy," Rowan offered. "Unless work gets in the way, it sounds lovely."

Rowan hoped Dottie didn't see or hear the lie. It wasn't that Rowan had anything against churches or Easter, but she wasn't really a religious person. Beyond the fact that she hadn't been since she was a child, she wasn't sure she wanted to go. Billy mentioned going to church with his parents from time to time but it wasn't something he did on a regular basis as far as she knew. Special occasions, she thought.

Easter was certainly a special occasion. How long was the service? An hour? She could do that if it made Dottie and Wyatt, Billy's father, happy. Billy parents had always been especially kind to her. This was the least she could do.

Dottie clasped her hands in front of her. "Wonderful! You haven't been to church with us since you were a child. This way you can see what a beautiful chapel we have. It's truly lovely. Dorothy Steele's younger daughter is getting married there in May." Her eyes lit with the news. "The fellowship hall is a perfect reception room, too. You just won't believe how lovely it looks when decorated for a wedding." She stopped and rubbed at her forehead. "I think Reverend Brickman mentioned having a Saturday left in July that's not scheduled for a wedding already."

Rowan closed her mouth, hadn't meant for it to drop open. "Wow," she said in an attempt to cover her surprise. "I can't wait to see it."

What else could she say?

Dottie sighed. "I've been to every wedding held in that church and they have all been spectacular."

"Who's getting married?"

Billy walked in, his hair damp from his shower. He'd pulled on jeans but no shirt. Rowan blinked, reminded herself not to stare with such lust since his mother stood only a few feet away.

Dottie rushed over to her son for the expected hug and peck on the cheek. "Dorothy Steele's younger daughter—you remember Lacy, don't you? She's getting married at the church in May."

Rowan's face ached from holding an exuberant smile in place. "Dottie was just asking if we might be able to attend the Easter service next month. She wants me to see the chapel."

"Oh yes," Dottie urged. "It's perfect for a wedding. You know what I mean. You were Charlie Reed's best man at his wedding. Remember how lovely everything was?"

Billy met Rowan's gaze, his expression tight with the same discomfort as hers. "I do remember."

"Everyone would love to see you, Ro." Dottie turned back to her. "We're all so excited that you and Billy are officially a couple now."

"What's that awesome smell?" Billy said, raising his head and sniffing the air the same way Freud might.

Rowan bit her lips together to prevent a grin while Dottie described the casserole she had made from scratch.

Thankfully the agony didn't last much longer. As they walked Dottie down, Billy promised he and Rowan would attend the Easter service with the caveat that work could get in the way.

At the door Dottie hesitated. "At our last Friends of the Library meeting, we discussed whether you might be willing to speak and sign copies of your book,

Rowan. I know the book has been out for a while, but you've never done a signing here and the library would just love it if you could do one there."

*The Language of Death.* Rowan's one and only book—nonfiction, of course—had been released more than a year ago, a few months before her father's murder. She'd written about her life growing up in a funeral home and her work with the Nashville Metropolitan Police Department. The book had been an unexpected success. It had also, she firmly believed, been the trigger that set off Julian's rampage.

Rowan swallowed back the answer she would have preferred to give and said, "Yes, of course. That sounds like a wonderful idea."

Dottie hugged them both before leaving. Rowan stood at the door while Billy walked his mother to her truck. He was a good son. Rowan was well aware he would make an amazing husband and an incredible father.

But she couldn't think about that right now.

Julian was still out there. And if she had dared to allow the danger he represented to fade to the back of her mind the slightest bit, the call about Josh was reminder enough not to be so careless.

Certainly Josh had made plenty of enemies in his career with the Bureau who might seek revenge, but this wasn't about just any enemy. This was about Julian.

Rowan knew it with every fiber of her being.

She waved as Dottie drove away. Before she could help herself she wondered if the woman would be so eager to marry her son off to Rowan if she fully understood how close evil lurked to her. That it was possible the bastard's sinister blood ran through Rowan's veins.

Rowan didn't have children, maybe she never would, but she felt certain she would not want any of her children involved with someone like her.

Clearly Billy hadn't told his mother everything.

He sauntered toward her and Rowan's heart skipped a beat.

"You should tell your mother more about me," she offered. "Maybe then she wouldn't be so determined to plan our wedding."

Billy smiled and Rowan's heart melted a little more. "I've told her everything that matters."

He stopped in front of Rowan, leaned down and brushed a kiss across her lips.

When they had closed and locked the door. He draped his arm around her and coaxed her toward the stairs. "I say we eat and then we—"

"Josh Dressler is missing."

Billy stopped, turned to her. "What happened?"

Rowan passed along all that April Jones had relayed, which was precious little. The news battered her emotions again as she retold it. No matter the differences she and Josh had, this was wrong. This was nothing more than additional proof that Julian was capable of anything.

She should never have allowed herself to slip into complacency.

"This is what he does," Rowan reminded Billy. "He goes after the people who are connected to me." She pointed at the door. "That woman who just left—your mother—doesn't want to lose you, Billy. I don't want to lose you. Being here, being with me, puts you in danger. The worst kind of danger."

Billy drew in a big breath, then let it go. "You're right

on both counts, Ro. I know this." He reached out, traced her cheek with his fingers, then curled them around the nape of her neck. "But don't ask me to leave because I won't. I'm staying right here with you. Addington isn't dictating what I do."

Before she could argue, he went on. "And don't ask me to stop feeling the way I feel, because I can't. This is us, Ro. All of this. The good, the bad and the uncomfortable. We just have to deal with it."

She pushed her arms around his waist and pressed her cheek to his bare chest. Tears burned her eyes and she wanted to scream at herself for being so weak. So damned weak. If she was completely honest with herself, she didn't want Billy to go. Ever. She didn't want him to stop feeling what he felt for her.

And the very idea scared her to death.

# *Four*

The body had been stretched out atop Norah DuPont's grave.

Crouched next to the dead guy, Billy shook his head. *Four months.* He and Rowan had enjoyed four months without any trouble related to Addington or any of the other ugliness associated with the history between him and her folks. Until the call about Dressler last evening, Billy had even dared to believe that maybe the ordeal was over. That Addington had crawled off into some hole and died either due to complications resulting from the injury Rowan had inflicted or from a heart attack or cancer or some other fatal illness.

But they weren't that lucky. Whatever the hell the bastard had started, it was still alive and well. Apparently, so was he.

The killer—Addington or one of his associates—had put a single bullet in the back of the man's skull. Judging by the entrance wound and the lack of an exit wound, Billy estimated the weapon used was a .22 or something along those lines. An up close, professional-style hit. No indications of a struggle. Considering how heavily muscled the victim was, whoever had put him down no doubt caught him by surprise or drugged him first. Otherwise, Billy was having a hard time with the idea that the shooter had overtaken the man without a serious struggle. Unless maybe he was outnumbered; even then Billy doubted he would have gone down without a fight.

Billy would rather walk barefoot across hot coals than to have to tell Rowan about this. He studied the man who lay atop her mother's grave, his arms folded across his middle as if he'd been posed in a coffin. If all that wasn't enough, there was the fact that the victim appeared to be the same man who'd rescued Rowan last October when she was abducted by Wanda Henegar and Sue Ellen Thackerson. Whether he was or not, he damned sure looked like the forensic artist's rendering of the bald guy with the mustache and the long beard. The victim's jeans were dingy, well-worn. He wore leather biker boots and a wallet chained to his belt. The wallet was empty as were his pockets. No ID, no loose change, no nothing. The T-shirt beneath the leather bomber jacket sported a well-known motorcycle logo.

"Run his prints," Billy said to Clarence Lincoln. Lincoln was his right hand and the best detective in the department. Billy counted on him and Lincoln had never let him down. "See if he's in the system."

"Looks kind of like—"

"I know," Billy said, cutting him off. "Let's not put that part in the report until we have more information."

"Got it," Lincoln assured him. "No need to stir up that hornet's nest just yet."

Billy had no intention of bringing Rowan into this until he had no other choice. The fact that the guy was stretched out on her momma's grave sort of negated any possibility that this wasn't connected to her or to Addington, but Billy could always hope. The case had lingered in the news for the better part of a year. Could be a copycat going for attention. It happened.

Now he was just grasping at straws.

Lucky Ledbetter, the assistant coroner, arrived to take possession of the body. Seemed strange not to see Burt next to him. Burt had been a fixture in this county for all of Billy's life. Not having him around would take some getting used to. There was also the question of who would finish out his term.

The sheriff and a judge would have to work out that quandary. Maybe a special election. Until then, Ledbetter would be in the hot seat. Billy had no idea if Ledbetter had any aspirations of taking over the position, but if he did, Billy was good with that. Ledbetter was a good man. Billy had never known him to be anything less than thorough when he and Burt were called out.

Since Addington had a habit of leaving notes tucked into his victims' mouths, Billy had Ledbetter check. The victim was in full rigor already. Opening his mouth was no easy task but Ledbetter knew all the right techniques to loosen things up. The extra effort was for naught since the guy's mouth and throat were empty.

"Thanks anyway, it was worth a try," Billy offered.

"I'll get him to the lab," Ledbetter said. "I assume you need whatever they can give you ASAP."

"That would be nice." Billy wasn't holding his breath. His department wasn't the only one who needed results ASAP. "Do me a favor, Ledbetter."

The deputy coroner glanced up at him. "Sure thing, Chief. Name it."

"When you prep him for shipment look him over for any potentially identifying marks or tattoos and pass anything you find along to me. That'll save us the wait for the official report to learn anything like that." Part of Ledbetter's prep would include bagging the victim's clothes and personal effects for evidence and a thorough documentation of the body's condition.

"Will do."

Leaving Ledbetter and his assistant to the task of bagging the body in preparation for transport from the scene, Billy headed toward the main gate of the cemetery. This was the oldest and most popular cemetery in the city. It was reasonably large for a town the size of Winchester. The brick wall that circled the perimeter of this section of the cemetery was the original one built nearly two hundred years ago. Vines and ivy had claimed a good portion of it, leaving little of the brick exposed.

The forensic folks were scouring the area for footprints or any other evidence related to whoever had brought the body to the cemetery and placed it on that grave. With no blood at the scene, the victim had obviously been murdered elsewhere. His being dumped here was to send a message to Rowan.

Billy gritted his teeth to prevent roaring his outrage. Why the hell after all this time would the son of a bitch do this? Had his injury kept him out of commission for the past few months? Or had it taken him this long to find the bearded man who had kept Rowan from becoming a victim of two desperate women?

Maybe the FBI wasn't the only law enforcement agency monitoring that old cell phone number of Addington's. He may have known that Rowan was in that shack all those months ago and had sent someone for her but the bearded man got to her first. Addington would have been outraged. If that was the case, he would have wanted to exact his revenge.

Billy had toyed with the scenario that Addington had sent the bearded man to prevent Rowan from being injured or worse. But he wasn't giving the bastard that kind of credit. Especially now with that same bearded man dead and presented like a trophy after a deadly hunt.

Lincoln caught up with Billy on the sidewalk outside the cemetery wall. "Got the prints loaded. As soon as we have a hit—assuming we get one—Saunders will let me know."

Milly Saunders was one of their newest recruits. She was damned good with all the electronics and software. Billy hoped she would help bring the department up to par on using the latest technology in their investigations. He was grateful to have Saunders on their team.

"Good," he said to Lincoln. "The sooner we know who this guy is, the better I'll feel." If Billy's suspicions were correct, he would need to notify the task force. Since Dressler was out of pocket, he would reach out to Detective April Jones.

Lincoln looked up, scanned the gathering clouds. "Looks like the storm is starting to gear up."

Billy removed his hat and shoved his fingers through

his hair as he surveyed the darkening sky. "They still saying we'll get high winds?"

Lincoln nodded. "With that unseasonable warm front moving in, conditions will be ripe for tornadic weather."

"Let's hope not." Billy settled his hat back into place. It had been a while since a tornado had hit the area, but when one came, lives were nearly always lost. Sometimes because the storms were particularly bad, other times because people didn't pay attention.

Ledbetter and his assistant rolled the gurney loaded with the bagged victim out of the cemetery. Beyond the yellow tape Billy spotted Audrey Anderson speaking to one of the officers guarding the perimeter. Audrey was the owner of the *Winchester Gazette*. She had folks who monitored the police scanners to ensure she didn't miss out on a breaking story. She was a nice lady and a good newswoman, but Billy wasn't giving her anything right now. Not until he had more about this bearded man and his connection to Rowan.

He moved back to the DuPont family plot. DuPonts had been buried here for a century and a half. The name was engraved in white marble beneath a towering angel statue. If Addington or his minion had been searching for the right place it wasn't difficult to find.

"Chief."

Billy turned to find Lincoln hustling to catch up to him. "You heard back on the prints?" That would be a record. If Saunders could work this fast, Billy might need to give her a promotion ASAP.

Lincoln grinned. "Saunders is good. Our vic is Crash Layton, sixty years old, retired army."

Billy frowned. "Is that his real name? The Crash part, I mean?"

"That's what's in the system. If there's any other name, it's not documented."

"Criminal record?"

"Assault and battery when he was thirty. Nothing before or since."

"Anything else we might find useful? Last known address? Next of kin?"

"That's the really weird part, Chief. His address is listed as Tullahoma."

"Tennessee?" Of course it was, but Billy had to ask.

"The one and only."

Frankly, Billy didn't know why he was so surprised. Just when he thought he had a handle on what was going on in his town he was tossed another curveball. "So this guy has been living fifteen or so miles away all this time?"

Lincoln nodded. "That's the only address in the system."

"First the Santos guy with all those crazy tattoos right here in Winchester and now the bearded man right down the road in Tullahoma." Billy shook his head. This case was getting stranger all the time.

"It's weird for sure," Lincoln agreed.

The trouble was, how many more of these guys were hanging around, watching Rowan, waiting for whatever it was they needed to do?

And who the hell was giving the orders?

"See what you can dig up on this Crash Layton from his neighbors."

Lincoln nodded. "Will do."

Billy moved through the cemetery again, going over all the entrances and exits. Hoping for a missed tire impression or anything out of the ordinary. His officers had scoured the area and were canvassing all those who lived nearby or who had businesses across the street.

There were plenty of streetlights, but folks weren't usually outside on the colder evenings and last night had been fairly chilly. The chances that anyone saw who came into the cemetery and dropped off a body were fairly slim, but they had to ask.

*Cover all bases.* That was Billy's motto, no matter how tedious or seemingly pointless. Sometimes you had to dig through a lot of haystacks to find the one needle that made the difference.

"Chief!"

Billy paused and waited for Officer Gordon Sails to catch up with him. Maybe they had gotten lucky and discovered a witness.

"A lady across the street," he explained between pants for breath, "says she saw a man in the cemetery last night. She claims she got a good look."

"Take me to her," Billy said. This could be the break he'd been hoping for.

The small house with its plate glass–front living room that had served as a beauty parlor for going on thirty-five years sat directly across the street from the main cemetery entrance. Shoehorned between the monument warehouse and a floral shop. Delilah Dixon, the current owner, had inherited the live-work shop combo from her mother, the beautician, who passed away a few months back. But Delilah had decided the salon business was not for her and she'd transformed the place into a fortune-telling shop. Shelves filled with potions and charms now lined the walls of the space where hair dryers and styling chairs had once held court. The new owner intended to get her license this very week, she hastened to add.

"I'm not concerned about your lack of a license, ma'am," Billy assured the young woman, who was suddenly nervous. Since Lincoln hadn't left for Tullahoma yet, both he and Sails had showed up at her door with him. "I'd just like you to tell me about last night."

"My dog, Scooter—he's at the groomer right now— is a beagle and you know they get on a scent and they just take off." She shook her head. "Anyway, I let him out back last night to do his business and he took off across the street. I called and called but he didn't come back so I had to go after him." She shuddered. "It was really cold so I wasn't exactly expecting to run into anyone. I grew up in this house. Folks don't generally loiter around in the cemetery after dark. Kids mess around sometimes but, like I said, it was pretty cold so I wasn't expecting anyone." Her cheeks reddened. "I had my nightgown and housecoat on. It was kind of embarrassing."

Billy offered her a smile. "Been caught that way myself a time or two."

She laughed nervously. "Yeah. It wouldn't have been so bad if the guy hadn't been so hot."

"Guy?" Billy asked.

She nodded. "Anyway, I spotted Scooter at the DuPont plot barking like a fool. That's where I saw the man. I figured he was some friend or member of the family. Or just curious since that woman—the undertaker—has been all over the news for months."

"What time was this?"

Her brow lined in thought. "Gosh, probably around eight or eight thirty. I wanted to hurry up and get back to the house because my favorite show was coming on at nine."

"Can you describe the man? Did you speak to him?"

"I didn't really get to talk to him and it was kinda dark. There's the streetlights but it was still pretty dark," she said. "He was tall. Lighter hair. I think his eyes might have been blue but I can't say for sure. When I walked up, he just looked at me like he was as surprised to see me as I was him." She shrugged. "All I said was hello and he walked away. It was kinda creepy."

"Was there anyone else with him? Maybe nearby. Maybe injured."

She shook her head. "No. There was no body lying around when I was there. Not where you could see it anyway. Just that cute guy."

Anticipation seared through Billy. "But you got a pretty good look at him?"

She nodded. "Pretty good, I guess. Like I said, he was hot. A regular pinup guy like Liam Hemsworth."

"Hemsworth?" Billy figured the name was some celebrity but not one he recognized.

"Yeah. You know, that movie actor."

Billy must have looked as confused as he felt. Lincoln shoved his cell phone in front of Billy and said, "This is the guy she means."

Billy stared at the screen and recognition clicked. He pulled out his own phone and did an internet search. Several images populated the screen based on the search results. He selected the most recent of the bunch and showed it to Dixon. "Is this the guy you saw?"

She took the phone from Billy's hand and stared at the image a moment. "Yeah, yeah. That's him. He was out there." She thrust the phone at Billy. "It was totally weird. Especially the part where he just walked off without saying a word."

"Thank you, Ms. Dixon." He started to turn away, but hesitated. He said to her, "See Joe Wheeler about the business license. Tell him I sent you."

A big thanks followed Billy out the door. When he was on the street, he stood there, hands on hips, for a moment trying to come to terms with what the woman's identification meant.

Lincoln waited close by, his expression guarded. "Should I not ask who she ID'd as the guy she saw?"

Billy passed him his phone. Lincoln stared at the screen; his jaw sagged in disbelief.

"Yeah," Billy said. "She ID'd Special Agent Josh Dressler, who is currently missing in action."

Billy's cell rang with an incoming call. Lincoln passed it to him. Billy didn't recognize the number. He answered with, "Chief Brannigan."

"Chief, this is Special Agent in Charge Luke Pryor."

Billy had a feeling this day was not going to get any better. "What can I do for you, Agent Pryor?"

"You're aware that Agent Josh Dressler is missing and we're growing more concerned by the minute."

Fate had a twisted sense of humor when it came to timing. "Still no word from him?"

"Unfortunately not, but we have had a development."

Billy braced for the bad news.

"We finally received Dressler's phone records and it seems his final contact was an incoming call from your area."

"Do you have a name or number for the caller?"

"I do, Chief. The caller was Dr. Rowan DuPont."

Billy wasn't sure he heard right. What the man said

was impossible. Before he could demand a more detailed accounting, Pryor was talking again.

"We're going to reopen a temporary field office in Winchester. My team and I will be there before close of business today. I'll need to interview Dr. DuPont as soon as I arrive."

"I'm no expert," Billy countered, "but I'm sure you're aware there are ways to mirror a number. There's no way Dr. DuPont made that call."

"We are aware of the technology, Chief, but I assure you, the call originated from Dr. DuPont's cell phone and from a tower in your city. If she didn't make the call, the real question is who had access to her phone?"

The call ended but the conversation was far from over.

Before Billy could call Rowan his phone rang again. This time it was Ledbetter.

"Brannigan."

"Chief, you're going to want to see this."

Ice speared through Billy's veins. "What'd you find, Ledbetter?"

"I removed and bagged his clothes and the man's body is covered in tattoos. Some are crazy creepy. But the creepiest part is the one on his back. It's one we've seen before. The same rose vine tattoo that circles the name Norah."

Rowan pushed the key into the door and gave it a twist. The knob turned and she opened the door. Burt's home was a neat bungalow on High Street. Inside, the house smelled of his aftershave. She smiled. His office manager at the Winchester Vet Clinic had already come by and picked up his two dogs. She wanted to keep them at the clinic where the staff could feel Burt's presence. Rowan could only imagine how devastated the staff was by his sudden death.

Burt's sister, Sally, had called and asked Rowan to pick out a suit for Burt. She'd said no tie and Rowan agreed. Burt wasn't the tie type. She considered for the first time that she needed to leave instructions on how she wanted to be dressed upon her death as well as a list of her other send-off wishes. One would think that since she'd grown up in a funeral home she would have thought to do this ages ago. But taking care of others always seemed to get in the way of taking care of herself.

Pushing the depressing thought aside, she wondered why she hadn't heard from April Jones this morning. Hopefully Dressler had been found, alive and well. If not and if his disappearance had anything to do with Addington, she hoped he wasn't dead already. Dressler had made it a point this past year to go after Julian with a vengeance. Julian had noticed. He wouldn't take Dressler's personal vendetta well. Like Billy, Dressler had a large target on his back.

Burt's living room was reasonably neat for a man who lived alone. His wife's touches were everywhere. The doilies on the backs of upholstered chairs. The many potted plants and the stack of magazines about decorating, gardening and design. Glass-front cabinets stored all sorts of glassware and china. The lady had liked collecting china and none of it matched. Rowan smiled. She liked the quirkiness of the mismatched patterns. Maybe one day she would start a hobby that involved something that had nothing to do with work.

From the rugs on the wood floors to the wallpaper on the walls, the home was reminiscent of a bygone era. All that wallpaper was coming back in style. Rowan saw it in the magazines Charlotte brought to work.

Burt's home was charming with big windows that allowed in the light. To the right beyond the living room was the dining room and the kitchen. Like the living room, the rooms were clean and neat if a little out-of-date. She passed two bedrooms—one of which had been turned into a sewing room, the other an office—and a bathroom. At the end of the hall she came to the final bedroom. This was Burt and his wife's room. There were two small closets. His wife's remained jam-packed. Reminded Rowan of her parents' bedroom. Her father hadn't had the heart to part with her mother's things and Rowan hadn't managed to part with his. One day, maybe, when the whole Addington mystery was solved, she would undertake that massive and painful endeavor.

After riffling through the offerings, Rowan selected a blue suit and white shirt. A quick prowl through a couple of drawers provided the rest of the things she needed. She tucked all except the shirt and suit into the bag she'd brought. The shirt and suit she kept on the hangers. On second thought she added a pair of dress shoes. As she moved back down the narrow hall, she passed the office again and something on the bulletin board caught her eye. She paused at the door and flipped on the light for a better look.

At the center of the bulletin board was a photo of the funeral home. Rowan sat down the bag and the hanging clothes and walked into the bedroom turned office. Unlike the rest of the house the office was cluttered and dark. There were two large windows but both were closed tight with heavy drapes that blocked all

light. Bookshelves lined most of the wall. But it was
the bulletin board spanning the better part of one wall
that drew her like a moth to a flame.

Around the photo of the funeral home were smaller
photos. Photos of her parents, of her and even of Raven.
There was Herman and Woody, a former assistant at
the funeral home. A photo of Billy was just beneath
Rowan's. And there was a duplicate of the photo with
Santos and the unidentified man. There was even a
photo of Julian.

"What in the world?"

Rowan moved closer still. Read over the handwritten
lists Burt had posted. One list was nothing but names,
most of which Rowan recognized. The victims in Winchester that Julian had murdered were on the list. Any
close associates of her father's—of hers—were listed.
There was another list. This one of things, not names.
But not all the items made sense. Bones. Faces. Skins.
Necklace. Those things she understood. But other
things like three different cars, none of which she recognized. There was a photo of a house she couldn't
place. A couple she couldn't identify. And dozens of
names, none of which she recognized.

"What in the world were you doing, Burt?"

Her first thought was that he was conducting his
own investigation. She walked to his desk and sank
down into the chair he had used. The blotter on his
desk was filled with handwritten notes. She skimmed
through them looking for anything related to her family or Julian.

*She has no idea.*

Rowan leaned forward and peered at the words. Definitely Burt's handwriting. Still scanning the words—

some written hastily, almost desperately—she dug her cell from her pocket. Billy needed to see this…this whatever it was. Apprehension swelled in her chest.

Before she touched the screen to call Billy, it vibrated with an incoming call.

*Billy.*

"I was just about to call you." She surveyed the room, shuddering at the bizarre find. Why hadn't Burt told her about this?

He had been trying to text her when he died. Maybe he'd come to the point in his research that he'd been ready to tell her.

"Where are you?"

She frowned. Billy sounded worried or troubled. "I'm at Burt's. I came for a suit but…" She shook her head. "You're not going to believe—"

"Stay right there," Billy urged. "I'm on my way."

# *Five*

Rowan was still seated at Burt's desk when Billy arrived.

"Ro?" he shouted from the front door.

She grimaced. Evidently she'd forgotten to lock it. "Back here," she answered. "Down the hall, second door on the right."

She stood as Billy made his way to her. She'd expected him to show up with the cavalry in tow. Forensic techs, at least one detective. But he was alone.

"You didn't lock the door."

"Sorry. I was…" Her words trailed off as his focus settled on the bulletin board. For a long moment he stood in the center of the room, his hat in his hand, and stared at the bulletin board with all its notes and photos.

"Well, Jesus Christ."

"That's what I thought when I first saw it." Rowan moved to his side. "Maybe this was what he wanted to show me."

"Guess so." Billy stepped closer to the bulletin board. "You know all these people?"

"Not all of them." She joined him at the board she'd

reviewed over and over since finding it. "This one." She pointed to a photo that was partially tucked beneath another. "I think he's the man in the photo with Norah and Santos." She turned to Billy. "I wonder if Burt got this photo from Herman somehow or if he actually did know the man."

Billy shrugged. "I sure as hell don't and no one else we've asked has admitted to knowing him." A frown furrowed his brow. "Did you ask Burt about him?"

Rowan nodded. "I did. He just shook his head, said he couldn't be sure. I can't believe he would lie to me. But then…" She gestured to the board. "Look at all this."

"Maybe he wasn't as much lying as trying to figure out the best way to approach the truth. Then again, he may have been attempting to come to some conclusions before he shared whatever he'd found."

Rowan had been certain she did not possess the wherewithal or the desire to smile and yet somehow she smiled. Billy was right. Burt was her friend. He had known her for her whole life. There was a perfectly reasonable explanation for why he had been doing all this. She refused to believe otherwise. At least, not at this point. For now, she only knew that they needed to find that reason. She couldn't bear the idea of adding another name to the betrayal column.

"You're a good man, Billy Brannigan. You see the best in everyone. Thanks for the reminder." She needed to see the good right now. There were so many layers of lies and secrets and tragedies hovering over and around her and the people she had thought she knew. Heaping any more onto the pile was simply more than she could bear.

"Keep in mind I'm not letting him off the hook that easily, but I'm all for going with giving him the benefit of the doubt until we see differently. Burt was a good man."

"He was." She had already taken a photo of his board and a close-up of the man who was in that photograph with her mother she had found at Herman's house.

She had ensured the lists of names and other notes were legible in the photos she captured. No matter how she looked at it, this didn't feel right. Burt was generally brutally honest. Why would he hide any of this from her? Why not discuss his thoughts or the names he'd listed? This—she peered at the barrage of photos and notes—was not his style.

"Ro, we need to talk."

Pushing aside the troubling thoughts, she turned to Billy, hadn't realized until that moment that he was staring at her. "Sorry. I was lost in thought."

The worry on his face sent a new ache piercing through her. She really had brought so much trouble to his door. She thought of his mother and how badly she wanted a wedding and grandchildren. Rowan could hardly see how the woman still wanted any of those things with Rowan involved. She had been nothing but trouble for Billy. And yet his family continued to treat her as if she was part of them.

"What's happened?" His hesitation rather than launching into whatever they needed to talk about amped up her anxiety even more.

"This morning a jogger discovered a body in the cemetery."

Dread welled inside her. "A murder victim?"

He nodded. "Male. No ID on him. But he looks familiar. I'll need you to confirm, but I believe it's the bearded man who helped you out of that situation with Henegar and Thackerson. If it's not him, this guy damned sure looks like the one in the drawing."

Images from that night flashed like a bad movie in Rowan's mind. She had been certain the bearded bald man had come to kill her. That Julian had sent him to do what he was too much of a coward to do himself. Instead, the man had killed the two women who had abducted her. He'd rescued her from certain death. The two women had already been guilty of murder and they were desperate. Desperation had made them even more reckless and dangerous. That desperation had also gotten them killed.

"Someone killed him?" Rowan had assumed she would never see the bearded bald man again. The artist rendering had garnered no hits anywhere. The image hadn't matched with any found in their accessible databases.

"Someone put a bullet in the back of his head. God only knows where since the killing didn't happen where we found him. The shooter brought him to the cemetery and left him lying across your momma's grave."

With all that had happened in the past year, Rowan had felt reasonably confident that nothing else could shock her and yet somehow this news did. "Do you think it was Julian?"

Saying his name aloud made her throat tighten. She had asked herself a hundred times already when he would stop. When he would come directly after her and stop killing others to get her attention or to accomplish some end only he could see.

Deep inside where she still felt compelled to keep

things from Billy she knew the answer. Julian was never going to stop until someone stopped him. Rowan had no doubt that the someone would have to be her.

"More likely one of his thugs," Billy said. "This guy—Crash Layton—wouldn't have been easily overtaken. I can't see Addington, at his age, putting himself in a position like that with a guy as capable as Layton."

"If this Layton had a record, why didn't we get something on him before?"

"It was an old A and B charge, from when he was thirty. He had hair and no beard in the mug shot so there was no face match. We didn't have prints or a name."

Rowan squared her shoulders and asked the next relevant question, the one that had dread expanding even wider inside her. "Did you find a note?"

Julian had placed notes to Rowan in plastic baggies and shoved them deep into the mouths of victims. The memory sent a shudder through her.

"Not in the usual place. I asked Ledbetter to look him over closely before shipping him off to the lab." Billy held her gaze. "He called a few minutes ago to let me know he'd found something I needed to see. This Layton character has the same sorts of tattoos Santos had, including the one with your mother's name."

The dread slipped away only to be replaced by an icy awareness. "I need to see him."

Rather than start for the door, Billy hesitated. "There's more."

Rowan felt the bottom drop out of her stomach. "Let's hear it."

"When my officers were canvassing the folks who live or operate businesses near the cemetery, they found a witness who saw a man in the cemetery last evening. When she spoke to him, he reacted by rushing away."

Rowan held her breath. "Was it Julian?"

Billy gave his head a negligible shake. "The witness ID'd a photo I pulled up from an internet search. If she's right, the man was Dressler."

Rowan held up her hands. "Wait. You're saying Dressler was here. In that cemetery last night?"

He nodded. "Standing at your family plot."

"Where the body was found?" The answer was one she already knew, but at the moment she didn't trust her reasoning powers.

"Yes. But the body wasn't there when the woman saw Dressler so we can't be sure he had anything to do with it."

This made no sense. "Why would he come here without contacting one of us? Why would he be hiding out from his own people?"

The answer slammed into her chest before Billy could say a word in response.

"We were right." She held his gaze, the same certainty in his that she felt deep in her gut. "There is a leak in his office and he knows it. He's fallen off the grid to get the answers he needs."

"That's my guess." Billy stared for a moment at his hat. "The man in charge now, this Agent Pryor, he insists that the final call made to Dressler's phone before he disappeared was from *your* phone."

The meaning behind the statement didn't sink in at first, then it abruptly did—like a sledgehammer blasting into a wall set for demolition. "He thinks I called Dressler?"

"I told him he was wrong, that there had to be another explanation, but he says the cell phone records show the call came from your phone and a tower in Winchester."

"He's either lying or the records are wrong." Her phone had not been out of her sight in the past twenty-four hours. Except for when she took a shower. A frown nagged at her brow. And when she went down to let Dottie in with her casserole. But Billy had been right upstairs in the shower. She said as much to him now.

"We can't rule out the possibility that someone got in somehow or that there's some sort of technology someone outside the funeral home could have used to somehow piggyback off your phone to make that call. The feds will have to figure out that one." He exhaled a heavy breath. "Whatever they have planned to get to the bottom of the call, Pryor and his people are on their way to Winchester. They're reopening a field office and he wants to see you first thing when he arrives."

"Again?" They did not need Pryor and his people nosing into every step she or Billy or his team made. She especially did not need another federal agent making her feel guilty for something she didn't do.

"Unfortunately." Billy was clearly not happy about the news either. "For now, let's get over to the morgue and have a look at Layton. Then I'll go to Tullahoma and have a look around his place."

"You have an address for him?"

Billy grinned. "I do. And I also have justifiable cause to enter the premises."

Rowan grabbed her bag. "I'm going with you."

"I'll just deputize you en route—that way we won't have any issues come up later about scene contamination or anything annoying like that."

Rowan was the one grinning this time. Billy was a quick learner. She'd pulled that on him before. Told him she couldn't enter a scene without risking later ramifications. He'd promptly deputized her.

Whatever worked.

The hospital was only a few minutes away and the morgue was on the lowest level. Rowan made pickups here. No one liked having a patient die in the hospital but it happened. Unless foul play was suspected or an autopsy was needed for some other reason, the funeral home picked up the deceased directly from the morgue.

Lucky Ledbetter met them at the door marked Morgue.

"Hey, Chief, Dr. DuPont." He opened the door wide for them to enter. "This way."

Rowan had been to the morgue, but she usually didn't have to go inside. She let the attendant know she was outside, and he brought the body to her. Just down the corridor on the left was the pickup and delivery entrance. It was a similar setup to what she had at the funeral home.

The morgue was small with only the basic equipment. More a holding area before the deceased moved on, either to the lab or to the family's preferred funeral home. While she and Billy stood by, Ledbetter pulled the gurney from the small refrigeration unit. Judging by what she saw beyond the open door, the unit was about the same size as the one in the funeral home.

"I told Ledbetter," Billy said, drawing her attention to him, "we'd need to do more than peek into the bag at Layton."

Billy was right. Rowan would want to take photos as well. Comparing them to those Santos had sported was imperative. Having Layton on a gurney would work far better.

Ledbetter pulled the drape down to the man's waist. "There aren't any below this point." He gestured to the tattoos around the victim's navel.

The markings on his skin were very similar to the ones she had discovered on the body of Santos, the man—killer, presumably—who had curated all those faces and skins.

Rowan removed her phone and started snapping pics immediately. She imagined that as soon as Pryor's people found out about this guy they would take control of the body. The tattoos were almost identical to those on the body of Santos. They were different but she would need to compare the photos to determine exactly how. When she had finished with those on the front of his torso, Ledbetter rolled him onto his side so she could photograph the back.

For a moment Rowan could only stare. The vine tattoo extended over his shoulder and down his back just as it had on Santos. Her mother's name, Norah, was encircled by that thorny vine of roses. What did this mean? Were Santos and this man, Crash Layton, somehow connected to her mother through some vow or alliance? Former lovers? Members of the same bizarre killing club?

When she'd finished, Ledbetter eased the man down onto his back. "I did find one other thing, Chief."

As Rowan and Billy watched, Ledbetter moved the man's right arm and pointed to a small mark on his side.

"Someone Tasered him," Rowan said almost to herself.

"Sure looks that way," the deputy coroner agreed.

"Thanks, Ledbetter," Billy said. "Now I know how the shooter disabled him without the usual signs of a struggle."

If only the rest of this mystery would be so easily solved.

Before leaving, Rowan moved through her photos until she reached the ones she had taken in Burt's home. She might as well follow up on this photo while she was here.

"Lucky, do you know who this man is?" She showed him the photo she had snapped of the photograph on Burt's board. "It looks fairly old. There was no date or name."

Ledbetter studied the screen for a moment and then nodded. "I don't know much about him, but I remember that when I first came to work with Burt, this guy would drop by the clinic once a week or so with information."

"What sort of information?" Billy asked, joining the discussion.

"Where he saw stray animals, dogs, cats, whatever, in need of help. Any he spotted that were being abused. He kept Burt informed about animals all over the city." Ledbetter grinned. "Back in the day, Burt would show up wielding a baseball bat and demand to take custody of the animal. If I remember correctly, this guy would help him. I think he was homeless. Lived on the streets so he saw things maybe others didn't."

Billy and Rowan exchanged a look.

"He didn't work for Burt?" Rowan asked. "Here or at one of the veterinary clinics?"

He shrugged. "I'm pretty sure he didn't. I think Burt gave him money for food and bought him clothes sometimes. That was about it."

"You don't remember his name?"

"Burt just called him Tex. I'm not sure if that was part of his real name or just a nickname."

"When was the last time you saw Tex?" Billy asked.

"It's been a while. At least a couple of years. He might have moved away. The homeless do that, you know. Or he could be dead. Burt never mentioned him."

"Thanks, Ledbetter," Billy said. "Maybe you can check with some of the folks at the clinics and see if they remember him or know what happened to him."

"I'll do it, Chief."

When they were in the corridor once more, Rowan said, "I think Burt was trying to help and he was waiting until he had something worth showing or telling before he came to me with it." The conclusion made far more sense than anything else.

"I agree."

As they exited the building Billy resettled his hat into place. "Let's find out what Mr. Crash Layton kept around his house."

Rowan couldn't help hoping that this time they would find some definitive answers rather than more questions.

The trailer park wasn't actually in Tullahoma but it had a Tullahoma address. This particular area fell within Franklin County borders. Billy had called Sheriff Colt Tanner and given him a heads-up on what he was doing. Finding the exact location for the trailer park wasn't quite so easy. Thank God for GPS. No matter that Billy had been forced to turn around several times when even the GPS got confused, Rowan doubted they would have found the place without the device.

Rowan surveyed the small neighborhood that was no doubt one of the oldest surviving trailer parks in the tricounty area. At least one junked car sat in each of the gravel drives alongside what appeared to be a working vehicle. Trash cans were overflowing. And most of the metal box homes on wheels were in sad need of a paint job or other repairs.

Not exactly home sweet home but it was far and away better than a place like tent city.

Layton's home was the fourth on the left. Looked like the typical midcentury mobile home. Approximately ten feet wide and four or five times that in length. The mint-green paint, obviously not the original, was peeling or missing altogether revealing the original tan color.

There was no vehicle in the drive. No way to know where it ended up. According to the DMV, Layton owned a motorcycle and a vintage truck. Billy had put out an APB on both. If Layton had been in his truck when he encountered the shooter, the truck may have been the primary crime scene. Based on what Billy had told her, the cemetery certainly was not.

"Stay in the truck until I see what we have here," he ordered.

Rowan started to argue with him but understood that it would only waste time. Billy was hardheaded when it came to her safety. Instead of protesting, she powered down her window and said, "Fine."

Billy climbed out and walked over to the front door. There was no porch, just a small stoop. Standing to one side of the door, he pounded a couple of times on the door. He waited. Rowan strained to hear any noise beyond the thin metal walls.

Thankfully the neighbors had opted to stay inside their homes. Rowan hoped they stayed smart that way. The knocking stirred up a couple of dogs in the neighborhood.

Another couple of knocks went unanswered. Rowan was biting her lower lip by the time Billy reached for the knob and gave it a turn. The door opened and he glanced back at Rowan.

His weapon drawn, he peeked inside and shouted, "Anybody home?"

Rowan's nerves jangled when he disappeared through the door, leaving it open. She clutched her phone, ready to call for help if necessary. Finally, he reappeared at the door and motioned for her to join him.

Rowan scrambled out and hurried to the door. "You see anything?"

"Not on my initial sweep. Let's walk through a little slower. Do some poking around."

He passed her a pair of latex gloves and she pulled them on while he did the same.

"I'll start in the back," Rowan offered.

Billy gave her a nod and started looking through the one bookshelf in the small living room. The home was sparsely furnished with nothing more than a couple of upholstered chairs, a small table and a bookcase in the living room. A small box-style television sat on the counter that divided the living room from the equally small kitchen.

Down the hall, Rowan spotted three doors. The first was a tiny bathroom. She stepped inside and checked the medicine cabinet. No prescription drugs. A bottle of over-the-counter aspirin and a packet of antacid. Two drawers under the sink. She opened both and checked inside. Toothbrush and toothpaste. The only other storage in the room was a small cabinet over the toilet. Toilet paper and a towel along with a cheap bottle of aftershave.

The shower was empty save for generic shampoo and a bar of soap.

Rowan moved on to the next room. This one contained only one thing: a weight lifting bench. An extra small closet was empty. She removed the register and checked in the hole in the floor that allowed warm or cold air to circulate in the room. Nothing there.

The next bedroom was slightly larger. This one actually had a bed. The sheets were tousled, and the comforter was thrown aside. One thick pillow was wadded as if whoever had slept there last had bunched and squeezed it repeatedly in an effort to get comfortable.

A single bedside table with only one drawer. She checked the drawer. Reading glasses. A comb. Lip balm. She placed the items on top and pulled out the drawer to have a look at the bottom. Clear. Then she moved on to the built-in dresser. Socks, boxers and tees and nothing else. Rowan checked the bottom of each drawer and then on to the closet. Three pairs of jeans were folded and stacked on a shelf. She felt in the pockets of each pair. Examined the outer pockets and inside the sleeves of the one jacket and the one button-down shirt. There was a pair of hiking boots and she thrust her hand into each of those.

Nothing.

Nothing under the mattress or inside the pillowcase. Under the bed was clear as well. She moved to the only remaining place where the man could possibly hide anything in this room considering there was no carpet on the floor. Linoleum ran from one end of the mobile home to the other.

She pulled the register from the hole in the floor and looked into the sheet-metal-lined space. Brown paper. Hope daring to sprout, she reached into the hole and tugged out the package.

Not paper. An envelope that had been folded and was a little crumpled. Rowan sat back on her heels and opened the envelope. A photo of her came out first. She considered the setting and how she was dressed and realized this was a photo of her visiting her father's grave. Maybe shortly after his death. April or May of last year, perhaps.

She laid the photo aside and shuffled through the pages. Yellow legal pad paper. Handwritten notes filled the lines. Notes about Rowan. Where she had lived and worked in Nashville. Her work friends. Billy. There were lots of notes about Billy. Where he lived, where he had attended university.

She moved to the next page. The names of the victims in the Winchester area who had been murdered by Addington or one of his followers were listed. Dates and causes of death. Vague reasons for the murders. Most, Rowan noted, were accurate. Other names marched down the page.

*Josh Dressler.*
*Burt Johnston.*
*Charlotte Kinsley.*
*Dottie Brannigan.*
*Billy Brannigan.*

Fear pounded through Rowan's veins.

Dressler was missing.

Burt was dead.

Was something about to happen to the next person on this list?

# *Six*

Billy insisted on stopping for lunch after the visit to Layton's home, but Rowan hadn't felt like eating. She kept thinking about the list of names she'd found in that envelope.

She stood in the lobby of the funeral home now. Billy had headed back to his office to follow up with Detective Clarence Lincoln on where they were with the Layton murder investigation. Rowan locked the door and headed for the mortuary. Charlotte had received an intake and was currently starting the prep.

Freud followed close behind Rowan, but at the stairs that descended to the basement level she ordered him to stay. Allowing him in the mortuary room with Burt was an exception to the rules. For his own safety, she couldn't allow him to grow accustomed to that sort of leeway. Halfway down the stairs she heard the strums of Charlotte's favorite Bach tinkling from the mortuary room. The woman adored classical music.

Rowan had to admit there was something relaxing about the music. She paused at the doorway and watched her assistant. Obviously she had already cleaned and disinfected the body. Now she was setting the face using a photo provided by the family. One of the most important tasks in preparing a client was to make him or her look as natural as possible. The family needed that sense of normalcy.

Charlotte glanced up and smiled. Using her elbow she lowered the volume on her CD player. Charlotte was one of the few people Rowan knew who still wagged a small CD player around. She insisted she was setting an example for her kids—not every aspect of life required a cell phone or tablet.

"Remember Ms. Donelson? She and her sister came in two months ago and did the preplanning package?"

Rowan joined Charlotte at the mortuary table. At the time of their visit, Ms. Donelson hoped for six more months of life. "I do remember them. So the cancer won the battle a little earlier than expected?"

Charlotte nodded. "Unfortunately."

Faye Donelson and her sister, Kaye, were twins, like Rowan and her sister, Raven. The elderly women had never been married. They had lived together their entire lives. Despite the grim nature of their visit to the funeral home a few weeks ago they had laughed and told stories of their grandfather making moonshine and their mother working in a factory to fill in for her husband who was away fighting in the war.

"Charlotte, if you're at a good stopping point, there's something I need to speak with you about." Rowan's pulse reacted to the worry coursing through her. "It'll only take a moment."

Charlotte was young with a family that included two children. If being close to Rowan was a risk, she might want to rethink working here for a little while. Rowan had an obligation to discuss the situation with her.

Charlotte removed her gloves and apron. "Sure."

They walked over to the desk on the other side of the room. Charlotte had carefully filled out the whiteboard regarding the steps taken and chemicals used in preparing Ms. Donelson, just as Rowan had taught her. Rowan couldn't imagine facing the responsibility of running this funeral home without her. She was not only a top-notch assistant director, she was also a friend.

"What's wrong?" Charlotte's expression showed the same worry Rowan felt. "You haven't decided the promotion was a mistake, have you?" Her lips quirked with the need to smile at her own joke. "Because my husband is out of town the rest of the week and I've promised him celebration sex when he gets back on Monday."

Rowan laughed, despite the worry gnawing at her. "No, no. Of course not. That is the one thing right now that I feel completely confident about."

Charlotte frowned. "Is it about that body they found in the cemetery this morning? Are you worried this is connected to you know who?"

In Charlotte's opinion, even saying Julian's name out loud was bad luck.

Rowan nodded. "The killer had stretched the man's body out on my mother's grave. Obviously the act is somehow related to *him*." She gave her assistant the other relevant details known at this time. "Billy and I went to his place of residence and I discovered a photo and some notes he had made. The photo was of me, but the notes included a list of the people closest to me. Your name was on that list, Charlotte."

Fear widened the younger woman's eyes. "Should I be worried?"

"Josh Dressler is missing and Burt is dead. Those are the two names above yours. I believe you should be very concerned for your safety under the circumstances."

Charlotte blinked, once, twice, three times. "But Burt died of a heart attack, right?"

"As far as we know. We have no reason to believe otherwise," Rowan said. "Hopefully we'll hear something about his blood work today or tomorrow. Either way, this could be a very serious situation. I keep thinking about all the people around me who have died in the past year. My father, Officer Miller, Herman, Woody, Burt… That doesn't even take into consideration the police officers and the women in Nashville who were murdered for the sole purpose of getting my attention."

Charlotte nodded. "I'm not going to lie, the idea is terrifying, but this is very scary for you, too."

Rowan shook her head. "I've worked with the police for years, Charlotte. I'm well trained with firing a weapon. I can take care of myself. Besides, this is about me. I have no choice but to be in the line of fire. You have a choice. I'm more than happy to give you a leave of absence until this is over. Your job, the promotion— everything—will be waiting when Julian is behind bars and you come back to work."

"No way." Charlotte moved her head side to side. "I love my work. I love working with you. I will not desert you when you need me most. The very idea is out of the question. Friends don't desert friends when they need them most."

Rowan closed her eyes and willed back the emotion crowding in on her. All she needed was another hero on her side. When she could speak again without her voice wobbling, she said, "I appreciate your wanting to support me, but you have to understand that if something happened to you, I would be responsible. I can't bear the idea."

"Let me show you something."

Before Rowan could ask what she meant, Charlotte reached down and pulled up her skirt far enough to reveal her thighs. Unlike Rowan, who preferred her jeans and tees when she worked with the dead, Charlotte always dressed in a skirt and blouse or a dress. She wore neat little low-heeled pumps and her hair was always perfectly styled—also unlike Rowan. Around her right thigh was a small leather holster. Ensconced in that holster was an equally small handgun. Rowan should have anticipated that Charlotte would own a handgun. A good many Southern women took their self-protection very seriously.

Charlotte slid the snub-nosed .38 from the holster and held it up. "I can hit a target center chest or center forehead from a fair distance. My husband says I'm a better shot with one of these than he is. I keep Shorty with me at all times." She smiled. "Shorty is the nickname I gave my gun since it's got this cute little stubby muzzle. You see, you don't need to worry about me, Rowan." She tucked her weapon away. "I can take care of myself, thank you very much."

What could she say to that? She would be a total hypocrite if she insisted Charlotte wasn't capable of doing so when Rowan argued this very point with Billy all the time. "In that case, I only have a few conditions."

Charlotte angled her head and narrowed her gaze. "Such as."

"Keep the funeral home's exterior doors locked at all times. When you're in here, close and lock this door as well. When you come and go anywhere, whether you're working or off for the day, stay alert. Keep your car locked. Do the same wherever you are and at home. Warn your children to be careful. And your husband."

Charlotte's eyebrows reared up. "Anything else?"

"That's all I can think of for now." Rowan placed a hand on her arm. "This is a serious situation, Charlotte. Don't be lulled into complacency when a day passes without trouble. Stay aware. Promise me that."

"I promise."

"Thank you." Rowan glanced at her watch. "If you have things under control with Ms. Donelson, I'm going on an errand."

Charlotte's gaze narrowed again. "What kind of errand?"

Rowan's guard went up. "Has Billy been talking to you?"

"He sure has," she confessed without hesitation. "If you're going somewhere, give me five minutes to get Ms. Donelson put away. I'll go with you. I can finish up later."

Rowan started to argue, but she decided maybe she should take her own advice. She should not be so complacent either. Besides, if Charlotte was with her, Rowan could make sure she stayed safe.

Maybe they could keep each other safe.

"You know, some people think she's a witch. Making potions and concocting spells from plants and bats and stuff like that."

Rowan laughed as she made the turn onto the narrow side road after having passed it twice. "Bats? Really?"

Charlotte chuckled. "That's what they say. Whoever 'they' is."

Ms. Beulah Alcott lived closer to Huntland than to Winchester. No one knew exactly how old she was. Older than dirt, Billy would say, though he made the statement with fondness. He was kind to everyone. Whatever her peculiarities, they had made Beulah Alcott a sort of dark legend in these parts. Some depended on her remedies while others felt certain she was a witch to be strictly avoided.

"Billy says she's more a botanist," Rowan suggested. "An herbal remedist."

Charlotte hummed a note of agreement. "That's one way to put it. I remember people going to her for all sorts of ailments and personal dilemmas. My momma always said that whether it was arthritis or a broken heart, Ms. Alcott had a cure."

Though she had never been a believer, Rowan vaguely remembered the stories about the woman. At this point, she was just desperate enough to look under that particular rock. The rumors about the lady included fortune-telling and tarot card reading in addition to the potions and remedies. The only time Rowan recalled seeing Ms. Alcott in person was when she made a rare appearance at a wake for an old friend. Rowan had been ten and standing at her father's side as he greeted visitors and reminded them to sign the guest book. She recalled vividly the whispers that had gone through the crowd in the parlor when the petite woman had appeared. Alcott had paid no mind to any of them. She'd gone right up to the casket and placed something inside.

Folks talked for months about how the old man who'd passed away had needed all the help he could get if there was any chance of him going to heaven.

That one time had made an impression on Rowan primarily for what happened after the woman walked out of the parlor. She had paused and looked directly at Rowan with her curious eyes. *Heterochromia.* One blue eye and one green eye. It was generally genetic but could be caused by another underlying problem. But Rowan remembered more than the difference in eye color. She remembered the way Beulah Alcott seemed to look deep inside Rowan before she smiled and walked on. According to what Billy had told her about his visit with Alcott a few months ago, she remembered Rowan as well.

Rowan parked next to the path of mossy stones that defied the overgrown yard and led to the little house that seemed to lean to one side. New sprigs of green were sprouting up amid the brown grasses and shrubs around the house. Daffodils spilled across the yard like yellow dots.

"Let's see if the legend is accepting visitors." Rowan opened her door and climbed out. Charlotte did the same.

Billy had said Alcott didn't have a phone. She also didn't have electricity. She preferred an oil lamp and a wood-burning fireplace. Since no smoke puffed from the chimney, Rowan had a feeling the elderly lady wasn't home. The weather was still a little cool to be without a heat source.

"Good grief, the sky is getting dark."

Rowan followed Charlotte's gaze to the storm clouds

churning overhead. "Maybe we can be back to town before the storm hits."

"That would be nice."

As they moved closer, Rowan recognized that the house was hardly more than a shanty. It could have been carved right out of the forest itself. Moss covered the roof and vines embraced the siding to the point it was barely visible. She stepped up onto the small porch, holding her breath in hopes it wouldn't fall in as she crossed it. Massive rosebushes seemed to support its corners. It was easy to envision all the colors that would spring to life a few weeks from now. The little house surrounded by the forest and all the blooms would look like something from a fairy tale.

Rowan knocked on the door. It was eerily quiet beyond the slab of aged and cracked wood. Then again, the lady didn't have electricity so she probably didn't have a television. Maybe a battery-powered radio.

"What's this?" Charlotte reached for the small leather pouch hanging on the doorknob.

"A previous visitor must have left her a gift." Rowan glanced around the yard. Definitely no one home. Frustration tugged at her.

Charlotte opened the pouch and peeked inside. She pulled a folded note free and opened it. She hummed a note of surprise. "I was expecting a rabbit's foot or a bat's wings."

Roman grimaced. At this point she hoped no one was home to see her nosy assistant poking around.

Charlotte made a face, then looked at Rowan. "Wow. It's for you." She offered the small piece of paper.

"What?"

"The note is for you," Charlotte repeated.

Rowan accepted the paper and read the words written in a shaky hand.

Dear Rowan,
Come back around tomorrow. I'll be watching for you then.
Beulah Alcott

Rowan had told no one she was coming here. In fact, she hadn't actually decided to come until after going to that trailer park with Billy. A cold chill danced along her spine. How could Ms. Alcott possibly have known?

Maybe there was more to her special talents than Rowan wanted to believe.

"You have a pen?" Rowan asked. She'd left her bag in her SUV.

Charlotte reached into the bag hanging on her shoulder and withdrew a pen sporting the logo of a local bank. "Here you go."

On the backside of the paper Rowan wrote: *See you then. Rowan DuPont.*

She tucked the paper into the pouch and hung it back on the doorknob.

Rowan handed the pen back to Charlotte. "Thanks. I guess we might make it back to Winchester ahead of the storm, after all."

By the time they reached the main road, Highway 64, big fat drops of rain splatted on the windshield. Rowan's cell rattled on the console and she allowed the call to come through the car's speaker so she didn't have to take her hands from the wheel.

"Hey, Billy, you're on speaker. Charlotte and I are en route back to Winchester. What's up?"

"Hey, Chief," Charlotte said, her tone teasing.

"Hey, Charlotte, Ro."

His deep voice had a calming effect on her. She was glad he'd called. Though she suspected the reason for the call would be anything but calming.

"Did Pryor arrive?" she asked. It was almost five o'clock. He should be in Winchester by now. "Or is there some other news?"

It was possible there was something new on the victim found in the cemetery this morning. *Crash Layton.* Even as the idea entered her mind she couldn't help recalling that night when he'd burst into the shack out in the middle of nowhere.

"He'll be here in half an hour. I can put him off until tomorrow if you'd prefer or you can go ahead and get this meeting over with."

"Why put it off? I'd rather do it and be done with him." She had met Pryor only once but already she didn't like him. "I'll take Charlotte back to the funeral home and then I'll be there."

"Drive safe. It's coming down here."

Even as he said the words the bottom dropped out and seeing through the downpour was a task.

Rowan ended the call and focused on staying between the lines. Thankfully traffic was light. Driving in a heavy downpour was one of her least favorite things to do.

When the roar of the downpour had lessened, Charlotte spoke. "Are you and Chief Brannigan serious? As in planning to make your arrangement permanent?"

Rowan had known there would be more questions like that one eventually. Burt had been the first to start nudging her. An ache swelled inside her. It was hard to grasp the idea that he was really gone.

"We're taking things one day at a time," Rowan said without saying too much. She still worried about ruining the friendship she and Billy had shared since they were kids. Whatever happened from here needed to occur naturally and without any unnecessary prodding.

"That's smart," Charlotte agreed. "The two of you are perfect together. I'm certain there will be a wedding before we know it."

Charlotte sounded like Dottie.

*A wedding.* Oddly enough, the idea was growing on Rowan.

Special Agent in Charge Luke Pryor was in his midfifties. He was short and thick in stature but fit-looking. Round, gold-rimmed glasses sat atop his broad nose. His suit was as fresh and unwrinkled as if he'd just put it on. Classic leather shoes were polished to a high shine despite the rainy weather. This was a man who liked making an impression. He wanted to stand out in the room.

For Rowan, he was basically a pain in the neck.

While Billy made the introductions, Cindy Farris, his secretary, brought bottled water to his office and the three of them—Billy, Rowan and Pryor—settled around his small conference table. Rowan had dropped Charlotte off at the funeral home where she would finish up with Ms. Donelson and then go home for the day. There were no viewings tonight. Ms. Donelson's would be tomorrow evening, then Burt's on Thursday.

First thing tomorrow morning Rowan intended to pay another visit to Ms. Alcott. A shiver crept through her at the thought of that odd note. Maybe the elderly lady had some way of knowing who had turned down her long driveway and had time to prepare the note. A reasonable explanation.

At least it was one Rowan could swallow.

With the pleasantries out of the way, Billy started the conversation with, "I take it there's still nothing new on Agent Dressler."

Pryor pursed his lips for a moment. "Unfortunately that is the case. We still have nothing. If he's able, he's made no attempt to contact us. Until your call this morning, I was convinced he was a hostage or…worse. Now I'm not so certain. Your witness saw him and he appeared to be moving about of his own volition. I stopped by Ms. Dixon's shop when I first arrived in Winchester and she was happy to answer my questions."

Whatever hers and Josh's differences in the past, Rowan wasn't ready to write him off as a turncoat so easily. "It's possible Agent Dressler is caught up in a situation where his restraints are not readily visible."

Pryor considered Rowan for a time. "A plausible explanation. We are, by the way, still attempting to determine how someone used your cell phone without your knowledge."

Rowan had checked her phone. There was no call to Josh or any unknown number in her history. "I'm afraid that one is above my pay grade since I can assure you the phone was never out of my possession and I'm no expert on the available technology that might fool your *experts*."

Pryor's gaze narrowed. He didn't like Rowan. That much was obvious.

As if to confirm her assessment, the agent tossed

out an accusation. "Detective Jones tells me that Agent Dressler was quite taken with you when the two of you worked together in Nashville."

Now he was really reaching. "First," Rowan said, "there was nothing remotely personal about my and Agent Dressler's relationship then or now. Second, whatever Detective Jones said, I'm confident the statement was not in the same context that you're suggesting."

Billy glared at the man but kept whatever he was thinking to himself. Most likely a good thing.

"Why do you suppose he came back to Winchester without telling anyone? Do you believe he's onto something? Perhaps following a lead he doesn't feel comfortable sharing at this time?"

Rowan smiled. "I'm certain you can read Agent Dressler's mind better than I can. Why don't you tell me because I have no idea?"

"Agent Dressler and I," Billy said, breaking into the thick tension, "discussed my concerns regarding a possible leak in his task force. Have you explored that possibility, Agent Pryor?"

Pryor continued to stare at Rowan for a bit before shifting his attention to Billy. "There is no leak in the task force, not on the Bureau's end in any event. Dressler mentioned your concerns, but he and I were on the same page on the matter. We believe Julian Addington had this man, Layton, watching Rowan, which would explain how he happened upon the scene last October."

Convenient, Rowan mused. Only Billy knew the message the bearded man, Crash Layton, had given her regarding who sent him. Of course, what he had said was impossible. Norah DuPont had been dead for going on three decades. She couldn't have sent him to intervene on Rowan's behalf.

"Under the circumstances," Billy said then, "it would seem we have nothing else to talk about."

Rowan divided her attention between the two men, curious as to who would back down first. Billy wanted this meeting over. Pryor wanted Rowan to confess to calling Josh and possibly knowing his current whereabouts.

She certainly wished she did have some idea where he was.

"Perhaps not," Pryor agreed. He turned his attention back to Rowan. "However, I am not convinced that you're sharing all you know with me, Dr. DuPont. If you are in contact with Addington or with our missing agent, you need to share that knowledge. Whatever situation Agent Dressler has gotten himself into, things could become deadly in an instant. We both know what Addington is capable of."

"I can't help you, Agent Pryor." Rowan stood. She wasn't going to keep going over the same questions. He had her answers. There was nothing else she could give him and none of the answers she had given were going to change.

Pryor sighed. "That's too bad, Dr. DuPont. I had hoped you would continue to be a team player."

Rowan had no idea what that was supposed to mean.

"Fair warning," Pryor added, "we will be watching."

She had expected as much. She shifted her attention to Billy. "If Agent Pryor is going to have someone watching me, that saves your resources."

She couldn't prove Billy had someone watching her, but she knew him too well to believe he didn't.

Billy stood. "We'll talk later."

She gave him a nod and left the office without another word to Pryor.

As she exited the building she noticed the officer sitting in a cruiser near her SUV. She climbed in and buckled up. When she drove away, as she expected, the officer followed.

Before she had traveled the short distance to the funeral home she'd already spotted the other vehicle following her. Probably one of Pryor's people. The man had made his decision about her before they had this meeting. No surprise there. And Pryor was wrong about Josh's conclusions about a leak in the task force. Perhaps he had changed his mind, but the last time he had spoken to Billy, Josh had been confident there was a leak.

It was possible Pryor was attempting to prompt reactions by tossing out misinformation. Now, apparently, he would have someone following her around.

"Lovely," she muttered.

If Josh or Julian was here, in Winchester, and needed to contact her, they were going to have one hell of a time getting close enough to get her attention without being spotted by one law enforcement agency or the other.

# *Seven*

Rowan picked up the next piece of the puzzle and taped it to the wall beneath the photos and lists that she had moved up to make more room. The stepladder she had used still stood in the center of the room. She might as well leave it there in case she had to move things around again. Freud was curled up next to her parents' bed. Outside it was still raining. The occasional blast of thunder and flash of lightning reminded her that the stormy weather the meteorologists had been calling for had indeed descended.

She stood back and studied what she had so far. The tattoos she had photographed on the bodies of Santos and Layton could possibly be pieces of some sort of puzzle. At first she had thought that might not be the case but then she'd magnified the images and looked more closely. That was when she noted the patterns. She'd enlarged and printed and enlarged and printed until she had the largest size possible while maintaining the details that worked for her needs. One by one she had cut out the images and now she carefully arranged and taped them onto the wall.

The patchwork looked oddly like a freakish quilt. There were numbers. Twenty-six. Finding that number had boosted her confidence that she was on the right track. Twenty-six was the number of faces and skin books and sets of remains found—all apparently victims of the first man with the tattoo of her mother's name on his back. Antonio Santos, aka Carlos Sanchez.

Perhaps the tattoos were nothing more than badges of proof that each serial killer had been exterminated. That appeared to be what Santos had been doing over the course of about three decades; many of the remains had dated back that far or longer. The question was how did he lure them in and what did her mother have to do with it?

Rowan picked up her glass of wine and downed a gulp. Since moving back to Winchester she most often drank beer with Billy, but tonight she had craved wine. A deep red that both she and Julian had loved. She shuddered at the memories of all the times they had talked shop over glasses of wine. Rowan had felt entirely at ease with him, trusted him completely. What a fool she had been.

He'd had his fun, showing the world what a fool she was. Stealing the life of her father. Why didn't he just tell her whatever else it was he wanted her to know? Why didn't he just do to her whatever it was he wanted to do?

Instead, she was left stumbling through all these pieces that meant nothing to her—or mostly nothing. She and Billy continued to burrow more deeply into their relationship no matter that the threat of whatever Julian had planned hung over them.

Part of her understood that this was in all likelihood exactly what Julian wanted. He was waiting for her to grow complacent. To come to care more deeply about Billy. He wanted to hurt Rowan with Billy the way he had hurt her when he murdered her father. She closed her eyes and held her half-empty glass against her breast. She could not allow that to happen.

Whatever she had to do, she had to find a way to stop this insanity before Julian had a chance to make another move.

There was just one question: How did she do that?

Billy had someone watching her. Pryor had someone watching her.

Pryor's arrogant insistence that she was somehow abetting Julian made her want to scream. The only thing she wanted from Julian was the truth and, at this point, she was almost ready to forgo that and just focus on killing him.

She and Billy would never be safe as long as Julian was breathing. That was the one undeniable, unwavering truth she understood with complete certainty.

Apparently neither would anyone else close to her. Charlotte's name on that list Rowan found in Layton's home was solid proof. To keep pretending otherwise would be foolish. Anna Addington, Julian's ex-wife, was wrong. Julian was obsessed with Rowan rightly enough, but he didn't want her to keep for himself. He wanted to torture her. To hurt everyone close to her before he ended her life. He wanted her to feel the pain, to pray for death. To want to end the pain. He had said those words to her all those months ago when this nightmare first started.

"Enough." Rowan grabbed the bottle of wine and headed up to the third floor. She was tired and she had no idea when Billy would be home.

Before going into the bathroom, she peeked out the window overlooking the front of the funeral home and its parking lot. Rain bashed the window but she could still see the one car that sat near the entrance. This one was Pryor's watcher. She went back into her bedroom—the one she shared with Billy—and looked out a window to the back of the house. Beyond the streams of water sliding down the glass she spotted the other vehicle—a Winchester Police Department cruiser—parked on the side street that ran along the west end of the funeral home property. That one would be Billy's watcher.

With a sigh she moved into the bathroom and turned the tap in the tub to hot. Freud curled up on the rug in the center of the room. As the tub filled with water, she poured another glass, then placed a towel on the bench next to the tub. She downed half the glass as she stripped off her clothes. Lastly, she removed the beautiful necklace Billy had gotten her for her birthday. By the time she was ready to climb into the hot water, she had poured her third glass and was finally feeling relaxed.

She placed her glass on the bench within reach and sank into the heat and closed her eyes, leaning back against the curved back of the slipper-style tub. Her tense muscles instantly started to loosen. She reached for her glass and brought it to her lips. She sipped more of the wine and let the alcohol do its work of sending her to that place where she wouldn't think of Julian or of death.

The glass almost slipped from her hand, but she caught it. Red wine spilled into the water. She watched it spread and dilute until the dark color pinked and then disappeared. Memories of her soaking in this very tub at thirteen and slitting her wrists because she didn't want to live anymore filtered through her mind. She squeezed her eyes shut against the images. Her father had been devastated. He had stopped the bleeding and sutured the wounds to prevent having to take her to the hospital and reporting the incident. He didn't want her to be humiliated later.

She had hurt him so badly with that act, but she had been severely depressed after losing her mother and her sister. She had only wanted to escape the sadness. Not even her loving father had understood the depth of her pain. The only person to whom she'd ever opened up fully was Julian. The bastard.

Besides Julian and her father, Billy was the only other person who had known about that horrifically bad decision as well as the one when she was in college when she'd taken all those pills. At least until she published that damned tell-all book. The world had learned the ugly truth about Rowan DuPont.

She wasn't nearly as strong as she wanted people to believe. As a teenager she had been broken and withdrawn…sad, so very sad.

Rowan downed the rest of the wine and carefully placed the glass on the floor next to the tub. She stared at the scars on the insides of her wrists. Every little detail of her sad childhood she had shared with Julian, first as his patient and later as his friend. How could she not have seen what he was? How he was using her?

She pulled her knees to her chest and lay her head there. Had her father been a fool where her mother was concerned just as she had been with Julian? As painful as learning that her friend and mentor had betrayed her, she could only imagine how badly her father suffered knowing his wife—the person with whom he shared every human intimacy—had betrayed him.

That was assuming her father hadn't known, hadn't been a part of whatever the hell this bizarre past of her mother's really was.

The room started to spin a little and she closed her eyes. She'd had too much wine. She should go to bed but the water felt so good she couldn't move.

Her worries faded and images of her sister filtered one after the other through her mind. Raven smiled at her and swam away.

Rowan was dreaming. She recognized the dream. Whenever she dreamed of Raven, her sister always came to her in the water.

*Come into the water, Rowan!*

Her sister would taunt her and swim away. Her pale skin and blond hair exactly as it had been the day she died. The day her bloated body was dragged from that lake.

In the dream, Rowan swam after her, though that was impossible because she never went swimming. She hadn't been in water beyond a shower or bath or rainstorm since she was twelve years old.

Her fear of water was unreasonable; as a psychiatrist Rowan understood this. But that knowledge did not abate the suffocating fear.

The next voice she heard in her dream whispered to her.

*I'm here, Rowan. Waiting for you.*

*Julian.* Rowan's head came up. Her breath snagged in her throat and the room spun a little.

A dream. Just a dream.

She shivered uncontrollably. A few moments were required for her to realize the water had gone cold. How long had she been dozing?

Freud lifted his head and whined.

"It's okay, boy. Just a bad dream." Rowan pulled the plug and the water growled loudly as it circled the drain.

She climbed out of the tub, still shivering, and quickly toweled off. Since only the ends of her hair were wet she used the towel to squeeze as much of the water out as possible rather than bother with dragging out the hair dryer. When she had pulled on a nightshirt and lounge pants and her necklace, she washed her face and brushed her hair. She gathered her stemmed glass and the nearly empty bottle of wine and went down the stairs to the kitchen.

She washed her glass and left the wine on the counter. She doubted she would finish it, knew without doubt that Billy would not. He hated red wine. Feeling restless, she decided to take a walk through the funeral home and check on things and to let Freud out to relieve himself. With her cell phone and keys in hand, she summoned him and headed that way.

At the second-floor landing she glanced at the banister and moved on. She hadn't dreamed of her mother in a while. Most of her dreams lately had only involved Raven. Dreaming of Julian was new.

And certainly not welcome.

Downstairs, she checked her office, the restrooms and the refreshment lounge. From there she moved back through the lobby, noting the mail lying on the table next to the main entrance, and walked through the chapel and the parlors. All clear, tidy and ready for tomorrow evening's viewing. She moved on into the corridor marked Employees Only. Numerous bouquets of flowers had already arrived for Ms. Donelson. They were stored in the small walk-in cooler. Beyond that cooler was the refrigeration unit. Ms. Donelson was there.

"Night," Rowan called out to her. Her father had always spoken to the clients when he entered or exited the room where they were. Never in front of anyone except Rowan and Raven, when she was still alive. Rowan suspected her father was only showing respect. She was relatively confident he hadn't believed they could hear him. She smiled at the memories. Though once or twice she had found him chatting away with a client he was preparing. The work was lonely. She caught herself doing the same thing on occasion.

She closed the door and locked the unit. Since the Santos body had been stolen she'd kept this unit locked at all times. To have anything stolen was bad enough, having a body taken was the worst possible scenario.

She grabbed the mail in the lobby and climbed the stairs once more. Any lingering effects of the alcohol were gone. She shouldn't have overindulged. Of all people, she knew how foolish too much alcohol and a hot bath could be, particularly with her home alone.

With the mail under her arm, she and Freud went back into the living quarters and locked the door. Billy's voice reminding her to keep all doors locked echoed in her head.

"Yes, sir," she murmured as she flipped the dead bolt.

Freud trailed her to the kitchen. She turned on the flame under the kettle. Tea would be nice. Maybe it would chase away the chill that still lingered from her dream and her snooze in the tub.

She rummaged through the mail. The usual flyers and invoices. A greeting-card-size envelope was tucked between the pile of sale flyers. She picked up the rose-colored envelope and read her name on the front. She turned it over, no return address. The postmark showed it had been mailed from Tullahoma.

Maybe an invitation or a belated birthday card. Having hit forty on her last birthday, she'd had no desire to celebrate—a smile spread across her lips—but Billy had planned a party without her knowledge. The cake had been beautiful, the food and drink and company splendid. He'd given her the stunning necklace. A plain platinum chain with a single teardrop-shaped diamond. She loved it. She fingered it now. Didn't like to take it off but she always did when she bathed and when she went to bed for fear of damaging the delicate chain.

She opened the envelope and removed the card.

*Deepest Sympathies*

She stared at the card. Would someone wait almost a year before sending a card regarding her father's death? She opened the card and a photograph fell onto the counter.

*Billy.*

Her heart crowded into her throat. In the photograph Billy was coming out of city hall, descending the steps.

She stared at the words written inside the otherwise blank card.

*Rowan,*
*You cannot protect him if you don't recognize the enemy.*
*Julian*

Her heart slid back down her throat and started to pound. "Son of a bitch!"

* * *

Billy was tired when he finally made it home. The briefing and conference calls with the task force had taken endless hours and had offered nothing new. How the hell could this many people be focused on finding one damned man and get nowhere?

The Julian Addington task force spent more time chasing its tail than making any headway on the investigation.

He locked the funeral home's main entrance and re-armed the security system. The night shift officer was still on the side street. Pryor's man was in the front parking lot. He'd waved to Billy when he arrived. Billy imagined Rowan was still livid about Pryor's innuendos.

She needn't worry, Billy had set him straight.

Rowan had no idea where Addington was and she had been just as surprised as Billy was to learn Dressler was missing.

As usual, the damned FBI was not only barking up the wrong tree, they were in the wrong damned forest.

Climbing the stairs zapped the last of his energy. He needed to see Rowan's face and then have a shower and a beer. Maybe food.

Freud met him at the door. Billy was thankful Rowan had kept that door locked as well. He wanted her safe. To make that happen, he needed her to cooperate.

Lately he'd been toying with the idea of finding a way to send a message to Addington. If he could lure the bastard into the right situation, he could finish this and ensure Rowan was safe. Except there was a law against vigilantism. Billy had been a lawman most of his adult life and still he despised the idea of the law protecting someone as depraved as Addington.

But the law protected all people and Billy had sworn to uphold it.

He peeked into the bedroom. Rowan was asleep. Her silky hair spread over the pillow. He smiled. She was so beautiful and he loved her so much. He thought of the ring he had tucked away in the glove box of his truck. He'd wanted to give it to her before now but the case had gotten in the way.

Something else that made Billy want to kill the bastard.

Freud climbed back onto his mat at the foot of the bed. Billy took the shortest shower in the history of showers, ate a peanut butter sandwich and guzzled down a beer, brushed his teeth and then climbed into bed with Rowan. He didn't feel complete until he had her in his arms.

He reached to turn off the lamp on the bedside table.

"You're home awfully late," she said softly.

He drew his hand back without turning off the light and peered down at her, couldn't help the broad smile that stretched across his lips. "You can thank our new friend, Agent Pryor."

Pryor had been in the background for the past year. He'd kept his finger on the pulse of the task force's investigation but never got involved on the ground. He outranked Dressler and the others on the task force. But with Dressler missing, Pryor had evidently decided he needed to be more hands-on.

Rowan rolled her pretty blue eyes at his comment. "I hardly know him and already I dislike him immensely."

Billy laughed. "I'm right there with you."

A soft hand settled on his bare chest. "Any updates I need to know about?"

"Not one thing. The entire evening was a monumental waste of time and resources. It's like they're going in circles. If Pryor has been running this show from behind the scenes all this time, it's no wonder Addington hasn't been found."

She frowned, those velvety fingers tracing the contours of his chest. "I've had my differences with Josh and the Bureau in general, but I've never known them to perform so inadequately. What we've seen the past few months feels unreasonably inept."

He reached down and trailed a finger along her cheek, loving the feel of her smooth skin. "Maybe there is a leak and that leak is somehow creating an information gap."

"I suppose that would do it," Rowan agreed. "Have them going in circles, I mean."

"Mmm-hmm." Billy's mind had shifted from work to other ideas.

"I went to see Beulah Alcott, but don't worry. Charlotte went with me so I wasn't alone."

"She wasn't home?"

"I knew you had someone following me." Rowan laughed, the sound rumbling against him making him want to roll her over and take her without any foreplay.

"I wasn't sure about her not being home. I only knew that you weren't at her house for long enough to actually have spoken with her. Ms. Alcott has her own way of getting around to things in a conversation."

Rowan sighed, her warm breath fanning over his skin. "She left a note for me to come back tomorrow. I have no idea how she knew I was coming but somehow she was expecting me."

"She has her ways." Billy didn't know why he bothered to say more. He knew the answer before he made the comment. "I suppose you're going."

Of course she was.

"I am. Charlotte will go with me."

"Okay."

Rowan rose up onto her elbows. "Okay?" She felt his forehead. "Are you ill? Where's the usual argument of why I can't go without you?"

He grinned as he lay back against his pillow. "You'll have plenty of backup."

She shook her head and folded her hands on his chest so she could rest her chin there. "True. So I guess you really don't have to worry about me anymore."

He chuckled. "Right."

She was silent for a moment and apprehension started its slow creep into his gut.

"There's something I should show you."

"Oh hell." One of these days maybe they would have five minutes of time together without Addington somehow managing to worm his way into the moment.

She sat up and reached for something on her bedside table. She thrust a sympathy card at him and a photo of him coming out of the office.

A frown worried his forehead. "What's all this?"

"Read the note in the card."

He laid the photo aside and opened the card. Fury bolted through him. "When did you get this?"

She was bad to keep things from him for a period of time. He had hoped she would stop holding back but he tried not to be too pushy on the subject. Rowan was an experienced investigator. She didn't need him telling her what she was supposed to do and when she should do it. She was well aware; she simply chose not to do them sometimes.

"It was in today's mail, but I didn't see it until tonight when I let Freud out."

He uttered a few choice words. Didn't do a damned thing to help the situation but somehow it made him feel better.

"My sentiments exactly," she agreed.

He placed the photo and the card on the table on his side of the bed and pulled her into his arms, her cheek resting against his chest. "We're going to get him. I promise you that."

"I know. I just worry that someone else will be hurt before that happens. I spoke to Charlotte about her name being on that list we found. She refuses to take a leave of absence." Rowan lifted her head so she could look him in the eyes. "Did you know she wears a thigh holster with a snub-nosed .38?"

"Seriously?" Billy laughed. "That's kind of sexy."

Rowan lowered her cheek back to his chest. "I suppose now you'll want me to start wearing one."

"You're as sexy as hell just as you are. But I am glad you keep your weapon with you. I don't want you to stop."

Her leg moved into the part between his and she eased her upper body farther up onto his torso. "I didn't know you thought I was sexy. You never said so before."

He forked his fingers into her hair and held her face so that she stared directly into his eyes. "You are the most beautiful woman I have ever met. Every part of you, every move you make, is sexy. Just watching you walk across the room makes it hard for me to breathe."

She kissed him. Slow and soft at first. Then she kissed him harder. He rolled her onto her back and took control of the kiss. If he died tomorrow he would die satisfied having made love to this woman. The one thing he wanted more than anything else was to show her how incredible she was…to show her how much he wanted her. He wanted to do exactly that for the rest of his days.

Later, she fell asleep in his arms and Billy was certain that nothing would ever feel as amazing as simply holding her close like this.

Fury burned through those softer emotions as he considered that Addington was still watching her. He was still close enough to strike. Too damned close.

Billy had to finish this. Soon.

# *Eight*

"You look just like her."

Rowan smiled no matter that she didn't feel like smiling. "I get that all the time."

Anyone who had known Rowan's mother swore Rowan was her spitting image. After her mother's death, the words had not warmed Rowan as they had previously. The one person who had never told her she looked like her mother was her father. Had he, too, resented Norah for how she had decided to leave them? After all, Rowan wasn't the only one Norah deserted when she hung herself.

Beulah Alcott studied her closely with her one green eye and one blue eye. "She loved you very much."

Rowan blinked, startled at the idea that this woman seemed to know what she was thinking. "I'm sorry. I was lost in thought. Who loved me?"

"Why, your momma, of course." Beulah chuckled. "She was too sensitive. Too caring. It was the death of her. You're like her in that way, too."

Rowan kept her lips pinched closely together. The woman was quite elderly. At least ninety, she would estimate. Silvery hair framed her dark face, the contrast as calming as it was eye-catching. The flannel shirt and long denim skirt swallowed her tiny body. Despite her small statue and her frail-with-age voice, there was something strong and powerful about her presence. The air literally vibrated around her.

"My mother hung herself," Rowan reminded the elderly woman.

"Sometimes sacrifices must be made, child," she warned. "Don't let all them book smarts get in the way of seeing what needs to be seen."

"What do I need to see?" Rowan tried very hard to keep resentment from her tone, but it was difficult.

"You can't forgive her for leaving you and she couldn't live with the idea that she hadn't left soon enough."

What was that supposed to mean? "I really have no idea what that means, Ms. Alcott. I do want to understand what motivated my mother, but I haven't discovered anything that suggests what she did was a selfless act."

"She blamed herself for Raven's death." Beulah nodded somberly. "She couldn't get past it. As much as she wanted to pretend it wouldn't happen again, she knew it would. So she did the only thing she could. She stopped fighting it. Took herself out of the equation. She really thought that would end it, but it didn't."

Frustration tightened its grip on Rowan. "End what?"

The older lady stared at her. "You know what. Don't pretend you don't."

Rowan summoned her patience. "If I already had the answers, I wouldn't have come to you with questions."

"I can't make you see what you don't want to see, Rowan. You have to see it with your heart, not with your eyes."

"Tell me what you saw in my mother."

Alcott stared at her for a long moment. "Your mother saw things." She shook her head and scrunched up her face. "Bad, bad things. Things no one should ever have to see. She tried to fix the trouble, but she only made things worse for her."

Rowan tamped down her frustration before it purged from her in a storm of fury. This lady was trying to help. Enough time wasted on the subject of her mother. Rowan opened the photographs app on her phone and moved to the older woman's side. She crouched down next to her chair and showed her the first photograph.

"There are tattoos on the bodies of two men who were somehow involved with Norah. Have you seen anything like these before?"

Alcott looked at the photos, one by one, taking her time. Rowan wasn't sure what to make of her not reaching for a pair of reading glasses. Most people her age had vision issues. Perhaps she only pretended to study the photos.

"This one—" she tapped a photo of Santos "—was very close to your mother."

Since there was no face in the photo, only the tattooed torso and arms, Rowan wasn't sure how Alcott made that call.

"How do you know?"

She pointed to the photo again. "The black birds.

They stay close and watch. He was more than a black bird. He watched, stayed close, but he also acted." She tapped the screen again. "The two circles intertwined. See them? They were linked. This one and your mother."

"What about these images?" Rowan slid the screen to another photo. "They look like the parts of a puzzle. They don't seem to have any other significant meaning other than the absence of the whole or a broken link. They go with something else and represent nothing in their own right."

"As long as the evil is broken, it is weak, but when it becomes whole, it gains strength. The pieces of evil have been shattered and scattered. They can never be pieced back together." Her gaze lifted to Rowan's. "But there is more. This is the reason you cannot falter."

Rowan held her gaze a moment. "Me?"

"You are the undertaker now. You help the dead make the transition from this life to the next. You are her daughter. Only you have the power to stop this."

"Do you mean him? Stop him? Dr. Julian Addington?"

"See," she mused. "You do have the answers. What you do with those answers is up to you."

Rowan thanked her and stood to go. She wanted to turn back to the woman and demand that she tell her more. What she had was nothing more than new riddles. So much talk but no explanations. No understanding of what any of this meant other than Julian was the enemy. Julian had to be stopped. She was the only one who could stop him. These things she knew.

Perhaps she did have the answers.

At the door she hesitated. She didn't believe in any of this. Not the tarot cards, not the fortune-telling, none of it. She believed in what was real. Actions, reactions. What she could see and touch.

Despite this knowledge, she hesitated, her hand on the door, and turned back to the woman. "I don't want to be the reason anyone else dies."

"Then look for the one who can help you stop him. No one else can do it. Only you, but she can point you in the right direction."

"The one?"

"She's here already. She came a very long way to find you. You'll see."

Once again, the lady said plenty and yet nothing at all.

Charlotte waited in Rowan's SUV. She had gone to the door with Rowan, but Alcott hadn't wanted to see anyone but Rowan. Since there was a cop and an FBI agent parked in separate vehicles right behind Charlotte, Rowan hadn't worried about her safety. To some degree she might have been safer out here than inside.

"Did you learn anything helpful?"

Rowan gave her a look that she hoped relayed the depth of her confusion. "I really have no idea." She started the engine and shifted into Reverse. The vehicles behind her were already backing up. "She said a lot but not much that told me anything."

"What now?"

Charlotte looked to Rowan. Rowan felt a weary smile nudge at her lips, but this was far from an uplifting moment. "You're sure you want to keep getting deeper into this? This is not a game, Charlotte. A lot of people have died. I'm worried there will be more before this is over."

She'd already warned her assistant and friend but the woman just wouldn't listen. Rowan supposed how she felt about Charlotte refusing to bow out was the same way Billy was feeling about her insistence on seeing this through. The difference was that Rowan didn't really have a choice. Charlotte could walk away without looking back.

Charlotte patted her thigh. "I'm not backing down, Ro. Besides, we've got our own private security parade."

Rowan glanced in the rearview mirror as she turned back onto the road. The WPD cruiser followed right behind her, the unmarked sedan next. "This is true."

"What's the deal with this FBI guy who's missing? Is he a friend of yours?"

Charlotte sat in the seat, her body angled slightly toward Rowan. From time to time she glanced behind them and then forward. Rowan had a feeling Charlotte was a little more anxious than she wanted to admit. Good. She should be afraid. This was a very dangerous situation.

"Josh Dressler." Rowan braked for the stop sign where this side road intersected with the main highway. Another left and they would be headed back toward Winchester. "I've known him a long time. We've worked together on several cases but nothing more."

"Oh."

With no oncoming traffic, Rowan pulled out onto the highway. "Oh?"

"I just meant that Billy sort of looked a little, I don't know, out of sorts about him."

"Josh may have asked me out a few times," Rowan said with all the nonchalance she could muster. "I always said no, but that didn't stop him from asking again."

"Josh." Charlotte nodded. "I see."

"No," Rowan assured her. "You don't see. There was no mutual attraction."

"So what now?" Charlotte said, repeating her earlier question.

"Since you mentioned Josh, I think we'll stop by the cemetery where he was allegedly last seen."

Charlotte faced forward. "You think all those cops and feds investigating the scene at the cemetery might have missed something?"

Rowan shook her head. "I think that's doubtful, but the lady who saw him may have left something out."

"How do you know that?"

"I don't know it. I'm following up on a long shot."

"This is what you did in Nashville. You worked with the detectives and offered suggestions on what they might have missed or where they might need to look next."

"Basically." Rowan glanced at her passenger again. "Did Billy tell you that?"

"No. Your dad. He was always bragging about you."

Rowan smiled. "Thank you for telling me."

No matter what secrets her father kept or what darkness he may have hidden, Rowan knew without doubt that he had loved her, that he was a good man.

Her mother was the questionable one.

Rowan parked on the street outside the main entrance to the cemetery. The DuPont family plot was still marked off as a crime scene. Didn't matter. There was nothing there that Rowan needed to see this morning. With Charlotte at her side, Rowan knocked on the shop entrance of the witness who had seen Josh.

When the young woman opened the door, Rowan asked, "Delilah Dixon?"

"I'm Delilah Dixon," she said, her voice steady but her expression wary.

"I wanted to ask you a few more questions about the man you saw in the cemetery night before last."

Dixon rolled her eyes. "Seriously? How many more people am I going to have to talk to?"

Rowan purposely hadn't identified herself in hopes the woman would assume she was another detective. "I assure you this is the only time you'll have to worry about questions from me."

"Fine. What is it you want to ask?"

Since she made no invitation to go inside but didn't refuse to talk, Rowan proceeded. "Did you see a vehicle you didn't recognize on the street or in the cemetery?"

Cars weren't supposed to enter at this entrance, particularly after dark, but people didn't always follow the rules.

"Like I told the others, I did not see any cars that don't belong in this neighborhood. Lots of times people park along this block to carry flowers into the cemetery or just to visit their folks buried there, but it doesn't usually happen so late in the evening. I guess that's another reason I was so surprised to see someone in there. There was no car."

"But he could have parked on another street and walked over."

She shrugged. "Sure."

"Did you notice anything odd about him?" Rowan asked next. "Did he appear nervous or shaken or scared? Anything like that?"

"He seemed surprised to see me walk up." She turned her hands up. She wore lots of rings, some on every finger as well as her thumbs. "Like he'd been lost in thought and I came upon him before he realized anyone was around."

"Do you remember what he was wearing?"

"It was kind of dark." Her face creased into a frown. "I think maybe he was wearing a suit." She tugged at the lapels of her sweater. "You know, a jacket and trousers. Dark. Maybe navy or dark gray. It was just too dark to say for sure. I didn't notice the color of his shirt."

Which meant it was dark as well. "You stated previously that he didn't say anything to you—have you recalled differently since you were interviewed?"

She wagged her head side to side. "He just walked away when he saw me."

"Which way did he go? Back toward the entrance or another way?"

She pointed to the entrance gate that faced her street. "He walked out that entrance."

"So you watched him for a moment when he walked away?"

Her frown reappeared. "Yeah, I guess I did."

"Which way did he go once he was outside the gate?"

"That way." She pointed south. "Toward the funeral home." Her gaze widened with recognition. "I know you. You're the undertaker. Rowan DuPont."

"Thank you, Ms. Dixon. We appreciate your help."

Rowan hurried away before the lady could think of anything else to ask.

"He was at your family plot and walked toward the funeral home," Charlotte said, quickening her stride to keep up with Rowan. "Sounds like he came here looking for you."

If he had come to see Rowan, he would have shown up at her door or at Billy's office. He hadn't been looking for Rowan. He was *watching* her.

But why drop off the grid to do that?

A man sat on the bench near the entrance of the funeral home when Rowan and Charlotte pulled into the parking lot. From half a block away when Rowan first spotted someone on the bench, she had hoped it might be Josh. That perhaps he was ready to tell her whatever was going on.

But it wasn't him.

*Owen Utter.*

The man who had lived next door to Antonio Santos. The Skin Man, as the FBI had dubbed him.

"Who's he?"

"A witness in the Santos case." Rowan shut off the engine. "You go on in and get started preparing for this evening's viewing. I'll see what Mr. Utter needs."

Rowan glanced in the rearview mirror and noted the sedan on the street. She didn't have to check to know that the WPD cruiser would be in his usual spot watching the back of the funeral home.

"You need to borrow Shorty?"

"No, thanks." Rowan picked up her purse from the floorboard. "I have my own shorty."

"Good for you."

They climbed out at the same time. Charlotte unlocked the door and went inside. Rowan sat down on the bench next to Mr. Utter.

"I thought you moved away," she said. He'd been MIA for months now. She'd tried to find him a couple of times to ask more questions about Santos—the neighbor he had known as Sanchez. No one seemed to have any idea what happened to the man. For such a small town, people seemed capable of disappearing quite easily.

"Nah, just found a new place to live. Too much excitement over there in Bell View. I needed someplace a little more quiet. I don't like too much attention."

Owen Utter was a short man, a little on the heavy side. Well into sixty. His gray hair was perpetually mussed. He'd led her and Billy into the woods to the place that turned out to be the burial grounds for all those remains. Twenty-six sets of human remains. More than two dozen murder victims right here in Franklin County they wouldn't even have known about if they hadn't found those faces and those books of skin in that low-budget little apartment rented by Antonio Santos, aka Carlos Sanchez.

"What brings you to see me?"

Rowan felt confident there was a reason Utter had shown his face again. He had to know the police had been looking for him. He was needed for further questioning related to Santos and all those dead people who had turned out to be serial killers. Not that he was really a suspect in their deaths but he had known the location of their remains.

"Someone gave me a message for you." He looked

directly at her now, his eyes wide as if the message was too much of a burden for him to continue carrying.

"Who?"

He shook his head and shrugged. "I don't know. He whispered it in my ear. I was sleeping but his voice woke me up."

There was a strong possibility that this man suffered from some sort of mental health issue or was on some sort of drugs, prescription or otherwise. Any number of things could have caused him to have hallucinations, which was why she didn't doubt that he believed someone had whispered a message to him. He assuredly would not have risked coming to see her otherwise. That said, whether there was any merit to his claim was a whole other story.

"All right, then. What did this unidentified person say to you?"

"It was a man." He nodded adamantly. "The voice was a man's. He whispered in my ear. Said I should give you a message."

Rowan nodded, hoping he would spit it out.

"He said to tell you that *he* was here."

Before she could stop the reaction, a shiver wiggled through her. Alcott had said someone was coming to see her but she'd said the person was a *she*. Maybe she'd only gotten half of her vision right.

Rowan barely resisted shaking her head at her own thoughts.

"Who is *he*, Mr. Utter? It doesn't help if you don't know who he is."

"He said you would know."

If anyone else told her she should already have the answer she was going to explode.

"Thank you, Mr. Utter. I appreciate you coming all this way to tell me. Can I take you home?"

If there was even a remote possibility that Julian had spoken to this man, Rowan needed to know where this happened. Julian could still be there. There was a very real possibility in Rowan's opinion that he was in the Winchester area. Alcott had as same as said he was here. The card he'd sent Rowan had a Tullahoma postmark.

Utter shook his head fast enough to give himself whiplash and shot to his feet. "No thanks. Take care of yourself, Dr. DuPont."

As he walked away it took every ounce of willpower Rowan possessed not to follow him. She watched him toddle along the sidewalk until he was out of sight. She needed to know where he lived. She needed to talk to people who lived around him. That would be just like Julian to hide out in plain sight among the least fortunate of people in the most unlikely of places.

Rowan walked back to her SUV and climbed in. The cop and the agent would follow her, but she didn't care. She called Charlotte.

"You still outside?" her assistant asked.

"No. I have an errand to run. Are you okay with the rest of the preparations for this evening's viewing? If you need me I can get back as quickly as possible."

"Don't worry. I've got this. Just be careful. Are those guys following you?"

Rowan glanced in her rearview mirror. "Oh yeah.

Make sure you lock the doors and arm the security system."

"Already done."

"See you in a bit."

Rowan ended the call and surveyed the sidewalks as she drove block after block. Where the hell had he gone? Someone must have picked him up. He could not have disappeared that quickly.

She would find him. She knew just where to look.

# *Nine*

Rowan started with the most likely places. The streets with the low-end rental houses and apartments. Bell View and neighborhoods like it. The few trailer parks scattered around town. She drove from Winchester to Decherd. No one she encountered admitted to knowing about a so-called tent city.

When she had driven every potential street in both Winchester and Decherd, she stopped for gas at a convenience store that also served as a sign-up location for homeless sponsors. A person in need could sign up for clothes or shoes, for example, and a customer shopping at the convenience store could "sponsor" that person and buy the needed items. The funeral home sponsored several people each fall to help with staying warm in the winter. Rowan's father had also donated annually to a shelter in Decherd that was the largest in the county.

Though Winchester and Decherd were different towns, it was difficult to tell where one ended and the other began.

After filling her gas tank, she wandered inside for a bottle of water. The man behind the counter glanced at the two vehicles that had followed her into the lot and asked, "Friends of yours?"

Rowan placed the water on the counter. "I guess I'm what you would call a celebrity."

The man grinned. "I know who you are." He hit the total key on the register. "One-fifty."

She handed him the cash. "See, I told you I was a celebrity."

He chuckled. "I knew your daddy, too. A fine man." He hitched his head toward the parking lot. "They following you around to protect you from that killer who murdered your daddy?"

Rowan nodded. "Sadly, yes."

"I heard about that fella they found on your momma's grave. That's some creepy stuff."

"It is." She picked up the bottle of water and decided to see if the friendly gentleman would be so talkative when he learned why she had chosen his store over numerous others. "Are you familiar with a place called tent city?"

He nodded. "I am."

"Do you know where it is?" Surely he did. The folks who lived there no doubt came to his store if for nothing more than to sign up for assistance.

"They move around a lot." He glanced at the parking lot as he said the words.

"I'm not asking to help the police cause trouble for them," she hastened to explain. "I'm looking for a man who lives there. I need his help and I can't find him."

He leaned on the counter, putting his face closer to hers. "DuPonts have always been generous to the homeless. That cause is close to my heart. I used to be homeless and someone helped me out and now I own this store."

"That's amazing. Congratulations. I'm certain you are an inspiration to all those in need." Rowan wondered if he'd ever done an interview for Audrey Anderson over at the *Gazette*. "Thank you for sharing your story with me."

"I tell you what, Dr. DuPont, you pledge to sponsor twice as many this year and I'll tell you what you want to know."

A smile slid across her lips. "You have a deal, sir."

He extended his hand. "Fletcher Holmes."

Rowan shook the offered hand. "It's a pleasure to meet you, Mr. Holmes."

"Fletch. That's what everyone calls me."

"Fletch. You should call me Rowan."

He nodded. "Well, Rowan, the place you're looking for is off Highway 16, Keith Springs Mountain Road. Just stay on that road until you see Old Rowe Gap Road. Drive slow along that road. You're looking for a yellow ribbon hung on a tree branch. Once you spot it, pull off the road. You'll have to walk from there."

"Thank you so much. I really appreciate your help."

"Take some cookies, candy bars or chips," he suggested. "They don't get snacks like that often. It might make what's following you a little less problematic."

"Good idea."

Rowan walked out of the store with four plastic bags overflowing with a variety of cookies, candy bars and chips. If he'd had any fresh fruit she would have bought that as well, but he'd sold out earlier in the day. She stowed the bags on the passenger side, slid behind the wheel and headed back across town. Keith Springs

Mountain Road was on the Huntland side of Winchester. The road rolled out into the country and then snaked up the mountain.

The trip took a full twenty minutes. Her security team followed right behind her. She imagined the officer in the WPD cruiser had already reported her movements to Billy. She'd likely get a call anytime now.

Once she'd made the turn onto Old Rowe Gap Road, she slowed down to a crawl and peered at the thick woods on either side of the road. He hadn't mentioned which side. Probably depended on which end of Old Rowe Gap Road you started at. The road snaked through the woods and came out on Keith Springs Mountain Road closer to the base of the mountain.

She missed the yellow ribbon on her first pass. But after turning around at the end of the road and retracing her path, she spotted it. Fortunately there was a decent shoulder to pull onto, rather than just a ditch. She parked and climbed out. With her cell tucked into one hip pocket and her key fob in the other, she slid her weapon in her waistband at the small of her back. After covering the weapon with her sweatshirt, she grabbed the bags. She bumped the door shut with her hip and hit the lock mechanism.

She was several yards into the woods when one of the men shouted, "Dr. DuPont!"

Rowan glanced back. The uniformed officer had gotten out of his car and was already following her, but the FBI agent didn't appear so inclined.

She paused for the officer to catch up. "Yes?"

"Can you tell me where you're going, ma'am?"

"To see a friend. No need for you to tag along."

The federal agent now leaned against his sedan and

had withdrawn his cell. He was probably calling Pryor. Nothing she could do about his actions.

While the officer seemed to contemplate what to do, she moved on.

The path wasn't exactly clear, but she spotted the occasional broken limb or trampled brush that suggested foot traffic had been through. She stayed with the vague path. She hadn't gotten far when the officer called out to her again.

"Dr. DuPont."

She paused and turned back once more. He wasn't far behind her. "Yes?"

"Would you like me to carry those bags?"

"As a matter of fact, I would." This was precisely why she had made the snack purchases. Well, this and to be kind. Of course, she couldn't take credit for the brilliant idea. That had been the store owner's. Since the officer was determined to follow her into the woods, it was imperative that he appear a friend rather than a foe.

She waited for him to reach her position, then she handed him the bags. "Thank you—" she glanced at this name tag "—Officer Gabrielle."

"No problem, ma'am."

Rowan picked her way along the path. Underbrush clawed at her jeans. Billy had told her Ms. Alcott's place was considerably overgrown, so both yesterday and today Rowan had dressed appropriate. Hiking boots, jeans and a sweatshirt. She'd tucked her hair into a ponytail. She had never been more glad to dress so casually than she was now.

"Does this friend camp out in these woods, ma'am? As far as I know no one lives out here."

"I was told he lives here," she answered without looking back. "I suppose we'll see if the information I was given is correct."

A partial view of the first gray top of a tent snagged her attention. Her pulse rate reacted to a blast of anticipation. As she moved closer, winding in the direction of the tent, more of the same came into view. The dwellers had positioned their tents more carefully this time. The colorful ones—reds, blues and yellows—were in the back nearer to the thicker trees and heavier underbrush. The sandy or gray ones that blended into the late-winter surroundings better were in front. All looked old, the colors faded with patches in the fabric here and there.

"Well, I'll be damned," the officer behind her muttered.

As they reached the small, main clearing, Rowan paused. "Officer Gabrielle, I'd like you to wait right here."

"Ma'am, I have my orders to keep you in sight."

"I think we can manage that without you following me any farther. The bags are for the people here." Rowan smiled at him and moved on.

He did as she asked, looking like a mannequin advertising a grocery store with those bulging bags in hand. She hoped the name of the convenience store stamped in blue on the white plastic would set the folks who lived here at ease.

Faces peeked from their tents but only two dwellers emerged. Both men. Both looked directly at her.

"You lost, lady?" the taller one asked.

"No, sir, thank you. I'm here looking for a friend." She tugged the cell from her pocket and pulled up a photo of Julian. Turning the screen so the two men could see it, she asked, "Have you seen him around here? He has dementia and I'm very worried about him."

The one who asked if she was lost shook his head. "I don't know him."

The other looked from the screen to her and back. "I can't be sure," he mumbled.

"What's *he* here for?" tall man asked with a nod behind her.

Rowan looked back. Officer Gabrielle was surrounded by children. Rowan did a quick head count. Ten kids. He was busy digging goodies from the bags and passing them out. She turned back to the two men. "He came to help me if my uncle grew combatant. He's very ill. You might not recognize the problem when you first meet him, but he can't conceal the trouble for long. He can be quite dangerous."

The two looked at each other. Rowan's anticipation climbed. They had seen him. That was obvious in their body language and in their vague answers. Her heart started to pound a little faster.

"There's a tent over that way." The shorter man hitched his head toward the north. "He stays away from everyone else. I didn't get a real good look at him, but that might be your uncle."

"I saw Mr. Utter earlier today," Rowan said. "Has he returned yet?"

"He came through a few minutes, maybe half an hour, ago," tall man said. "Went back to the tent he—" he nodded toward the other man "—mentioned."

"Thank you." Rowan turned and waved to the officer.

He handed the bags to the kids and headed her way. The two men who'd spoken to her ducked back into their tents. Neither wanted to risk the officer getting too close while they were out in the open.

"Yes, ma'am?"

"We're going this way," she said as she headed beyond the cluster of tents.

When they had moved beyond the main cluster of tents, she spotted a lone one thirty or so yards in the distance, tucked into the trees and underbrush. As she drew closer, it was obvious this tent was not like the others. It was new. Very sleek-looking. An expensive tent. Rowan instinctively reached beneath her sweatshirt and curled her fingers around her weapon.

Gabrielle tapped her on the shoulder. She stopped, turned to him, and he motioned for her to let him go first. She started to argue but he was the one with the most field training, so she relented. Besides, the officer would have to answer to Billy if she refused his offer and his chief found out.

They approached the tent as silently as possible considering the leaves and twigs layering the ground. Once again Gabrielle motioned for her to stay behind him. As annoying as it was, she did so. The entrance to the tent was unzipped.

"Police," Gabrielle announced. "Whoever's inside the tent, come on out."

Rowan held her breath. No sound. No movement.

Though every part of her understood that Julian likely was not in that tent at the moment, she was certain he had been here.

Standing back from the entrance, Gabrielle used the barrel of his weapon to push aside the flap. When there was still no sound or movement, he crouched down and had a look.

"Holy hell."

The horror in his voice sent a chill through her, sending goose bumps rising on her skin. Rowan crouched beside him to have a look.

Owen Utter was in the tent, his throat slashed, blood still oozing from the wound.

Gabrielle called for backup and emergency medical care while Rowan checked the man's pulse. Nothing. Skin was cold. His eyes were wide-open. She used the flashlight app on her cell to check for a response from his pupils. Nothing. A massive puddle of blood had pooled on the nylon floor of the tent creating an ominous circle around his body. He was dead. No amount of resuscitation attempts would help at this point.

She glanced around the interior of the tent and saw nothing but the blood. "There's nothing we can do for him, Officer Gabrielle."

He nodded somberly. "I'll need to protect the scene until backup arrives."

Rowan was aware of the routine, but he might not know she was an experienced investigator and she couldn't wait. "Do you have gloves with you? I need to check inside his mouth."

Thankfully without questioning her, he opened a small pouch on his utility belt and removed a pair of latex gloves. "Here you go, ma'am."

Rowan thanked him and tugged on the gloves. Before when Julian left a victim in a similar condition outside the funeral home, he also left Rowan a note. Usually tucked into a small plastic bag and inserted into the victim's mouth or into the wound itself. If there wasn't a note in Utter's mouth she would wait for the coroner to check the wound.

*Burt.*

Her chest squeezed. Burt wouldn't be coming. An ache pierced her.

Pushing aside the sad thoughts, she did a swipe through Utter's mouth. They hadn't found a note in Layton's mouth, but this time could be different. Her breath caught when she encountered an object. She pulled it from his mouth and it was a small plastic bag with a folded paper inside just like the previous ones.

Julian had been here.

And Utter had been foolish enough to do his bidding.

She removed the paper and unfolded it. Read the words scrawled in Julian's bold strokes.

*Rowan, sorry I missed you. See you soon. Julian*

She pushed to her feet and scanned the woods now seemingly closing around them. Fury bolted through her. "What're you waiting for, you son of a bitch?"

Her words echoed through the trees, made her flinch.

"Ma'am?"

She ignored Gabrielle. He didn't understand. He didn't get it. Another person was dead because of her.

Within half an hour cops were combing the woods. The residents of tent city glared at Rowan as if she'd brought a biblical plague down on them. What they didn't realize was that the plague had already been here and gone, leaving only one casualty. They were incredibly lucky only one of them had died by his hand.

Rowan stood on the fringes of the buzz of activity.

She felt cold and alone. How the hell did Julian keep eluding the police and the FBI? He was an old man, for God's sake. Why wasn't he exhausted from this deadly cat and mouse game?

She was worn-out from it all. She wanted it to end.

He had told her he would do this. He had promised that she would want the pain to end.

"You got what you wanted, you bastard," she murmured. "Now let's finish this."

"Ro."

She lifted her gaze to Billy's, at once grateful to hear his voice and dreading what he would say about her recent activities. Her statement had been given. Billy had asked the questions, but Pryor had been standing by. They knew about Utter's visit and his message. Gabrielle had filled them in on all the places she visited before coming to this location. The idea that many of the tent city dwellers were already taking down their tents to move sickened her. She had brought trouble to their door yet again. Forced them to move. Though it was mid-March, many of the nights were still cold. Finding a usable location where they wouldn't be discovered had to be difficult.

This, too, was her fault.

She summoned her failing wherewithal and responded to Billy, "Yes."

"Would you like Gabrielle to take you back to the funeral home?"

That was the last thing she had expected him to say. She had anticipated that he would scold her for all that she had done this day. Going off investigating without him. Getting into things that might get her hurt. Failing to keep him informed. But he said none of that.

"My car is out there. I can drive." She took a breath. "Ms. Donelson's viewing is tonight. I should get back, yes."

"I'll have Gabrielle follow you and finish out his shift."

She stared at Billy, couldn't help it. "Is that all?"

Maybe she felt guilty for letting him down yet again. Maybe that was the reason she couldn't be thankful he wasn't giving her hell for not being careful enough. She wanted him to yell at her. To be disappointed in her actions. To remind her that she'd disappointed him like a dozen other times.

He nodded. "That's all I can think of at the moment."

She blinked. Decided she had pushed him over the edge and he couldn't argue with her anymore. He was too weary of the battle to fight it any longer. Wow. She had really done it this time.

"Okay."

She turned and started back toward the road.

"Ro."

She paused, turned back to him.

"I'm glad you're okay."

She nodded. Couldn't speak without the risk of falling apart. Because she wasn't okay. Another man was dead. Billy was disappointed in her and Julian just wouldn't stop.

The walk back to her car felt like a death march. She sensed the homeless people staring at her. They knew what she was. She was the reason trouble had descended upon them. She was the reason one of them was dead. When she reached her car and climbed in, she fought to keep the tears at bay.

Julian Addington was not worthy of her tears.

She had cried because of him too many times already.

The victims were the ones who deserved something from her and it sure as hell was not tears. They deserved justice, damn it.

By the time she reached the funeral home she was so furious she could scream. She grabbed her bag and stomped to the door. Gabrielle waved as he drove on past the front parking lot to take his usual position. The nondescript sedan the FBI agent drove pulled to a stop on the street in front of the funeral home.

She unlocked the door and then relocked it after closing it behind her.

Freud and Charlotte met her in the lobby. "You okay?"

Rowan shook her head. Not trusting her voice. As if he sensed her distress, Freud trotted over to her and pushed his head under her hand. She scratched him behind the ears, tried to smile. Failed.

"Everything's ready," Charlotte assured her. "We have plenty of time. Why don't you go relax for a while?"

Rowan nodded and headed for the stairs.

"There was a woman," Charlotte said.

Rowan paused at the newel post and turned back to her.

"She stopped by a couple of hours ago and said she needed to see you. She said she had come a long way to find you."

Beulah Alcott's words echoed inside Rowan. She had said a woman was coming—one who had come a long way to see Rowan.

"I offered to call you," she went on, "but she said

she would come back tomorrow. She didn't leave her name or a phone number." Charlotte held out an envelope. "But she did leave this. Maybe her name and number are in there."

Rowan took the envelope, too tired to work up any specific emotion. She opened it and pulled out an old photograph. There was nothing else inside. The photograph was the sort taken with film and then developed. She instantly recognized one of the two women in the photo. *Her mother.* The other woman, a brunette, looked to be around the same age as her mother but she didn't look familiar. She held a single, long-stemmed red rose. The two smiled as if sharing a secret only they knew.

"Does this look like the woman who was here?" Rowan showed the photo to her assistant.

Charlotte studied the image a moment. "It does. Her hair was sprinkled with gray and she was older, obviously, but I think that's her. Yeah." She frowned and looked closer still. "Is that your mother?"

Rowan swallowed back the emotion crowded in her throat and nodded.

"She was beautiful."

"Thanks."

*She came a very long way to find you.*

Maybe this was the woman Alcott was talking about. Rowan would find out tomorrow.

And maybe no one else would be murdered between now and then. Not that she expected this woman to provide any earthshaking information that would help stop Julian. Alcott had said she could help but Rowan wasn't holding her breath.

So far no one had been able to help.

For the past four months she had grown complacent.

With no bodies turning up until the last few days, no contact, she had wrongly assumed Julian was dead or unable to continue his vengeful killing.

But she had been wrong.

He had likely never been far away. Just waiting and watching for the perfect moment to swoop in and shatter her world again. Rowan would see what this woman had to say and then she was going to take steps of her own.

It was time she did what she had known she had to do all along. Face him. Force him to finish this.

Except she was the one who was going to finish it.

# Ten

Billy's officers had stopped the exodus of folks who had been camped out in these woods and organized them into small groups to be questioned. None were happy about it, but he'd ordered a hot lunch for all who cooperated voluntarily. Most were agreeable to those terms.

Photos of Addington had been shown but only a few admitted to having seen him around the area. Several had known Owen Utter and insisted he had been behaving strangely since his friend died back in October. A handful of people saw Utter return to the camp, though none had seen him with anyone. Not a single person on-site had seen Addington today. No one admitted to having seen anyone leave the tent where Utter's body was found.

Whatever happened and whoever was responsible no one had witnessed the events.

Pryor drifted from one cluster of folks to the next, tossing out his own questions. From what Billy had overheard, his questions seemed to be focused more on Rowan's visit than the possibility Addington had been living among these people. The man was clearly more interested in building a case against Rowan than in determining if Addington might be active again.

The idea infuriated Billy. He wanted to punch the guy's lights out.

Pryor also showed a photo of Dressler but no one had seen the missing agent. Pryor wanted to tie Addington, Dressler and Rowan together with a nice, neat little bow, but that wasn't reality.

As if he wanted to see how far he could push Billy, the smart-ass federal agent marched up to him. Hands on hips, he surveyed the ongoing activities and shook his head.

"A waste of time," he announced. "This is a homeless encampment. This entire exercise is pointless."

"It's a murder scene," Billy reminded him. "A man is dead and we have an obligation to investigate his murder the same as anyone else's." Every hour he realized how much more he disliked Pryor.

"My mission here—" Pryor spat the words at him "—is finding Addington. We've wasted enough time with this investigation. Obviously Addington murdered the man. What else is there to establish?"

"If you're finished here, Pryor, by all means feel free to leave." What the hell was wrong with this guy?

"Actually…" Pryor rounded on him. "What I really want is to question Dr. DuPont further. You wrapped up that questioning and sent her on her way before I was finished. *She* should be the real focus in this investigation. Addington is here for her."

Now he was just trying to piss Billy off. "You questioned her," he argued. "What else did you want to know? I'm certain she'll answer whatever other questions you have. I'm just trying to figure out what else you could possibly want to ask."

Pryor's face darkened. Now he was the one pissed.

"Are you serious?" He shook his head. "Obviously, Chief, you don't understand how this works. DuPont is more than a mere pawn in Addington's game. She *is* the game."

"Why don't you explain what you believe that means?" Billy suggested. "Because I have a feeling that it means something entirely different to me."

*"Apparently,"* Pryor said, emphasizing the word, "your personal relationship is adversely affecting your ability to be objective."

Billy laughed. "Why don't you stop beating around the bush and just say whatever it is you have to say, Pryor. You're dancing all around it, and I'm here to tell you I'm not going to say it for you."

This was what he wanted. He wanted Billy to say the words suggesting Rowan was somehow a part of what Addington was doing. No way in hell he was going down that path. The man was out of his mind.

"This all started with her," Pryor said. "When she was a child. Addington has been obsessed with her all this time. They were close friends—perhaps more—for many years. Somehow we can't get a fix on where he is and yet he seems to reach out to her with ease—right under our noses."

"First," Billy said, struggling to control his anger, "Rowan is the victim. She is not facilitating him in any way. Let's not forget that Addington murdered more than a hundred people and your fancy Bureau had no idea who he was. He was out there, killing people, for decades before Rowan ever met him. Not to mention, her father was one of his victims."

"As far as we know," he argued. "We have no idea what really happened between those two."

Billy ordered his fingers to relax and uncurl from the hard fists they had tightened into. "You may not have any idea, but I do. I was here when Rowan was growing up."

"But you have no idea what she did all those years in Nashville."

Billy was finished with this conversation. "She helped find killers and I'm betting her success rate was a hell of a lot better than yours or your buddy Dressler's."

"Chief, at this point I'm convinced that your participation in this task force hinders more than helps the investigation."

"Lincoln!" Billy held the other man's gaze as he called to his detective.

Lincoln was at Billy's side mere seconds later. "Chief." He looked from Billy to the other man and back. "What's up?"

"Pryor here seems to think my presence is a problem. I'm putting you in charge of this scene. Don't take any orders or any BS from this guy."

"You got it, Chief." Lincoln turned his attention to Pryor. "If you've completed your questioning, Agent Pryor, I'm going to need you and your people to leave my homicide scene."

Billy didn't wait to hear Pryor's rebuttal. He walked away, leaving the ongoing activities in Lincoln's capable hands. Billy needed to talk to Rowan. But first he had a stop to make.

* * *

The Antebellum Inn was one of the oldest establishments still operating in Winchester. It had been in the same family all that time. The black sedan in the parking lot told him that Anna Prentice Addington, Julian Addington's ex-wife, was in. The lady had taken a room here last spring when her daughter's remains were found. She'd been in Winchester ever since, watching and waiting. Like Pryor and all the other FBI types in the investigation, the ex-wife felt certain Addington would keep coming back or would stay hidden in the area until he had gotten what he wanted.

Presumably Rowan.

"Over my dead body," Billy muttered as he climbed out of his truck.

As he entered the lobby the owner, Donna England, greeted him in her usual exuberant style. "Chief Brannigan." She flashed him a big smile. "How's Dottie?"

Ms. England and Billy's mother had gone to school together.

"She's doing great. Keeping Dad in line." He removed his hat and strode over to the counter. "How have you been? I hear you got engaged at Christmas."

England had been married before, had grown kids, but she had been single for as long as Billy could recall. His mother always said she was waiting for Mr. Right. Evidently, the one she'd been waiting for had shown up a few months back.

"I sure did." She held up her hand, wiggled her fingers to show off the huge diamond engagement ring. "Getting married in July right before my birthday."

"Congratulations," Billy said. "I hope he deserves you."

"He's wonderful." She sighed, her face beaming with happiness. "Speaking of happily-ever-afters, last time I saw her, Dottie mentioned you and that pretty Du-Pont girl were getting serious. You two planning nuptials yet?"

"Not yet." Billy thought of the engagement ring he'd bought. He'd intended to propose already but then Addington had resurfaced. The bastard.

"She's a lucky lady," Donna said with a nod. "You're a good man, Billy Brannigan. Remind your momma that folks have used this inn for weddings for more than a hundred years. You and your lady feel free to do the same."

"Thank you, Ms. England. I appreciate the offer. Is Ms. Addington in today?" He'd seen the sedan outside, but it was well after lunch. She might be out and about with her friend the private detective. Cash Barton, a former LAPD detective, had been working to help Ms. Addington determine what had happened to her daughter for nearly three decades. Eventually their relationship had turned personal. Now they were here, living in Winchester, waiting to see what happened with her ex-husband. Billy had spoken with the woman before. So had Rowan. The ex-wife was the one to reveal her former husband's infatuation with Rowan for longer than the FBI had known.

Coming by today might not garner him anything new, but Billy had to try. If Addington was back in town or if he'd been here all this time lying low, maybe the ex-wife had heard from him.

"She is," England confirmed. "You know the room number. Her driver is in the restaurant having a late lunch and that PI fellow left about an hour ago. Right after my police scanner picked up the news about that body being found over there off Keith Springs Mountain Road."

So Barton was lurking around the fringes of the crime scene trying to get the details. Billy wasn't surprised but he was annoyed that he hadn't noticed the guy. "Thanks, Ms. England. I'll just knock on her door and see if she's accepting visitors."

"You got it, Chief." England laughed. "And if her driver finishes lunch before you're done, I'll try to distract him for a while. That'll be my contribution to your investigation."

Billy winked at her. "You do that. I might have to hire you for my team. I'm always looking for a sharp detective."

England's laughter followed him up the stairs. At the door marked number three, he knocked.

He faced forward as the floor creaked. He imagined the lady on the other side of the door was checking the security peephole to see if her driver had returned from lunch. Billy figured the man had his own room, but he likely checked in with his boss whenever he came and went.

The lock rattled and the door opened. Anna Prentice Addington looked elegant as always. Her hair was pulled back from her face, fashioned in some style on the back of her head. Her eyes narrowed as if she had been expecting someone else and had no idea why Billy would stop by.

"Chief Brannigan, what a surprise."

"Ma'am." He gave her a nod. "I'd like a few minutes of your time."

She stepped back and opened the door wider. "Of course. Come in."

Billy walked into the room and waited while she closed the door behind him. When she faced him she asked, "How may I help you, Chief?"

"You've probably heard we found another body this morning. That makes two in practically as many days—both appear tied to your ex-husband."

She folded her arms over her waist and considered his question. Billy was surprised she didn't ask him to sit down. On his prior visits, she had always asked him to sit and offered refreshments. This time she seemed a bit offended at the topic or perhaps his use of "ex-husband."

"I have heard the news, yes. But I have not heard from Julian, if that's the reason for your visit. If I had heard from him, I would have notified you immediately."

Billy turned his hat in his hands and decided on a different approach. "Tell me, ma'am, why do you keep staying? Not that we don't appreciate your company, but it seems odd to me that you've stayed all this time. You've already taken your daughter's remains back home to LA and given her a proper burial. Why not go home and live your life free of this nightmare?"

"Like your friend," she said, obviously meaning Rowan, "I want the whole truth. I want to know who murdered my daughter. I want to be here when Julian is captured. I want to spit in his face and laugh at the shackles he'll wear."

Well, that was plain enough. "I can understand how you would feel that way."

"I can tell you another thing," she said then. "The

first body you found, the one on Norah's grave. He was close to Norah, just as the man you discovered in that shabby little apartment last October was. She spoke of her protectors."

Confusion joined his surprise at her statement. "Norah spoke to you about this?"

Addington threw her head back and laughed. "Of course she didn't speak to me. These feelings and confessions were in the notes Julian kept. If the FBI hasn't shared those case notes with you, you must insist. You'll find them most interesting. Norah was always very open with Julian and he lived for every moment of her attention."

Anna Prentice Addington had insisted that Norah was once a patient of Julian's. She claimed that was how their relationship had begun. The FBI had found notes but they weren't sharing. Considering Billy's current standing with Pryor he didn't see that changing.

"I'll do that," Billy said to her. "Thank you for your time, ma'am. I hope you will keep me informed. And do be careful, he may be close. You could be in danger."

"If I hear from him, you have my word that I'll let you know, Chief. As for being concerned for my safety, I stopped being afraid of him long ago. I'm reasonably confident I don't mean enough for him to go to the trouble of killing me."

Billy wasn't so sure about her word or the idea that Addington represented no danger to her. With one last word of caution and another thanks, he left.

Like her ex-husband, Anna Addington was difficult to read.

* * *

The viewing in parlor one for Faye Donelson was underway by the time Billy left the office. He and Lincoln had gone over every statement and each piece of evidence from the scene at the tent city. Ledbetter had packed up Mr. Utter and prepared him for transport to the lab. Cause and manner of death were obvious but there were other tests and examinations that would need to be performed.

Ledbetter had spotted the Taser mark on Utter's body. Like the other victim, Crash Layton, Owen Utter had been disabled before the fatal strike was delivered. In Billy's opinion, this confirmed the murders were the work of Addington. He typically used drugs or something along those lines to disable his victims. If Billy had been fairly convinced before today that the bastard was close, he was absolutely certain now.

Addington was close by and he wanted them to know it.

Pryor argued the point. Some of the comments he'd made when he showed up at Billy's office suggested he considered Dressler a suspect in these two murders. The idea was complete nonsense. Dressler was a pain in the ass and Billy didn't care much for the guy, but the man hated Julian Addington. He would never do anything to help him. His dropping off the grid could only mean one of two things: he had either lost his mind or he believed he could better contribute to the investigation this way.

Billy stood in the middle of the lobby, his hat in his hands, and realized that it had been a year since Addington started this bizarre game with Rowan. *A year.*

And they were no closer to catching him than they had been 365 days ago.

Were he and Rowan just supposed to keep putting off the rest of their lives?

He thought of the ring in his glove box. He had wanted to propose to her already. He had considered proposing at Christmas. But their living together arrangement had still been new and they had been working out the kinks. He hadn't wanted to push her too much at once. Rowan was terrified of putting him in danger. He sighed. Wished he could make her see that she was the one in danger. Finally, two weeks ago he had found the perfect ring. He'd been waiting for the perfect moment and then all hell had broken loose.

A couple entered the lobby, spoke to Billy as they passed on their way to the parlor. Judging by the number of cars in the parking lot he imagined that parlor had about reached capacity. The Donelson sisters were longtime members of the large Baptist church in town. Rowan had probably had to open the big doors between parlors one and two. Billy should sign the guest register and say hello to the family.

He was tired but he was never too tired to do the right thing.

He signed his name below those of the last visitors. He stepped into the parlor and, as he'd suspected, the two parlors were joined and Ms. Donelson's casket sat front and center between the two. The rows of chairs were filled with either people or their belongings. A good number stood in the aisles chatting quietly. Music selected months ago by the sisters played softly in the background. Rowan circulated around the room greeting visitors and checking with the family to see if they needed anything.

Billy watched her for a while, his heart beating faster each time she smiled. She wore that smoky gray suit he liked so much. She always wore a set of pink pearls with it. A smile tugged at his lips. He couldn't wait to strip all that silky fabric and those dainty pearls off her and to hold her close.

Her gaze met his and she smiled. The ability to breathe deserted him. She walked in his direction and he could have watched her do that all night.

When she reached him, she searched his face, the same longing he felt shining in her eyes. She said, "Hey."

"Hey." He forced air into his lungs.

"Anything new I should know about?" She asked the question casually but the wariness that slipped into her tone was unmistakable.

"A Taser was used on Utter the same way it was on Layton."

She nodded, then shook her head. "What does Pryor have to say about this? As if he didn't say enough at the scene."

"Yeah, well, if it makes you feel any better, I had to work extra hard at not punching the guy today."

Rowan put her hand to her mouth to cover her smile.

Billy looked down to hide his. When he had cleared his face, he voiced his newest suspicions about Pryor. "I think he's leaning toward framing Dressler for these two murders."

Rowan cleared her throat softly but the shock in her eyes was loud and clear. "I won't even go there. The man is obviously mad."

Billy glanced around the room. "I was thinking the same thing."

"I guess you're unhappy with me. I suppose you feel my going off into those woods was risky."

"I'm just glad you didn't ditch your surveillance team first."

She shrugged. "I like to think I'm a little smarter these days when it comes to protecting myself."

"Good. Make sure you stay that way."

"I think you're right," she said as she surveyed the room.

"About which part?"

"Pryor is looking for a scapegoat. We both know there's a leak somewhere on his side of this. I think Dressler might be his chosen sacrificial lamb. And me, of course. I'm an equally worrisome enigma."

"Don't worry about Pryor," Billy assured her. "I'll take care of him."

Whatever beef the man had with Dressler was between those two. But when he poked his suspicions at Rowan, he might as well be poking Billy.

Not a good idea at all.

# *Eleven*

*Thursday, March 12*

Rowan finished off her coffee and placed her cup in the kitchen sink. She watched Billy pace the living room, his cell phone pressed to his ear. Maybe there was a new development in the case. She hoped there hadn't been another murder.

He had told her about visiting Julian's ex-wife. Like Billy, Rowan couldn't reconcile the idea that Julian and his ex had not been in contact with all that had happened the past year. Julian had to be aware she was in Winchester and that her friend, Cash Barton, was following the investigation. Rowan knew Julian well enough to understand he would not appreciate the interference, much less the reminder of his failed marriage or his ex-wife's lover.

Then again, why would the woman lie? What did she hope to gain?

It was possible this game was as enticing to her as it was to Julian. She claimed Rowan's mother had destroyed her life by luring away her husband. But why wouldn't she be grateful? Julian was a serial killer. He had murdered more than a hundred people and he'd started long before he and Norah met. His ex-wife should appreciate that he had been lured away. Then again, she blamed Norah for the death of her daughter. Perhaps her insistence on seeing this through was exactly what she claimed—the need for justice to be served. Or maybe she simply wanted to watch Rowan squirm. Maybe she hoped if she hung around she would be able to watch Norah's only surviving daughter end up dead, too.

Whatever the case, it was a very strange relationship. Rowan wondered how Julian could have so carefully and so successfully kept that side of himself—his history—from her when she had spent her days helping to identify motives and track down killers. Had she needed him to be what she believed him to be? Had Rowan been so desperate to never be betrayed again— as she had been by her mother—that she overlooked the signs right in front of her?

Apparently that was the case. She had been so adept at recognizing evil during all those homicide investigations, yet she had not recognized the most depraved of killers in her personal life. But she recognized him now. Rowan rinsed her cup and wiped down the counter. Anything to keep herself occupied until she knew what Billy's call was about. Though he had discussed yesterday's events with her last night, she had sensed that he had kept some aspect from her. Something that disturbed him deeply.

Maybe he would tell her this morning.

She had been exhausted last night. The Donelson visitation had turned out far larger than expected. Ms. Donelson's sister had been very pleased with the attendance. The family was always happy when friends and neighbors made an appearance at a loved one's visitation. Memories were shared and reminders of the lives that had been touched were discussed. Rowan had appreciated those same aspects of her father's visitation and funeral.

She hardly remembered her mother's viewing. She'd been in shock, swallowed by grief and despair. Her father had stood stoically by his wife's casket and greeted the many, many visitors. Most had come to show their support for him. Her mother hadn't had that many friends. Many in the community had considered her a bit odd.

Rowan remembered standing beside him wearing that dark blue dress he'd selected for her. He'd said it wasn't right for a little girl to wear black. She hadn't uttered a word the entire evening. Not even when Billy and his family arrived. That was the first time she remembered him hugging her. He'd looked so dapper in his suit. Even then he'd been wearing cowboy boots. She might not have noticed except she had spent most of the evening staring at the floor to avoid eye contact with people. Deep down she had been glad Billy came even if she hadn't been able to interact much with him.

He appeared in the doorway now. Rowan blinked away the memories and produced a smile. "Everything okay?"

The question was a foolish one, but it was better than asking if someone else had been murdered.

"That was Pryor. He wants to talk to you again. I told him it would have to be tomorrow."

Rowan shook her head. "He just won't let the idea go that I'm working with Julian somehow."

Billy heaved a weary breath. "As much as I disagree with everything this guy says, I don't believe he's convinced you're working with Addington. I think he believes you're hiding information about him. Keeping relevant details to yourself."

They had been down this road before. "Is that what you think?"

He held her gaze for a long moment, his dark eyes as familiar as her own heartbeat. Finally, he shook his head. "No. In the beginning, there were things you kept to yourself, but you're not doing that now."

Her chest ached with the realization that he trusted her so completely when she wasn't sure she trusted herself. "How can you be so certain?"

He moved away from the door, put his arms around her waist and pulled her close to him. "I trust you completely, Ro. I know you wouldn't do that to me or to yourself."

She hugged him hard, then drew back. "Thank you. I needed to hear that."

He held on to her, searched her eyes as if he needed to be sure what he saw there. "What we have is the real thing. I hope you know that, Ro."

She made a face. "Of course it's real. Why would you think I don't recognize that?"

He shook his head. "No reason. I guess I just want to be sure we're on the same page."

Uncertainty swelled beneath her breastbone. "What page is that?"

"Moving forward with this..." He glanced around. "With us."

Was he having second thoughts? "Why wouldn't we be on the same page? We want the same thing."

"Do we?"

His question took her aback. "This," she insisted, "is what I want."

"Okay. Good." He gave her a sweet kiss on the nose. "I need to get to the office."

"Be safe," she called after him.

When the door had closed behind him she shut her eyes and fought the urge to cry. Something was off with Billy. He either suspected she wasn't being completely honest with him or he wasn't being completely honest with her.

Not possible. Billy Brannigan wasn't capable of lying.

Rowan tucked her cell phone into her back pocket and her weapon into her waistband beneath her sweatshirt. "Let's go, boy."

Freud followed her into the corridor and she locked the door, then headed downstairs. Burt's viewing was tonight. She wanted everything to be perfect for him.

So much had happened the past few days she hadn't had a moment to consider just how badly she would miss the man. He'd lived a good life and he'd lived it well. As grateful as those who knew and loved him were for that, he would be missed.

As they passed the refrigeration unit, she smiled and said, "Morning, Burt." Freud glanced up at her, recognizing the name. She reached out and scratched him behind the ears. "You miss him, too?"

She disarmed the security system and unlocked the back door so Freud could go outside. The WPD cruiser was parked on the side street. As much as Rowan had hated the idea of anyone watching her every move, she felt grateful now. Freud trotted across the yard, barking at a squirrel that raced up the nearest tree. A school bus rolled down the street, reminding her it was almost eight. Deciding to let Freud romp for a while, she locked the door and headed for her office.

A knock at the main entrance echoed in the air as she crossed the lobby. She walked to one of the front windows and checked the parking lot. An unmarked sedan was there, a woman seated behind the steering wheel. That would be Pryor's agent. Another car, this one sporting a Davidson County tag, sat nearer the lobby entrance. Another knock drew her attention to the door. A woman dressed in slacks and a sweater, her dark hair threaded through with gray, stood at the entry door.

Rowan walked to the door and went through the steps for opening it. As soon as her gaze collided with the other woman's, Rowan recognized her as the one from the photo with her mother.

The woman gasped. "My God, you look exactly like her."

Rowan steeled herself against the words. "May I help you?"

The woman thrust out her hand. "My name is Kara Solomon. I was a friend of your mother's. I wanted to speak with you if you have a moment."

Rowan considered the large shoulder bag she carried. "Do you mind leaving your bag in your car?"

Solomon glanced down at the bag she carried. "Sure. No problem."

She walked over to her car, unlocked it and dropped the bag onto the passenger seat. She reached inside and removed her fob, then locked the door.

Rowan stepped back, opening the door wider and inviting the woman inside. Once they stood in the silence of the lobby, Rowan asked, "What is it you'd like to talk about, Ms. Solomon?"

"Do you mind if we sit down?" She gestured to the nearest grouping of chairs.

Rowan moved in that direction as did the other woman. When they were seated Rowan waited for her to begin. She was the one who wanted to talk. Rowan had questions but she wanted to hear her out first.

"I've been watching you in the news the past several months."

"Year," Rowan corrected. "My father was murdered a year ago."

Solomon nodded. "Yes. I suppose I had hoped that would be the end of it and then Carlos died and now Crash has been murdered."

"You're referring to Carlos Sanchez and Crash Layton?" Rowan wasn't going to cut her any slack. She needed to get to the point.

"Yes. The two of them and I were friends just as your mother and I were."

"Perhaps you can shed some light on the nature of their relationship with my mother." Rowan used the coolest tone she possessed.

"All those years ago when your mother married your father and settled in Winchester, she and I became friends. I was living in Tullahoma and I was actually a friend of Julian's. He and I had known each other when I lived in Nashville. He asked me to become friends with her. He wanted me to watch her for him."

Rowan's pulse raced. It was true, her mother had known Julian before.

"How did he know my mother?" Rowan found herself holding her breath.

Solomon shook her head. "The only thing I know is that it had something to do with their childhood. Julian and Norah were both very tight-lipped about their childhoods."

Rowan shook her head. "I don't understand. My mother grew up in Memphis."

"This was before. As a teenager she lived in Memphis but not as a child."

"I'm not aware of her ever having lived anywhere else." The woman had to be wrong. Rowan would know where her own mother lived as a child. This made no sense. Even as the thought entered her mind, instinct warned her that the things she knew about her mother's childhood could be more lies.

"All I can tell you," Solomon said, "is that, according to Norah, she ended up with a foster family in Memphis when she was thirteen. By the time she was fourteen the family had adopted her, so she took their name, O'Brien."

"What was her name before that?" Rowan wasn't sure she was buying this story, but it wouldn't be completely impossible to confirm either way. There would be records somewhere.

"I have no idea. I only know that she was born in Alabama. Something happened when she was thirteen and she was put into the foster care system." Before Rowan could ask, she went on. "I have no idea what happened. Like Julian, she would never speak of it."

"Assuming any of this is true and not just another of her stories, why would she need these so-called protectors?" Rowan blocked the images from the October night at that shack in the middle of nowhere when Crash Layton had appeared and rescued her from certain death. When she'd asked who sent him, he had said her mother—which was impossible...at least, she'd thought it was impossible. Now she wasn't so sure.

*Don't be ridiculous, Rowan. This is just another trick no doubt inspired by Julian.*

Solomon turned her hands up. "I wish I could tell you more. I only know that whatever happened when she was a child, it was like something from a horror movie. Those two, Crash and Carlos, would have done anything to protect her. Whatever Julian would have you believe about your mother, it's probably lies. He was obsessed with her. He used me to try and get to her."

"How did she become involved with Julian?"

"I don't know. She wouldn't speak of that either. The one thing I am certain of is that when I met her all those years ago, she did not want Julian to know where she was. Obviously something had happened between them before that time."

"You're saying that when she settled here in Winchester with my father she wanted nothing to do with Julian."

"She hated him. And she was terrified of him."

Rowan leaned back in her chair for the first time since they'd sat down. "I don't understand. Both Julian and his ex-wife insist that Norah was having an affair with him before my sister and I were born. That it went on for years."

Solomon shook her head. "They're lying." She spoke with such vehemence that Rowan drew back. Solomon held up a hand. "I apologize, but I know those two and you cannot trust them."

Rowan put her hand to her mouth and tried to think where to go from here. Her first thought was to call Billy.

"I'm sorry if I've upset you but I only came because I'm afraid for your life."

"Why now?" Rowan didn't trust Julian or his ex-wife and she damned sure didn't trust this woman who suddenly came out of the woodwork with this bizarre story. "Why allow me to flounder all these months and then suddenly show up and tell me this story?"

"Until your father was murdered, I had no idea you even knew Julian. Even then, I swore I wouldn't get involved." She looked away. "I was afraid."

"But you suddenly grew a conscience and decided to pay me a visit?"

When she said nothing in response to the accusation, Rowan stood. She had heard enough. "Thank you for stopping by, Ms. Solomon."

The woman stared up at her. "He murdered the

only man I've ever loved." Fury tightened her face. "I couldn't let him get away with it."

Obviously she wasn't talking about Utter, and Sanchez had died of a heart attack. "Layton?"

Solomon nodded. "We couldn't be together. He said I'd never be safe, but I still loved him."

"How does this help me, Ms. Solomon? I know Julian is a monster and I assumed his ex-wife wasn't to be trusted. But what am I supposed to do with the rest? You insist my mother never spoke of her childhood. How will this headline help me without the story?"

"The answers you need lie deep in the past. Find those answers and you'll know what to do now." She stood. "She wouldn't speak of it, but she often told me that she wrote of those days. She said it was the only way to purge herself of the demons that haunted her."

A tale about a young girl whispered through Rowan's mind. There was a story about a child amid all those ramblings in her mother's journals. Anticipation awakened inside Rowan. She needed to get to her mother's journals.

"Thank you, Ms. Solomon. I appreciate you coming forward to help."

They chatted a moment longer about what a wonderful person Norah had been as Rowan ushered her toward the door. When Solomon was out the door and Rowan had locked it and rearmed the security system, she headed up the stairs but then remembered Freud was still outside.

After letting Freud in, the two of them hurried up to the second floor. Rowan went to her mother's desk and pulled out all the journals. She skimmed one after the other until she found the one about the child.

Rowan started to read and she couldn't stop.

The little girl's name was Nina Mulligan. She'd lived in a tiny village near the river and her family had been monsters.

Journal in hand, Rowan rushed up to the third floor and opened her laptop. She opened a screen and entered the name Mulligan and Alabama into the search box. Hundreds of entries filled the screen. Slowly but surely she weeded through the extraneous. When she had sufficiently narrowed down the results she was left with shocking headlines.

The blurry photo of a young girl could have been Rowan or her sister.

Her heart thundering, her fingers touched the screen. "Momma."

Rowan studied the image of her mother and the house behind her. Her breath caught. The house was the same one in the photos she'd found in Burt's home office.

"Oh. My. God."

Another photo showed a middle-aged couple. The woman had long blond hair; her features were familiar—too familiar. Her heart started to race. The man was taller, lanky with darker features—the murdered Mulligans.

This was the couple in the photo from Burt's house.

"How did you find them?" she murmured.

Rowan printed the article and the photo. After folding both, she tucked them into the journal. She grabbed a bag larger than the one she usually carried and stuck her gun, her phone and the journal inside. She changed her sweatshirt for a pullover sweater and swapped her house shoes for a pair of sneakers.

She gave Freud a treat and a hug. "I'll be back, buddy."

On the way down the stairs she called Charlotte.

"I'm just pulling into the parking lot," her assistant said.

"I'll talk to you outside."

Rowan disarmed and unlocked the door and hurried out to meet Charlotte.

"I'm so sorry to do this to you again," she said in a rush. "But I have to make a quick trip into Jackson County."

"No problem," Charlotte assured her. "Everything's done. Take your time. I won't let Burt down. I'll make sure it's the best viewing ever."

Rowan grabbed Charlotte and hugged her. "Thank you so much for all you do."

Charlotte returned the hug and then drew back. "Now I'm worried."

Rowan laughed. "It's okay. And don't worry, I'm not going alone. I'm calling Billy right now."

Charlotte took Rowan's bag. "Call him before you go. I'll feel better."

Rowan made the call to Billy. She told him about the woman who'd visited her and who the people in the photo from Burt's home office were. She explained that the house was where her mother grew up. He told her to sit tight; he was on his way.

For the next five minutes Rowan fought the need to cry. Was it possible her mother was not the awful person she had believed? Was she, too, a victim of Julian's?

Rowan decided right then that she would not stop until she had the truth, and somehow she would see that Julian paid for what he had done to her family... and to all the other families he had damaged by murdering a loved one.

Every instinct warned she was getting closer.

# Twelve

The drive to the destination took forty-five minutes. Rowan spent the first several minutes of that time filling Billy in on the Solomon woman's visit and the information she had relayed. Then she'd explained what she'd found during her internet search. By the time they had reached ground zero, both she and Billy felt certain everything was about to change.

The house was relatively easy to find. The village of Princeton, Alabama, was more a ghost town. According to the man they'd asked for directions, at one time there were several stores, in addition to the post office and a school. Other than the post office, it was all gone now. The buildings were falling into disrepair. Even the school had been closed. Many of the residents had moved away to find jobs. The vast acres of mountain land had been overtaken by hunting clubs.

As the man had instructed they'd driven past the now closed school and into the area known as Lick Fork. The driveway to the old Mulligan place was the final one before reaching a fruit jar curve. Not that any of these were marked by road signs, but they had figured it out easily enough.

The Mulligan house in the background of the newspaper photo of Rowan's mother still stood. The white clapboard siding could use a coat of paint. The front porch leaned a little to the right. And the metal roof was on the rusty side. A long, narrow drive cut through the woods until it reached the small clearing where the house stood. The yard might have been bigger at one time, but the woods had begun reclaiming it decades ago.

Several yards from the end of the driveway a gate extended across it. A length of chain and a padlock prevented opening the gate and driving beyond that point.

"The house is most likely locked, too," Billy pointed out.

"Most likely," Rowan agreed.

"We can call the number listed there." He nodded to the metal sign attached to the gate. A maintenance company and telephone number were stamped into the metal.

Rowan dragged her cell from her back pocket and checked the screen. "We'll have to go back out to the main road to get service."

Billy glanced back down the drive. "Let's do it."

The drive was far too narrow to attempt turning around and there wasn't a single spot for doing so along the way. Billy put his truck in Reverse and rolled out tailgate first.

"I'm glad you could do that," she said with a laugh. "There would be no paint left on the sides of the truck if I was the one driving. I would be scrubbing trees on one side or the other the entire distance."

"That's because all your crime scenes were in the city." He flashed her a smile. "You never had to go after a meth operation or a hunting incident in the middle of nowhere like this."

"You have me there."

Back on the main road she placed the call the instant a bar or two of service appeared on the screen. The voice that answered was female. Rowan explained she was interested in viewing the property.

"The property isn't for sale," the woman who turned out to be a real estate agent stated, her attention clearly somewhere besides this phone conversation. It sounded as if another conversation or conference were going on in the background.

"I don't want to buy it," Rowan explained. She looked at Billy as she embellished the rest. "I'm here with the chief of police from Winchester, Tennessee, and we'd like to see the property as part of an ongoing investigation."

An impatient sign whispered across the line. "Are you suggesting that some aspect of a crime in Winchester, Tennessee, involved this property?"

"We're only trying to rule it out," Rowan assured her.

A pause, then, "I'm going to need to see a warrant."

Rowan closed her eyes and went for broke. "My name is Rowan DuPont. My primary reason for the visit is that my mother grew up there. I just want to see the house. If you could call the owner and ask permission to show it to me, I would really appreciate it." If the woman refused, she and Billy would have to track down the owner themselves.

"So there's no criminal investigation?" The woman sounded annoyed now.

"There is," Rowan said, "and we're trying to retrace the history of one of the people involved."

"Your mother?"

"Yes."

Another extended pause. "Though it goes against my better judgment, I'll make the call. Should I call you back at this number?"

"Yes. Thank you. I'll be waiting to hear back from you."

The connection ended. "I should have let you talk to her," she said to Billy. "I'm sure you would have charmed her into an immediate yes."

Mere psychology couldn't compete with cowboy charm.

Billy laughed. "She didn't sound like the type easily charmed."

Silence settled between them. Rowan felt as if a rug had been pulled from under her feet. It wasn't like it was the first time she'd learned some shocking secret about her mother. This was different, though. This meant that her mother's entire past had been a lie.

"All this time—" Rowan shook her head "—I believed my mother's parents lived in Memphis and died while she was in college."

"The parents who adopted her did live in Memphis and both had passed away by the time she was in college. Maybe she didn't see the people who lived here as her parents," Billy suggested, ever the optimist when it came to her family. He wanted to believe the best.

Rowan had given up on that months ago.

"Why wouldn't she want us to know about her childhood? I wonder if my father knew." She shook her head. "This is like a bad movie. All the secrets and lies...the darkness. I knew my family was dysfunctional, but I had no idea I didn't even know them."

Billy reached out and squeezed her arm. "I'm sure we'll find a good reason for why Norah didn't want you to know any of this."

Rowan understood that it was possible her mother's history was too painful. She may not have been able to bear sharing it. Except in her writing. A chill sliced through Rowan at the memory of what she had read about the little girl named Nina.

"What she wrote in her journal was considerably different from the article that ran in the local papers." Rowan wasn't sure which to believe.

"If she hoped to turn her childhood into a book she might have added to the truth to make it more interesting. More shocking."

He was right. Rowan had no way of knowing what was truth and what was fiction. The newspaper article had basically hit the highlights of what appeared to be a family tragedy—a double homicide. Nina Mulligan's parents had been murdered with an ax. Both had suffered dozens of blows. The ax had been found at the scene but it had been wiped clean of prints. The girl, Nina, had been missing and presumed kidnapped by the murderer or murderers. Two days later she'd been found wandering and nearly frozen to death in the woods. The girl had remembered little of that night. Only that she had been told to run—presumably by one or both parents or perhaps her brother. She'd gotten lost in the woods and would have died if she hadn't been found by the search team. There was an older brother, Richard, but he was never found. The case remained unsolved but the prevailing theory was that the brother had killed the parents and then run away.

The brother could be the reason the girl was taken to another state and her name changed when she went into foster care. Maybe she had been afraid he would find her and chop her to pieces the way he had their parents.

"The weirdest part," Billy said, "is that Burt somehow figured this out."

Rowan agreed. "This must be what he was going to share with me."

Her phone vibrated with an incoming call and she jumped. It was the Realtor. "Rowan DuPont."

"Ms. DuPont, the owner has agreed to allow you to see the property. I've sent the caretaker to unlock the gate and the house. He'll be there shortly. He lives in the area."

"Thank you."

"Good luck with whatever it is you expect to find." The Realtor severed the connection.

Rowan hadn't bothered asking her the owner's name. Not that she would have provided any personal information without a warrant. Didn't matter since according to the property records it was owned by a company based in Birmingham.

The caretaker arrived and instructed them to follow him. Rowan sat in the passenger seat and tried to calm the racing in her chest. The questions buzzed around in her head like flies around a rotting carcass and she couldn't help wondering if she would finally learn some portion of the answers she sought or if she would only uncover more questions.

Every layer she peeled back exposed more darkness. She shivered.

The caretaker stopped at the gate, unlocked and pushed it open. Then he drove on through. Billy followed. The driveway ended abruptly in the front yard. There was no garage or carport. Beyond the house was an old barn that looked ready to fall in on itself. When she'd climbed out of the truck, Rowan stood very still and listened. What was that sound? A distant, dull roar.

"The river," the caretaker said, noting her expression. "It cuts through the back of this property."

Now one of the articles she had read in the newspaper made sense. "That's why they were looking for those children in the water."

The caretaker held her gaze a moment and then he moved on to the front door. Judging by the look he'd shot Rowan, he didn't want to talk about the home's history.

After unlocking the door he stepped off the porch and strode toward them. "Just lock the door when you're done. I'll come back over later this evening and make sure everything is secure."

"Thanks." Billy extended his hand and shook the other man's. "We appreciate you going to all this trouble. Have you worked for the owner long?"

"About thirty years." He removed his baseball cap and scratched his head. "My daddy did before that. I took over after he passed away."

"So you know the owner?" Billy asked.

Rowan held her breath in anticipation of a name.

The caretaker glanced at Rowan before answering. "I work for the real estate agent. She pays the taxes and does all the official stuff. You'd have to ask her for information like that. I just take care of the place. Gotta paint the house this year."

Disappointment speared Rowan. The man was certainly old enough to have known her mother. "Did you know the Mulligans?"

This question got the man's attention. His gaze snapped to hers. His expression promptly cleared of any emotion. "I was a kid when they got killed. I didn't really know them. They kept to themselves. The girl, she was real quiet. Not like her brother. He was kind of a smart aleck."

"He was older," Billy commented.

The man nodded. "Yeah. He was always reading and hiding out in the house. Kind of weird. No offense."

"They say he's the one who killed his parents," Rowan said.

The caretaker stared at her a moment, then shrugged. "Who knows? If he didn't, I guess whoever did took him off and did no telling what to him."

"What was your name again?" Billy asked. The man hadn't given his name.

"Eddie Proctor."

Billy gave him a card. "If you think of anything else about the family who lived here, I hope you'll give me a call."

Proctor took the card and tucked it into his shirt pocket. "Happy to." Before he climbed into his truck, he looked at Rowan again. "You look like her."

Rowan managed a smile but couldn't dredge up a response.

When he'd driven away, she walked toward the house. Billy matched her stride, moving beside her. There were two steps up to the porch. The boards creaked as she crossed to the door the caretaker had unlocked. Though she had never been here, the place felt eerily familiar. Was it possible her mother had brought her here as a small child? She and Raven may have played on this porch.

The windows were covered in plastic that had deteriorated with age, shredding it like fringe. Rowan wasn't sure whether the plastic was covering broken glass or served as a windbreak for a poorly insulated house.

No matter that she couldn't be sure of what any of this meant, emotions churned inside her. Trepidation. Anticipation. With a little fear tossed in. This was strange territory for Rowan. Not a place she ever expected to be. Her mother was a part of her distant past. Now she was suddenly here in Rowan's face, in her present, pulling her into a dark past.

The living room was exactly as her mother had described in the Nina Mulligan story. The walls and trim were white. A stone fireplace took up the better part of the far wall. An old sofa upholstered in a faded gold crushed velvet stood in the center of the space. Scarred end tables and a chair covered in a floral textile that had long ago lost its sheen flanked the sofa. The wood floors were worn and the rug gracing them was as faded as the rest. A single bulb metal light fixture hung overhead. A ceramic lamp sat on one of the end tables. Beneath the front window stood a console television.

The room could have been in the home of any family from the mid to latter part of the last century.

"I expected cobwebs and dust," Rowan admitted.

"I guess the owner wants the place kept in livable condition. Maybe the insurance requires it." He flipped a light switch. "Power's on."

"But no one lives here." Rowan moved on to the kitchen. A wood heater and flue stood in one corner.

The cabinets and appliances, table and chairs were from the same era as the other furnishings. She opened a cabinet door to find dishes. "Strange."

The light inside the refrigerator came on when she opened the door but there was nothing inside. The interior was cool but only slightly so.

They wandered back through the living room and to the hall beyond.

"There are no photographs on the walls." She surveyed the hall. "No personal items at all other than the furniture and not much of that."

"Maybe it's a rental property for hunters." Billy opened the first door on the right to a small bedroom.

A twin-sized bed, small dresser with mirror and a tiny closet that was empty beyond a couple of mothballs in the corner. The walls were a dark gray. Not very feminine.

They passed a bathroom complete with claw-foot tub and pedestal sink. The window over the tub looked straight into the woods that crept almost to the very back of the house.

The next room was like the first. Twin bed. Small dresser with mirror. Tiny closet. No mothballs this time, but this one was a very pale lilac. Could this have been her mother's room? Another of those bone-deep shivers went through her.

The final room was larger and empty. Another fireplace, this one smaller, stood on the back wall.

Other than the linoleum in the kitchen and bathroom, the same wood floors ran throughout the house. The finish was worn from the wood in places and it squeaked here and there, but in this room it was different. Two large, dark stains were visible in this room. Rowan moved closer and inspected the first one.

*Blood.* She had viewed far too many homicide scenes not to recognize the deep, dark stain created by pooled blood left to stand on wood for a while.

"The bed would have been here," Billy said. "The stains are on either side."

He was right. The article had said the Mulligans had been dragged from their beds and murdered. She studied the stained area again. Hash marks in the wood had her drawing back.

Billy crouched down for a closer look. "He chopped them up right here on the floor in their bedroom."

A shudder quaked through Rowan. "First, he must have landed a fatal blow for each one while they still lay in bed," she suggested, "or surely one would have gotten away or tried to stop him."

"Most likely."

All the furniture had been removed from the room. Blood had likely splattered across the space in all directions. She stared at the window. On the curtains. She blinked. She stared at where the bed had stood. All over the linens. Shaking off the images, she moved to the closet and opened the door. It was empty as well.

"There's no basement or root cellar."

Rowan turned back to Billy. "There has to be an attic."

"I think I saw the access in the hall."

They moved back into the hall. The small framed square in the ceiling was eight feet off the floor.

"There probably isn't a ladder around here." Disappointment tugged at her. She had expected to find something that would fill in the missing details. It had been a foolish notion, but she'd hoped anyway.

"I might be able to reach it with one of those chairs from the kitchen."

Rowan wasn't so sure. She chafed her arms to ward off a sudden chill. While Billy brought a chair from the kitchen, she paced the hall, trying to block images of a teenage boy wielding an ax and chopping his parents to pieces. Screams echoed in her head. The screams of a thirteen-year-old girl. She could only imagine the terror of waking up to that nightmare.

Had she run out of the house and hidden from the horror…from her brother?

"It's my lucky day."

Rowan looked up to see what Billy had discovered. Beyond the access panel was a pull-down ladder. The sound of the wood-on-wood slide of the ladder scooting down splintered the air until it settled on the floor. Billy climbed up and poked his upper body through the access hole into the attic.

The first box he brought down had Rowan's heart pounding again. While he went up for the second, she dropped to her knees and sorted through the contents of the box. An old shoebox full of photos. The deed to the property, recorded to Virgil and Patricia Mulligan. Property tax records.

Rowan removed the lid from the shoebox and riffled through the photos. Many were black-and-white. There were dozens upon dozens of photos of Nina—Norah. From infant to the summer she was twelvish. There were a couple of photos that showed the brother but his head was always turned away from the camera. It was as if he purposely ensured the camera didn't capture his face. Amid the photos was Nina's birth certificate. Same birth date as Rowan's mother.

Billy sat down on the floor beside her. "My God, she looks just like you did as a child."

If there had been any question in Rowan's mind whether or not this Nina was actually her mother, she had none now. This was Norah as a child.

She turned to Billy. "I'm going to snap pics of some of these."

He nodded. "You might be interested in this box, too."

The second box was smaller. The contents were obviously Nina's toys. A doll, a teddy bear and a couple of dresses from when she was small. There was a handheld mirror. Rowan's breath caught. It reminded her of the one she had at home only smaller. The one at home had been her mother's mirror.

One by one she snapped pics of the photos. Billy helped her put them back in the box and then she hoisted each one up to him as he stashed them back in the attic.

"You're sure there's nothing else up there?"

"Nothing but wiring, dust and a little insulation."

When the ladder was back in place and the access panel replaced, Billy put the chair away and dusted off his shirt.

"You want to have a look around outside?"

She nodded, not trusting her voice at this point. Rowan peeked in the barn as they walked past it. An old tractor and a few other farm implements sat amid the cobwebs. Beyond the barn was another building that had collapsed in on itself. About all that was visible was the metal roof.

At the edge of the woods they found a family cemetery. The roar of the river was louder here. A short iron fence surrounded the cemetery. Rowan opened the gate and walked inside. Apparently at least a couple other generations of the family had lived here. There were eighteen headstones. Several smaller homemade wooden crosses marked the graves of pets. Names were scrawled on the crosspieces. *Shaggy. Trixie. Toto.* It was the lone headstone in the back corner that drew her attention. She crouched down in front of it and read the name and dates.

The child died at four years old.

*Nora Mulligan. Our Angel.*

If the little girl hadn't died she would have been the same age as Nina. Had the same birthday. Rowan reminded herself to breathe. *Twins.* Nina and Nora were twins.

*Nora. Norah.*

Her mother had been a twin.

But was she Nina or Nora?

# *Thirteen*

Billy had suggested they look up the cops who investigated the murders. They had decided to start with the sheriff.

Rowan was thankful the man wasn't dead. After half a century it was more likely than not that most of the people who had known the Mulligans at the time of their murders would be gone.

The newspaper article cited Robert "Bob" Mount as the Jackson County sheriff at the time of the Mulligan murders. Discovering that he was still alive was only half the battle. Locating him hadn't been easy since his wife had died a decade ago and their children had grown up and moved away before that. Luckily, one of the deputies had remembered Bob and was certain he lived in an assisted-living facility in the Goose Pond area. There was only one facility in that area, which made tracking the place down far easier.

Lake Grove sat in a picturesque venue just outside Scottsboro proper, just a short drive from the Goose Pond neighborhoods. The facility was made up of a large building that included the offices, the game room and lounge, classrooms for dance, art and music classes and a variety of small restaurants, three of them. It was more like a resort than an old folks' home. The living spaces appeared to all be single-story apartments that surrounded a graciously landscaped common area. Each had a rear patio with a view to the lake. Sheriff Bob, as he was known by the staff and other residents, was only too happy to invite Rowan and Billy into his home. According to the resource coordinator, Sheriff Bob liked nothing better than talking about his days as sheriff of Jackson County.

Rowan hoped his memory was as good as his physical health appeared to be.

"Mercy, that was a good while ago." He studied the copy of the article Rowan had brought with her. "This county never had a murder like that before or since." He shook his head. "Awful business. Just awful. Reminded me of that Lizzie Borden tale." He passed the article back to her. "What would you like to know?"

Rowan had asked Billy to lead the interview. She hoped the lawman bond would prompt greater cooperation.

Billy said, "Do you mind walking us through what happened starting when you received the call? Maybe you can also tell us something about the family."

"I can do that," Bob agreed. He tapped his right temple. "Mind is like a steel trap. I haven't forgotten one thing about the cases I worked, especially the ones like this."

There was a long pause as if the former sheriff was gathering his thoughts.

Rowan still felt shaky after the visit to the house and the unexpected finds. There was a hollowness echoing inside her. She had so many questions. How was it that each new discovery only added more questions? Her life felt as if it were spinning out of control from the past forward.

"I turned thirty-two that year," Bob said. "I was a newly minted sheriff. I'd been with the department for a dozen years." He sighed. "Things were different in those days. Folks respected a man who wore the uniform. The law meant something." He shook his head. "I didn't know the Mulligans personally. They lived in the valley on the other side of the mountain. Lot of the folks who lived around that river were cliquish. Kept to themselves. You know what I mean."

Billy nodded. "We have our share like that over in my county. They operate under a different set of rules."

"You're not kidding." Bob drew in a big breath. "When the call came in, I was out in the woods. It was deer hunting season and I intended to nail me a big old buck. I'd been laid up after a car accident the previous season." He paused again. "Took me nearly an hour to get back to my truck and then drive over into the valley. The man and woman had been dead better than twenty-four hours. Coroner estimated thirty-six or so. The house was ice-cold. We don't get snow often, but it had snowed the night before. The fires they'd used for heat had long since gone out, slowed the decomp process a little, but God Almighty, it was the most unnerving thing you've ever seen."

During the lull that followed, Billy asked, "Who found them?"

"We had one of those rolling stores. Pete Toliver drove the truck all over the valley, on the mountain, too. He said Patricia, the wife, had ordered some oranges from the school. The seniors were selling them that year to raise money for their class trip. Pete's daughter was a senior. Anyway, he stopped to drop off the box of oranges and found the front door standing wide-open. He stuck his head in and called out, but no one answered. Snow had blown across the porch and into the living room. No fire in the fireplace. He worried there had been trouble so he went on inside. That's when he smelled the blood."

Rowan's stomach churned. She knew that smell. She'd walked into her share of homicide scenes with the coppery odor so overwhelming she'd had to hold her breath.

"When I got there, my deputies were already processing the scene. Pete told me there was two kids, a boy and a girl, so we started a search party to look for them. We never found the boy but we did find the girl. She was about frozen to death and covered in blood. She was in the hospital for several days. Didn't speak for weeks. When she did, she couldn't remember a thing about what happened."

"Sheriff Bob," Rowan said, "do you know what happened to Nina's twin sister?"

"Well, in the beginning I didn't know she had a sister. Like I said, I didn't know the family at all. But during the investigation we learned a good bit. The parents, Patricia and Virgil, were an odd sort, according to the few who had any dealings with them. They kept to themselves. Lived off their land mostly. Cultivated a big garden every year. Had chickens and pigs. A few cows. You probably saw the barn—there used to be a farrowing house farther on down from the main house but it fell in years ago. They must have had a hog killing right before they got murdered—the farrowing house was covered in blood." He shuddered. "Course that was the way of it. Most folks shot their hogs once in the head and then cut their throats to let them bleed out. It was always a bloody mess. This was unsettling since that bedroom looked pretty much the same way. But you were asking about the little girl who died—the coroner checked his records and said it was pneumonia that got the little girl. She was about four, I think."

Rowan's chest felt so heavy she could hardly breathe. "The girl, Nina, she never remembered anything."

Bob shook his head. "She swore she didn't remember anything. Considering what few clues we had pointed to the boy, Richard, being the possible murderer, the state decided it was best to take her away from here before placing her in a foster home. In case he tried to come back and finish what he started…killing his family."

"Is there anything else about the family that those who knew them found particularly odd?" Rowan asked. A theory was beginning to develop and she needed more information. She felt ready to shatter with this band of tension tightening around her chest. Her mind kept conjuring images of little girls and dead hogs and blood everywhere.

Bob's brow furrowed with concentration. "Let's see. There were a few things. Most of the women who ran into them from time to time said the husband, Virgil, liked to look a little too long. The wife was always very friendly, always inviting people over for tea. None ever went, considering the husband made them uneasy." He rubbed at his chin. "There were a lot of strangers—out-of-towners—in and out of their place. Several neighbors mentioned the number of people who visited the Mulligans. I think they had big parties for hog killing. I guess that's why there wasn't much meat in their freezer. I think they shared with all those visitors. Maybe did some bartering. Lots of folks traded for the things they didn't have back in the day."

The conversation went on a little longer, but the former Jackson County sheriff had shared the known relevant facts with them as well as his conclusions. There was nothing else to tell, he affirmed. Just one of those unsolved tragedies that haunted the investigators for the rest of their lives.

Rowan mulled over all that she'd learned as Billy drove the long twisty road toward home. Now that she understood the events that had molded her mother, it was easier to see why she had been the way she was. Overcoming that sort of trauma would have required serious counseling. She wondered if any had been provided.

"I'm thinking the missing brother could be Addington."

Rowan turned to Billy. "You read my mind. It makes sense. If they were brother and sister, that would explain the connection. With what we know happened, this could also clarify why my mother needed protectors. Maybe she was afraid of Julian. The story about an affair may have been nothing more than Julian's way of hiding the truth while explaining their relationship."

"Maybe his parents were his first kills." He glanced at Rowan.

She nodded. "I was toying with that conclusion. And what was the deal with all those people coming in and out? Strangers—out-of-towners, as he called them. Maybe the Mulligans were dealing in more than livestock and homegrown vegetables. They could have been growing and selling marijuana or some other drug."

"In a remote area like that, they could've been growing anything."

Rowan felt giddy with possibilities. "The first time I dreamed of her, my mother said something to me—in the dream—that fits with this theory." Billy braked to a stop at an intersection and set his gaze on hers. "I asked her why she left me and she said she couldn't stay."

Norah couldn't stay because she had thought leaving this world would end Julian's obsession.

She couldn't have known he would only transfer it to Rowan.

Billy turned on the blinker to make a left turn. "She thought she was helping you."

Rowan's heart felt ready to crack open. All this time she had believed her mother hadn't loved her enough to stay.

Maybe she had loved her *too much* to stay.

"I need a bottle of water, how about you?"

Rowan blinked, turned to him. "Yes. Sure."

Billy went into the only convenience store between Skyline and Winchester. Rowan waited in the truck and decided to make a few notes about all they'd seen and heard while it was still fresh in her mind. She touched the screen of her cell intending to use the notepad. Instantly the battery died. Warnings had been popping up for the past hour.

"Damn it." She tossed it aside and opened the glove box to looked for paper and pen. Even an old envelope or cash register receipt would work. She prowled through the loose papers and vehicle manuals. Her fingers curled around a small box. Something soft. She pulled it out of the pile.

*Ring box.*

The bottom dropped out of her stomach.

Biting her lip, she opened the box.

A brilliant princess-cut diamond winked at her. It was beautiful.

The air fled her lungs.

"Oh no."

The sound of voices in the parking lot had her closing the box and shoving it back under the manuals and papers in the glove box.

Two men had exited the convenience store. Not Billy.

Rowan sank into the seat and tried to slow her racing heart.

What did this mean?

*Don't be stupid, Rowan!* Billy had decided to propose. For a while now she had felt their relationship was heading in that direction. She had hoped for more time. She had really hoped this wouldn't happen until the Julian thing was over.

*What if it's never over?*

Julian could disappear again and orchestrate his devious plans from afar.

"But he can't live forever," Rowan mused.

He was on the back side of his sixth decade of life. Seventy was looming just a few short years down the road. Yet even a few more weeks was enough time for him to destroy everything left that mattered to Rowan.

Billy opened the driver's side door and slid behind the wheel. He passed a bottle of water to her and then opened his own. When he'd had a long swallow, he placed the bottle in the cup holder, fastened his safety belt and headed back onto the road.

Rowan could only stare at him.

When she'd summoned enough courage, she asked, "Do we need to talk about anything?"

He glanced at her as he reached for his water once more. "You want to talk more about today?"

"No." She tried to focus on the road rolling out in front of them. Looking at him was too difficult. "I meant regarding us. Are we okay? Is there anything we should discuss?"

Billy blew out a big breath. "What did I do?"

No matter that her heart was pounding and her nerves were jangling, she laughed. "I'm serious, Billy. Is everything okay with us? Or is there something you need to talk about?"

"Actually, there is something."

Rowan held her breath.

"Since Pryor has basically kicked me off the investigation, I was thinking of taking some time off. Like today, and doing our own investigation full-time."

The announcement startled her almost as much as what she'd found in the glove box. "Are you serious? When was the last time you took time off?"

No sooner than the words were out of her mouth the answer popped into her head. He'd taken time off when her father was murdered…to be there for Rowan. To help with the arrangements and to just keep her from feeling so alone.

They exchanged a glance as if he understood she'd just realized the answer.

She nodded. "I would appreciate that."

Burt's viewing was held in the chapel. Rowan had known there wouldn't be enough room in all the parlors put together.

The entire community had come through the funeral

home tonight. Rowan had said hello to people she hadn't seen since she was a child.

It was a bittersweet event. In her heart she knew that Burt would have loved the attention. But right next to that knowing was a hole left by his departure from this life. She thought of her mother and she wished she hadn't spent all these years disliking her so much. Maybe it was premature, but deep inside where pure instinct existed, she believed the dream she'd had was accurate.

Norah couldn't stay.

# *Fourteen*

Rowan cradled her mug of coffee while Billy readied to go to the office. She had hardly slept last night. She couldn't stop worrying about the decision he'd announced yesterday. With Burt's viewing last night there hadn't been time to revisit the idea of his taking leave so they could pursue a personal investigation. After the viewing, they'd both been physically and emotionally depleted. But she couldn't let him go to the office this morning and do this thing he had planned without further discussion.

"You're sure this is what you want to do? Taking personal leave during this investigation may be seen as indifference toward your official obligations."

He picked up his hat, settled his gaze on hers. "This is what I want to do. The people in this town know me. I'm not worried about anyone misconstruing my actions. This is not the big city, Ro. This is our hometown. People know us. They care about us."

Worry twisted in her belly. "I really don't want *this* to damage your career."

His hat went back on the table next to the door. "Ro, the bottom line is that as much as I love my work, you mean more to me than anything else. Right now, it's important for me to be with you until we finish this."

She placed her cup on the counter and moved toward him, searched his eyes for any glimmer of regret that he'd mentioned taking this step. "It has been a year since my father was murdered and I discovered what Julian was. What if another year passes and we're still trapped in this place? In this *in-between* position of not knowing where he is and what he might do next? Are you prepared to take that much time off? The citizens of this community depend on you, Billy. Do you really want to risk jeopardizing your career? Can't you see that's what Julian wants? He wants to break us down and then, when we have nothing left to lose except each other, he'll finish the job. This is what he does. He hurts people and then he kills them."

"We're close, Ro. He's running out of time and options. He's growing more desperate. He'll have to make a move soon. I plan on being next to you when he does. He is not going to win this time."

As much as she wanted to tell him that he was wrong, some part of her recognized that he was not. Julian was growing desperate. He would either have to make a move or disappear completely fairly soon. His options were vanishing.

"Okay. Do it. But promise me you won't allow Julian to take over your life the way he has mine."

Billy reached out and touched her cheek, smiled

sadly. "We are not going to allow him to control our lives. Not anymore."

He kissed her lips and then he was gone.

Rowan wandered back to the kitchen, still uncertain about the decision Billy had made. She rinsed out their coffee cups and dried her hands. Burt's funeral was at one. She and Charlotte—mostly Charlotte—had everything prepared already. Maybe Rowan was the one who needed to take a leave from her work. Charlotte was carrying most of the weight anyway.

It was true, Julian had taken over their lives. Rowan thought of the ring she'd found in Billy's truck. The bastard was a part of every day of their lives. Their decisions and plans revolved around what was happening with the case. How could they possibly move on with him hanging over their lives, orchestrating events from wherever the hell he was?

Just like now, Rowan realized. He ruled her every thought.

"Enough."

She grabbed her cell and headed down to work. Freud followed. Like Billy, he didn't like when Rowan was out of his sight. He'd been immensely happy to see her when they'd arrived home last night.

Charlotte was coming in the front entrance as Rowan descended the stairs.

"Good morning." Rowan realized as she moved down the final step that her mother's suicide hadn't entered her mind this time. She glanced back up at that second-floor banister. She searched her emotions and found no sense of anger or disappointment or any of the other hurtful ones she'd experienced her entire adult life just coming back to this place…just descending those stairs.

"Good morning," Charlotte responded. "How did it go yesterday? Did you find anything useful?"

"Yes." Rowan understood only just now that she had found more than she realized. "I found forgiveness for my mother."

The two of them ended up walking around the yard, admiring the early-spring blooms—no matter that it wasn't officially spring yet—while Rowan filled Charlotte in on what they'd found in Jackson County. This was another first. Since coming back home she hadn't taken a moment to just be, to simply enjoy that moment.

"That's amazing," Charlotte said. "All these years you had no idea why she did what she did and now you have some closure."

"There's still a lot we don't know, but I am beginning to see the reasons she made the decisions she made." The relief was indescribable.

"I'm so glad to hear this. You were due some good news. Well, maybe not *good* news but informative news." Charlotte made a face. "Excuse me a moment." She took her cell phone from the pocket of her wrap dress and answered a call.

Rowan decided to go inside for a vase and a pair of clippers. There were hundreds of daffodils blooming. A big bouquet would be beautiful in the lobby. With Burt's funeral at one, it was a perfect time to pick them now.

"Ro."

She turned back to Charlotte. "Yes?"

Charlotte extended her cell toward Rowan. "It's for you."

Why on earth would anyone call her using Charlotte's phone? Billy? Her heart stumbled as she accepted the device. "Hello."

"Rowan, it's Josh."

Her knees felt weak with relief that the caller was not Billy...or Julian. "Where are you?" She glanced at Charlotte, who immediately strolled away to give her privacy.

"We need to talk face-to-face, Rowan."

"Are you safe?" Her next thought was that Julian was forcing him to make this call. No matter that Pryor had seemed to move past the scenario, she had still feared that Julian was behind Josh's disappearance.

"I'm fine, but I need your help."

Rowan braced. "What can I do?"

"No one can know I've contacted you. We need to talk face-to-face—alone. Do you think you can make that happen?"

She moistened her lips, thought of how disappointed Billy would be that she'd kept something from him yet again. "I can make that happen."

"I regret the need to ask you to do this, Rowan, but I have to know you won't tell Brannigan."

"For now," she qualified, "I won't tell anyone."

"You'll need to make sure you aren't followed."

Rowan considered her options. "I can do that."

"I'll meet you in the parking lot in front of the local hospital."

"I'll be there."

The call ended and Rowan searched for an excuse to give Charlotte. As she walked toward the younger woman, Rowan decided she didn't need an excuse.

"Thanks." She handed the phone back to her.

Charlotte smiled but the questions were obvious on her face.

"That was Special Agent Josh Dressler."

Charlotte's eyes widened. "The guy who's missing?"

"Yes. He wants to talk to me. But no one can know."

"Do you trust him?" Worry immediately kicked aside the surprise in her expression.

Rowan was fortunate to have such a dedicated employee. Not just an employee, a friend. "I do. We haven't always agreed on certain aspects of cases, but I've never really had a reason not to trust him."

"What about Billy? Are you going to tell him?"

"I will. Just not right now."

Charlotte nodded. "Okay, then. Let's do this."

"I have to go alone."

"If you're going, I'm going. I'm sure you can explain to this Dressler guy that you didn't have a choice. It's not like I'm going to tell anyone."

Before Rowan could protest, she added, "Besides, how would you get past that cop and that FBI guy watching you?"

"I see your point."

"If I pull my minivan under the portico you can go out that entrance and get into the backseat without anyone seeing. You stay low and I'll drive away as if I'm going on an errand."

"I think you might be enjoying this cloak-and-dagger stuff a little too much."

Charlotte smiled. "You're a good teacher."

While Charlotte moved her van, Rowan went upstairs and got her handgun. She tucked it into her waistband at the small of her back and arranged her sweater over it. By the time she reached the portico entrance, Charlotte was behind the wheel and ready to go. Rowan armed the security system and locked the door. With a quick glance around, she slid into the backseat. She huddled down in the floorboard and waited while Charlotte drove out of the parking lot.

Charlotte waved to the agent parked out front. Rowan smiled. She was definitely a bad influence on this woman.

After a few minutes of driving, Charlotte said, "We're clear."

Rowan sat up and straightened her sweater. "Thanks."

"Where are we going?"

"Front parking lot at the hospital."

The drive took only a few minutes. Charlotte parked and Rowan surveyed the numerous vehicles in the lot. She had no idea what Josh would be driving.

"You see him?"

Rowan shook her head. "I don't see anyone, do you?"

"All the vehicles look empty."

A rap on her window made Rowan jump. Charlotte squealed. Twisting around toward the window, Rowan reached for her weapon.

It was him.

"Damn it, Josh, you scared the hell out of us."

He opened the rear passenger side door and climbed in, settled in the seat next to Rowan. At least two days' beard growth darkened his jaw. His clothes were rumpled. The whole image was very un-Dressler-like.

"I thought you were coming alone." He glanced at Charlotte, who had turned in the driver's seat and was staring at him.

"I wouldn't let her," Charlotte said before Rowan could.

His gaze bored into Rowan's. "We need to talk. Privately."

Charlotte grabbed her purse. She handed Rowan the fob. "I have a friend to visit. Hit the panic button if he gives you any trouble."

"Thanks, Charlotte."

"Yeah," Josh echoed sarcastically, "thanks, Charlotte."

She ignored him and climbed out, closing the door behind her.

Josh watched her walk away. "You're sure you can trust her."

"Yes."

He nodded, watched until Charlotte entered the hospital.

"What's going on, Josh? Are you in trouble?"

"No." He shrugged then. "I don't know. Maybe."

"What happened?" They needed a starting place; otherwise, this conversation would never get underway.

"Too much information was leaking to Addington. He seemed to always be one step ahead of us."

This was true. Billy and Rowan had thought for a while that there was a leak in the Bureau. She said as much to Josh.

"You're right. There is a leak. I'm just not sure I can get him before he gets me."

"Who are we talking about?"

"Pryor."

Rowan had expected some low-level player easily manipulated by Julian. But Pryor was anything but that.

What was she thinking? Julian would never deal with anyone who didn't have sufficient power to do his bidding.

"Are you sure?" It wasn't that she didn't believe it possible to turn a senior agent—of course it was—it was just that a move like that took time. The building of a relationship over a period of months or years. Had Julian been involved with Pryor all this time?

"I'm positive, I just can't prove it."

That was a problem. "Do you have any evidence at all?"

"I overheard his end of a phone conversation but that is nothing more than my word against his. The real evidence is something else I can't prove. I made the decision to see if my suspicions were correct, so I mentioned that you were planning to go back to Nashville to have another look around Addington's office. That same night his office was broken into. Drawers of files were destroyed. There was no way to determine all that was missing."

Rowan hadn't planned a trip to Nashville but she understood his strategy. "Did you discuss your concerns with anyone at the Bureau?"

He shook his head. "I need more than what I have to take that step. But he was growing more and more suspicious of me. I knew I had to do something drastic or he'd have me arrested by planting some sort of evidence before I could prove it was him who was leaking intel to Addington. I have a feeling he's been doing it for years, which may explain why Addington was never under suspicion, much less caught."

Rowan considered what the witness had said about Josh the night she saw him in the cemetery. "Why did you go to the cemetery?"

"I wanted someone to see me." His gaze connected with hers. "I wanted you to know I was here. I wanted *him* to know."

"Okay. So what now?"

"He's here, Rowan. He's close. You can't let down your guard for any reason."

She nodded. "I'm aware."

For the next several minutes she briefed him on what she and Billy had found in Jackson County.

"I agree with your and Brannigan's conclusion that Addington is your mother's brother. I'm not surprised that he grew up in an environment like you described." Josh rubbed his temple as if he had a headache. "Whatever happened in that house or during those hog killings, Addington's hidden dark proclivities were triggered somehow."

"If we're right," she said, "he may have killed his parents to gain his freedom." Fledgling killers often took extra measures to emerge from their cocoons.

"His sister—your mother—probably escaped while he was in his killing frenzy."

Rowan thought of the little girl covered in blood running through the woods in the middle of winter. Had she tried to help the first parent he killed? Was that why she was covered in blood? Had she realized she might be next and run for her life?

"What will you do now?" As annoying as this man could be at times, she didn't want him to go down in flames because of a case that involved her. She couldn't bear yet another life destroyed by Julian's obsession.

"I'll be watching for an opportunity. He's here, Rowan. Just waiting for the right opportunity to strike.

I don't require you to help me in any way. I just wanted you to understand what happened."

"Billy and I both knew you hadn't turned. We were certain you had good reason for dropping off the grid."

He exhaled a breath of relief. "Thank you, that means a lot to me."

"Do you have a place to stay?"

"I've got that covered."

"I have a funeral in a couple of hours, but after that I'm going to see Julian's ex-wife. I find it hard to believe that she knows nothing about his childhood and family. She's had that detective looking into her daughter's case, including her ex-husband, for decades. She must have had him investigate Julian. It's difficult to swallow the idea that a veteran detective wouldn't have come across some aspect of what Billy and I have found."

"Good idea. Maybe you'll have more success talking to her with this new information. She certainly wasn't forthcoming in my interviews."

Rowan searched his face for a moment. "Are you armed? Do you have all that you need? Clothes? Money?"

"I have everything covered but I appreciate your concern." His usually charming smile was filled with regret and a hint of sadness.

Just then sitting in the backseat of this minivan in the hospital parking lot Rowan couldn't help wondering if this would be the last time she would see this man.

He was desperate, just like her. He didn't want to give up, it seemed. Also like her. He had never once given her reason to doubt him. He could be arrogant and self-serving but he had always been loyal to the Bureau...to the case.

"You should be careful, Josh. Pryor isn't going to go down so easily. He's older, close to retirement. He has a lot to lose. And we both know where Julian is at this point. Desperate, even more determined. He may have gone over the edge. He could do anything."

"I intend to." A faint glimmer of a real smile appeared. "Don't worry about me. If you need to get a message to me, call or text the number I used to reach your friend. It's a burner phone."

Rowan nodded. "I will."

"Be careful, Rowan. It's never been entirely clear whether Addington wants you for his own entertainment or if he wants to watch you die. At this point, maybe both."

"You be careful," she countered. "It may be me he wants, but he will go through you or anyone else to accomplish his goal."

He reached for the door but hesitated. "One other thing. Pryor is determined to tie you to Addington. I think he's planning to use you to save himself if this thing blows up."

Bastard. "Thanks for the heads-up. I was reasonably confident he had a plan that involved me somehow. I just wasn't sure why."

"Goodbye, Rowan."

"Goodbye."

She watched him go and that hollowness expanded inside her.

Slowly but surely Julian Addington was taking her world apart.

Obviously he was saving her for some big finale.

"Get on with it already," she muttered.

The driver's side door opened, and Charlotte slid

back behind the wheel. "Everything go all right?" She glanced at Rowan in the rearview mirror.

"I think it did." For the first time since this nightmare began, she felt the situation might be about to take a turn.

She hoped.

# Fifteen

By three the last of the guests had wandered away from the burial. A blanket of flowers had been placed over the freshly covered grave. The tent and the chairs were being removed. The funeral had been beautiful. The church filled to overflowing, the prayer at the graveside shared with a massive crowd. Rowan hadn't been able to stop surveying faces. Billy had stayed by her side, only stepping away long enough to give his mother a hug when she and his father readied to leave. Rowan had remained with Burt's sister.

Alone now for the first time since noon, Sally Jernigan hugged Rowan. "Thank you so much for everything, Rowan. Burt truly adored you. He would have been so proud of how beautiful this day was."

"And I adored Burt. I'm grateful I could have some part in this final celebration of his life."

Rowan walked Sally to the limousine where Charlotte and the driver waited. "Charlotte will ride back to the funeral home with you. Please call me if you need anything or have any questions."

Charlotte picked up the conversation from there as

she helped the older lady into the car. Rowan waved as they drove away.

"It won't be the same without him."

Rowan looked up at Billy, who'd joined her on the sidewalk. "It absolutely will not."

They stood for a moment and stared out over the cemetery. Her parents were buried here as were numerous other DuPonts. She supposed that one day she would be buried here. If Julian had anything to do with it that day might come sooner rather than later.

But not today.

"I want to pay a visit to Anna Addington."

Billy turned to her. "I didn't spot her in the crowd."

"Me either. I know what a master of disguise and duplicity Julian is. I didn't recognize what he was and I'm a trained psychiatrist. But the ex-wife has had someone investigating him for decades. Someone who wasn't emotionally involved with the situation. How could Barton not have discovered that Addington wasn't even his real name? I think they've been holding out on us."

Billy settled his hat into place. "I say we ask her. Barton, too, if he's there."

Rowan smiled. "If he's not there, she'll know where he is."

As they walked to his truck, she asked, "How did it go at the office?"

"Besides taking some time off, I did something I'd intended to do for the past year, since Hargrove had his accident."

Thomas Hargrove was deputy chief of police. He'd been in a terrible car accident early last year, before Rowan moved back to Winchester, and he'd been off work since. For his family's sake and the purposes of health insurance, Billy had kept Thomas on the payroll until he reached full retirement age just last month. Clarence Lincoln had basically taken up the man's slack, working directly with Billy most of the time.

"I'm sure he and his family appreciate what you did for them."

At his truck, Billy opened the passenger side door. "It was the least I could do after the man put in forty-odd years with the department."

"Did you announce his permanent replacement?" Rowan settled into the seat.

"I did. I thought Deputy Chief Clarence Lincoln was going to cry." Billy grinned as he walked around to the driver's side.

"I wish I could have been there." Rowan fastened her seat belt. "He's a great detective and a really great guy."

"He is." Billy started the truck and headed out of the cemetery.

The meeting with Josh had been weighing heavy on her all afternoon. She couldn't keep this from Billy. "I met with Josh this morning."

Slowing for a traffic light, Billy shot her a look. "Dressler showed up at the funeral home? Where the hell has he been?"

"He didn't exactly show up. He called me on Charlotte's phone and asked for a private meeting."

Billy exhaled a weary breath. The light turned green and he rolled through the intersection. "And?"

"Charlotte took me so my—" she cleared her throat "—followers wouldn't realize I'd left. She and I went to the location he gave me, the hospital parking lot, and met him."

Billy frowned and made a disagreeable sound. "What was he doing at the hospital?"

"I suppose he thought no one would be watching the hospital."

"What did he want?"

Billy didn't ask why he called Rowan instead of him or one of his Bureau buddies. He was well aware Josh *liked* her.

"He wanted to warn us that he believes Pryor is the leak."

"Ironic," Billy said with a heavy dose of sarcasm. "Pryor believes Dressler is the leak."

Rowan ignored the comment that was made more out of jealousy of any connection she had with Josh than with doubt about his suspicions. "He's convinced Pryor has been trying to set him up. He disappeared to avoid what he presumed to be the inevitable—being arrested and detained. He wanted to keep looking for Julian and the only way to do that was to prevent Pryor from making a move. He dropped off the grid, leaving Pryor with no proof of whether he vanished of his own accord or was taken."

She told him about the test Josh did to see if Pryor was the leak. This got Billy's attention.

"Pryor didn't mention anything about that to me. Of course, he's taken me off the task force so I don't suppose he was required to brief me on anything related to Addington." He glanced at Rowan. "Have you heard any news from Detective Jones?"

"The last time she and I spoke, she left me with the distinct impression that she couldn't discuss details of the case with me. April is a friend. I know she would share with me if she could but she's also a very loyal detective and rarely breaks the rules."

"If what Dressler says is true, it looks like Pryor is closing ranks. Keeping us on the outside."

"Which means we have to find what we can on our own." Rowan didn't like this.

"It appears we might just be in luck. Barton's sedan and that car the ex-wife gets hauled around in are both here." He came to a stop in the Antebellum Inn parking area and shut off the engine.

Since there was only one other vehicle in the lot, Rowan assumed that one belonged to the owner or whoever was working behind the counter today. The inn didn't serve dinner so the kitchen staff would be gone by now.

"You should probably do the talking," Rowan suggested as they emerged from the truck. "She likes you better than me."

Billy laughed. "It must be my small-town-cop charm. They probably don't have that in LA."

"I'm certain. I'm also sure there are many differences between life here and life in Los Angeles."

Anna Prentice Addington had moved out to LA with her daughter many years ago after she and Julian decided to end their marriage. Julian had remained in Nashville supposedly because he'd grown up there. He had inherited his grandmother's Victorian home. A home in a highly sought-after area. He had renovated the ground floor into an office and had passed on numerous very generous offers from developers.

How much of that could be true considering what Rowan now knew?

She reminded herself that she might not ever know

everything or even a reasonable portion of everything about her mother's and Julian's pasts. But she had to keep trying to find the answers. At least for now. Allowing this to consume her life couldn't go on forever. She glanced at Billy. She wanted more.

In the lobby Rowan was surprised not to see Donna England behind the counter. She was always here. At the moment, the lobby was oddly empty.

Billy climbed the stairs beside her. They'd barely made half a dozen steps toward the room when Billy stopped, his hand coming out to prevent Rowan from moving forward.

She started to ask what was wrong and then she saw it, too. The door to the room was ajar.

Billy reached beneath his jacket and withdrew his weapon. He motioned for Rowan to stay back.

She flattened against the wall, her heart pounding, and watched as he moved toward the door.

When he pushed it inward, she held her breath.

He stood in the doorway and swore.

Before Rowan could ask what was going on, he disappeared into the room. She pushed away from the wall and went after him. Rowan stalled in the open doorway. Bodies were strewn across the room. The ex-wife. Barton. The driver—what was his name? Garrett something or something Garrett.

Billy was crouched next to Anna Addington. "Call Lincoln," he said. "Tell him we have three dead."

Rowan made the call, her instincts automatically kicking in and prompting her to back away from the door. She stood to the side so she could see into the corridor, watching for anyone who might suddenly appear. Whoever had done this could still be in the building.

After checking the en suite bath, Billy came back to where she stood. "I'm going downstairs to look for Ms. England. Lock this door and stay right here until I'm back."

Rowan shoved her phone back into her pocket. "I'm going with you."

Billy started to but decided not to argue. There wasn't time. Before they reached the stairs, they checked that the rest of the rooms on the second floor were locked. It didn't take long. There weren't that many.

Downstairs, the area behind the check-in counter was clear. No sign of a struggle. No blood.

They moved through the dining area. Clear. And then to the kitchen. The kitchen and adjoining storage room appeared to be undisturbed. Like the door to Addington's room, the rear entrance stood ajar.

"I'm going out this way," Billy said, "to have a look around. I'll come back in through the front. Wait in the lobby."

Rowan nodded and headed back the way they had come. In the lobby she considered if there was any area of the inn they might have missed. Wait. There must be a restroom down here somewhere.

She walked around the staircase, past the hall tree. There it was, tucked beneath the staircase. The sign on the door read Powder Room. Rowan reached for the knob, gave it a turn, suddenly wishing she had her weapon. But she'd been with Billy so she hadn't bothered. Tucking it into the waistband of this skirt wouldn't have worked; the jacket was too formfitting.

Slowly she pulled the door open, her breath held deep in her lungs.

A woman, not Ms. England, sat on the floor, her head

leaning against the vintage pedestal sink. Blood leaked from her abdomen.

Rowan fell to her knees and quickly checked her pulse.

*She was alive.*

Rowan snatched out her cell and called 911. They needed an ambulance. Now!

She set it to speaker and placed the phone on the floor. Moving quickly, she eased the woman onto her back and tore open her blouse to get a look at the wound.

The dispatcher's spiel echoed in the small room.

"This is Rowan DuPont. I'm at the Antebellum Inn and we have a female gunshot victim who is still breathing. We need an ambulance."

The dispatcher confirmed the address and said, "Help is en route, Ms. DuPont. Can you answer a few questions for me?"

"Yes." Rowan reached for the stack of paper hand towels on a shelf above the sink. She used them to help staunch the flow of blood from the entrance wound as the dispatcher fired off her questions. "The gunshot is on the left side of the abdomen. Victim is unconscious. Pulse is weak but steady. She looks to be about thirty. I am attempting to staunch the bleeding."

There were a few more questions Rowan couldn't answer, like the woman's name and how the injury happened.

Billy appeared at the door. "Oh hell." He knelt at the woman's feet. "This is Laura Brewer."

"Maybe you can reach someone in her family," Rowan said as she kept one hand on the wound and checked her pulse with the other. "Have them meet the ambulance at the ER."

Billy made a call to his office. His assistant would locate a name and number and call the family. Sirens in the distance sent relief coursing through Rowan. This woman needed the kind of help Rowan or Billy couldn't give and she needed it quickly.

Billy rushed out to meet the ambulance and guided the paramedics to the powder room. Rowan stepped out of the way and allowed the paramedics to do their work.

Clarence arrived along with four others from the department. Rowan went outside and found a water spigot. She checked to ensure there were no footprints around it and that the ground wasn't damp, indicating the faucet had been used recently. The last thing she wanted to do was contaminate any potential evidence.

She washed the blood from her hands and shook them dry. There was blood on her skirt and some on her sleeve. Didn't matter. The only thing that had mattered was keeping the woman alive.

"Okay." She took a deep breath and then another to clear the smell of blood and death from her lungs. "Get back in there."

She started for the steps. The paramedics rushing out with their gurney stalled her. She watched as they loaded the victim into the waiting ambulance and drove away. Rowan hoped the woman would make it. There was no way to know just looking at her what sort of internal damage had been done. Two uniformed officers had started rolling out crime scene tape. The inn was now an official crime scene. If there were other guests arriving today they would need to find someplace new to stay for the next couple of days.

Climbing the steps she heard another vehicle pull into the lot. She glanced back expecting to see Pryor or some of his people but it was the forensic techs. As she went on inside she wondered why Pryor's agent hadn't followed her from the cemetery. She'd spotted today's surveillance detail when they first arrived at the cemetery. Strange.

Billy had ended the department's detail since he intended to be with her at all times. She wasn't sure how that was going to work out, but he wasn't going to change his mind.

She climbed the stairs and walked along the corridor until she reached the room where three people had died. How in the hell did Julian do this? He obviously had one or more hired killers working for him. He couldn't possibly have executed all of this mayhem himself. He was an old man, for Christ's sake.

Not so old, she reminded herself. Sixty-seven. But he was in outstanding physical condition, better than most forty-year-olds.

"Better than you," she muttered to herself.

Today she felt a hundred.

Next to the door of the room, an officer was stationed. He nodded to Rowan. She paused at the door and surveyed the scene inside. Clarence and another detective were with Billy. They studied the positions of the victims and discussed the possible weapon used. Billy checked Anna Addington's fingers and bent her arm, assessing the state of rigor mortis. All things the deputy coroner would do when he arrived.

*You're missing all the fun, Burt.* Rowan closed her eyes against the thought.

She didn't go into the room. Wouldn't be a good idea. Scene contamination and all that. No matter that she'd been in there before, at this point she could have

the Brewer woman's blood or some trace evidence from
the powder room or elsewhere in the inn on the bottom
of her shoes. Billy and the others had donned shoe covers and gloves. Rowan was only too happy to let them
do their jobs.

The two forensic techs hustled up the stairs. Rowan
moved aside and they entered the scene. Lucky Ledbetter hurried along the corridor next. He nodded to
Rowan before rushing through the door.

Rowan backed up, leaned against the wall on the
other side of the corridor. She was so tired of the killing. Of the devastation.

The pounding of footsteps echoed from down the
hall once more. Rowan turned her head in that direction just in time to see Pryor and two of his colleagues
striding toward the primary crime scene.

Pryor paused to glare at her. "You shouldn't be here."

There were a great many things she wanted to say
to the man but she decided it was better not to say anything at all. Not just yet.

He shifted his outraged glare from her to the law-
men in the room. The officer at the door held up a hand.
"This is an official crime scene."

Openly hostile to the young officer, Pryor and his
team dragged on shoe covers and gloves, then filed
into the room.

Pryor's first act on the scene was to order Billy off
the premises.

"This is a triple homicide in my jurisdiction," Billy
reminded the arrogant man. "Until we've confirmed
these murders are a part of your investigation, this is my
crime scene. Until then, you need to step back, Agent
Pryor."

If Rowan had thought Pryor was angry when he arrived, he was beyond pissed off as he tramped away, his colleagues following. They wouldn't go far. Maybe to the parking lot where they would simmer until they had the go-ahead to take over.

A few minutes later Billy came out into the corridor. "Lincoln has everything under control. We can go. He'll keep us up to speed on anything he finds. I briefed him on how we came to be here and all. He'll come by to take our official statements later."

"There's something else I'd like to do." Rowan had been mulling over the idea for the past several minutes.

Billy glanced at her as they descended the staircase. "I'm listening."

"I'd like to visit the hospital near Nashville where my mother was a patient. Maybe there's something in her records or someone who remembers her."

It was another long shot but it was worth a look.

Billy nodded. "We'll drop by the funeral home and change clothes. You should call the administrator and see if we can speak to someone today. It's going to be close to six o'clock before we can get there."

"Good idea."

Pryor stared at them with utter disdain as they loaded into Billy's truck.

"There's one other thing," Rowan said as Billy drove away from the latest scene of devastation.

"What's that?"

"Maybe nothing." She drew in a deep breath. She hoped it was nothing. "When I talked to Josh this morning I told him what we discovered about my mother's childhood and the possibility that Julian is her brother."

"You told me you brought him up to speed." Billy

parked in front of the funeral home and waited for her to go on.

This felt like a betrayal but it had to be said. "I mentioned that I intended to see Anna Addington today to question her about Julian's childhood."

"Did anyone else know you planned to pay her a visit?"

Rowan shook her head. "No one else."

# *Sixteen*

The Serenity Center was outside Nashville, nearer to Franklin. A peaceful setting in a wooded area amid horse country certainly lent itself to an atmosphere of tranquility. Nightfall was nearly an hour away but the dense woods surrounding the landscaped property had shadows of gloom reaching out toward the brick-and-stone building.

Ivy climbed the walls of the three-story structure, threatening to overtake the windows. The vines reminded Rowan of the ones growing on the old cemetery wall back home. A broad portico provided a drop-off and pickup point for patients. Early blooming shrubs filled landscaping beds around the parking area. But it was the eight-foot iron fence that surrounded the property that made Rowan feel as if she were in a prison disguised to look like a house.

She was grateful Billy was with her. Whatever she learned here—if anything—she wouldn't have to analyze and deal with it alone. They were in this together. She'd always felt confident in her work, with her colleagues. But this was different. This was intimate and personal. She glanced up at him. For the first time in her life she was certain she could spend the rest of her life and never tire of sharing every intimate and personal detail with him.

She wondered if, after all Norah's childhood trauma, she had felt this way about Edward. Had Rowan's father been her safe haven…at least for a little while?

Inside, the lobby was quiet and empty save for the woman behind the desk. She smiled as they approached her. "Good evening. Are you here to see a patient? Visiting hours are over at eight."

His hat in hand, Billy explained, "This is Dr. DuPont and I'm Chief of Police Brannigan. We're here to see Dr. Winslow. He's expecting us."

"I'll let him know you've arrived."

Billy thanked her.

When the receptionist had made the call, she replaced the phone in its cradle. "Dr. Winslow's office is down the corridor on your left." She gestured in that direction. "It's the fourth door on the right, office 8B."

"Thank you." Billy gave her a nod.

Rowan kept pace with him as they made the short journey down the corridor and to the door specified by the receptionist. It opened as they approached.

"Chief Brannigan," the man said to Billy, then turned to Rowan. "Dr. DuPont. Please come in."

Winslow's office was moderately sized and well equipped, though lacking in any sort of warmth. The walls were beige as was the carpet and the furnishings. There was no art on the walls, only the framed documents detailing his credentials. Nothing, Rowan concluded, to give away his personal story.

"Have a seat." He moved around behind his desk and settled into his chair.

Rowan took the first of the two chairs flanking his desk, Billy took the other.

"Can I offer you something to drink? Coffee? Water? A soft drink?"

Both she and Billy declined.

"We appreciate your time, Dr. Winslow," Rowan said.

"I'm afraid your mother's file has been archived," Winslow said, "and it would take several days to retrieve it, but I do have some rather general information I was about to download from our system."

"Whatever you have could prove useful," Rowan assured him.

He provided the date and length of her admission. This would have been when Rowan was about three, which explained why she didn't remember. She could imagine her father had been a bit overwhelmed with a funeral home to run and twin daughters to see after.

"She was admitted for clinical depression. Based on the brief overview of the case, she had wrestled with depression since her twins were born. One of our fourth-year residents took a special interest in her case and wrote copious notes about how she presented with multiple personality disorder. However, the program director as well as the psychiatrist assigned to Mrs. DuPont's case disagreed with his conclusions. You know, the residents can get a little overzealous sometimes."

"Can you tell us who that resident was?" Obviously it was Julian but Rowan needed confirmation.

"I fear you'll recognize the name. He was all over the news last year. Julian Addington." He shook his head. "It's an utter disgrace for the medical profession. We were all quite stunned to hear the news. Though I will say that many of us had our reservations about him."

There it was. A mixture of anticipation and regret churned inside Rowan.

"Dr. Winslow," Billy said, "can you elaborate on those reservations?"

Winslow pursed his lips for a moment. "He was rather a cocky sort, which, as you can imagine, didn't sit well with those tasked with guiding him. He had no friends among the staff. They disliked him immensely. But it was the lengths he would go to prove he was right that unsettled me. I was also a resident at the time. Addington was not above devious methods for getting what he wanted. That's all I'll say."

"You worked with him?" Billy asked. "Closely?"

Winslow shook his head. "Fortunately I was assigned to a different group. But I heard plenty of rumors."

Rowan wasn't surprised. "Is there anything in her record that explains why my mother was brought to this hospital in particular?"

"Actually," Winslow said, "she first arrived at Cumberland Heights, but she was transferred here two days later. I assumed her family decided they preferred a private hospital."

Certainly there was no way to prove it but Rowan would wager that Julian had discovered she was at Cumberland and finagled the move. It was possible he may not have known where Norah was until that point. This hospitalization may have been the beginning of the end for her.

An ache pierced Rowan's heart. "I realize this was a very long time ago, but is there anyone we might be able to speak with who worked with my mother while she was here?"

It was another of those long shots Rowan had been going after recently.

Desperation did that.

Winslow scanned the meager file in front of him. "Yes, all right. There is a nurse who was assigned to your mother. She's long retired, of course, but she still volunteers twice a month. Beatrice Reinhold. She was one of the best nurses I've had the privilege of working with. At seventy-five she is still quite amazing."

"Dr. Winslow," Billy spoke up, "do you think Ms. Reinhold would speak with us?"

"I can certainly give her a call and see. I have no idea what her weekly schedule is like. But we can try."

Rowan twisted her hands together as he made the call. He chatted for a moment, exchanging the usual pleasantries. Then he asked if she would be willing to speak with Rowan and Billy via a phone call.

Rowan held her breath. Winslow made agreeable sounds. Uttered the occasional "Yes" or "I see." Finally, he thanked the woman and said goodbye.

He clasped his hands on his desk. "Ms. Reinhold's hearing isn't what it once was and she is not a fan of phone conversations."

Rowan's hopes deflated.

"But she said she would be happy to speak with you

in person if you'd like to come by her home. I told her I'd discuss the possibility with you and let her know."

"I would love to do that." Rowan hoped this might be a major break in their investigation. "When would she like us to come?"

"Now if you'd like. She said she is home and would be happy to see you."

Rowan couldn't believe her good fortune. "Perfect." She glanced at Billy and he agreed.

Winslow called Ms. Reinhold once more and gave her the news, then he provided Billy with directions to the woman's home. Rowan thanked Dr. Winslow. He wished her luck with finding whatever it was she sought.

As Billy backed out of the parking slot, Rowan surveyed the hospital. All those years ago her mother had been here. Afraid and uncertain of what her future held. Rowan could only imagine how she had felt when Julian showed up. Her worst nightmare had come true.

But then, what if Rowan and Billy had it all wrong? Perhaps her mother hadn't been afraid of Julian. The idea could very well be wishful thinking on Rowan's part. The Solomon woman may have been another liar sent by Julian to confuse Rowan. Either way, perhaps she would know soon.

Beatrice Reinhold lived in a neat little duplex in Spring Hill. It was dark, just past seven, when Rowan and Billy arrived. They parked on the street and emerged from the truck. The neighborhood was quiet and well lit with carefully placed lampposts. A cobblestone path led to the narrow front porch. There were no steps. Just a straight shot to the front door.

Billy pressed the doorbell and the chime echoed inside.

Rowan felt suddenly cold, her determination turning tentative. If this woman remembered Rowan's mother, she could tell her things she wished she hadn't learned. The past year had been filled with information she wished she had never discovered.

And yet if she hadn't dug so desperately for the truth, she would never have known her mother had not left her because she didn't love her enough.

If Rowan hadn't written that book, *The Language of Death*, would Julian have ever slipped up and revealed himself to her? Would some other thing Rowan might have done in the future have tripped the trigger that set him off?

The answers to those questions she would never know, but what she had learned—the hard way—was that he was capable of anything. No matter how seemingly horrific. Julian Addington sat at the very top of the evil scale.

"You okay?"

Rowan produced a smile for Billy. "I am. Maybe a little tired."

He reached out and squeezed her hand. "I know."

The door opened and a woman with silvery-blond hair and a trim figure dressed in a very stylish jumpsuit smiled as if long-lost friends had appeared at her door. "Hello! You must be Rowan—" she looked from one to the other "—and Billy. Come in, please."

Her home was warm and full of eclectic treasures.

A cross between country and elegance. Lots of white contrasted with rustic touches. She guided them along the foyer and to her open concept main living area.

"Do have a seat and tell me your pleasure. I have coffee, tea, soda, beer—" she grinned at Billy "—and just about anything else you could desire. I'm a firm believer in being prepared for unexpected guests."

"We don't want to put you to any trouble, ma'am," Billy assured her.

She waved him off. "Come on. Allow an old lady to show off."

"In that case," Rowan said, "I would love a cup of tea."

Her face full of glee she turned to Billy. "How about a beer?"

"Yes, ma'am, that would be nice."

"Make yourselves at home and I'll be back in two shakes."

They settled on the sofa. Billy placed his hat next to him. "I should probably call Lincoln and see how things are going."

"I'm curious about that myself."

Billy jerked his head in the direction they'd come. "I'll just step into the foyer in case our host returns."

Rowan nodded and watched him until he'd disappeared into the front hall. Her father had never mentioned her mother's problems with depression. It was possible Norah had been particularly good at hiding her feelings. Some people were. Sometimes family and friends just didn't notice or didn't want to notice until something drastic happened. Denial was a powerful emotion. It was far easier to see a person as you expected them to be.

"Here we go." Reinhold breezed in carrying a tray laden with refreshments. She glanced at the empty seat next to Rowan as she lowered the tray to the coffee table. The low murmur of Billy's voice coming from the foyer was explanation enough of his absence.

"I took the liberty of adding a few snacks. I thought you might be hungry." She passed Rowan the tea. "It was my day to host Bunco so I have lots of scones and tea biscuits left over. Cheese straws and absolutely marvelous spiced crackers." She placed three small snack plates on the table, arranging them for her guests and herself. "If I don't share them, I'll eat them all."

"That's very kind of you." Rowan sipped her tea. She wasn't sure she could eat a single bite if her life depended on it but she wanted the lady to cooperate. The best way to ensure that happened was to indulge her. Rowan reached for the smallest of the tea biscuits. She hummed her satisfaction. "Delicious."

"I had to make a call," Billy said as he walked in and resumed his seat.

"Crime never takes a vacation for a chief of police." Ms. Reinhold passed him the longneck bottle of beer. "Enjoy this little break."

Billy thanked her, turned up the beer and had a swallow.

"You want to know about Norah." Reinhold's gaze settled on Rowan. "Looking at you is like looking at her."

Rowan managed to keep her smile in place. "You

spent a good deal of time with her during her stay at Serenity?"

"I did. I liked her and she trusted me." Reinhold picked up her own cup of tea. "There were few she trusted. She was afraid most of the time."

The knowledge found its mark and twisted like a dagger in Rowan's heart. "Did she speak to you about her childhood?"

Reinhold held her gaze for a long moment. "She didn't like to talk about it. She repeatedly resisted speaking about her early years in her sessions."

"Was this part of the reason for her depression?" Rowan was aware there were a wide variety of underlying issues that contributed to depression. Childhood trauma was merely one of them.

"In part, I think." She sat her teacup and saucer aside. "But it was more about her children."

A new tension bumped against Rowan's breastbone. "In what way?"

"She was afraid that her heritage—her childhood—would come back to haunt them. She was desperate to protect you both and she felt she had failed."

The heaviness on Rowan's chest increased. "Did she explain why?"

"She would never say." Reinhold shook her head. "She was just a beautiful, creative woman who had suffered greatly as a child. She refused to go into the details."

"She was here for three weeks," Rowan said. "Was any headway made at all on the underlying reason for her depression?"

"Not really. She agreed to try medication—something

else she feared greatly. The one thing that became clear during her stay was that she despised Dr. Addington."

Rowan winced before she could school the reaction. "Did she say anything specific about him?"

"She wanted nothing to do with him. She refused to speak when he came near her. She complained to the point that he was reassigned from her case. Addington insisted she was suffering from what they called split or multiple personality disorder in those days, but he was the only one who saw this alleged side of her."

"What were your personal impressions?"

Reinhold studied her for a moment. "There was something in her childhood—something very dark that she blocked with every ounce of determination she possessed. Whatever it was, it terrified her and she fought hard to keep it buried."

"Had she been successful to that point? Was her stay at Serenity the first of her hospitalizations?"

The older woman nodded. "There was no history of previous hospitalizations. As a psychiatrist you know that for some the darkness they hide is far more difficult to contain. It keeps digging its way out. Keeps showing up."

"Ms. Reinhold," Rowan said, "did you at any time feel that Dr. Addington and Norah had been involved before? Were connected somehow?"

Something changed in the other woman's eyes. "I felt there was something, yes." She drew in a big breath. "But Norah would never confirm. She wouldn't speak of him just as she wouldn't speak of her childhood. It was the tension between them that told me there was a history there. Whatever it was, it was intense and very painful for Norah."

"After her release," Billy asked, "did you ever have any dealings with Addington and other patients?"

Reinhold shifted her attention to him. "Being at the same hospital during his residency, of course I ran into him from time to time, but he was always careful to avoid me. I had already spoken with the administrator and asked not to be assigned to the same patients as Addington. The administrator was a longtime friend, so he indulged my request."

"Why do you believe Addington avoided you?" This piqued a new curiosity in Rowan.

"I think he knew I saw through him. Of course, it was nothing I could put my finger on and certainly I had no evidence of wrongdoing, but I sensed a kind of darkness in him as well. But his darkness was different from your mother's."

Rowan angled her head. "How so?"

"The darkness your mother kept hidden was a product of fear and desperation. His, on the other hand, was spawned by something sinister and malevolent. Obviously I was right to feel that way."

"Thank you, Ms. Reinhold." Rowan stood and offered her hand across the table. "If you think of anything else you believe I should know, please call me. Dr. Winslow has my contact information."

The woman shook Rowan's hand and pushed to her feet. "Good luck to you, Dr. DuPont."

Billy exchanged handshakes with the woman and she walked them to the door.

As they drove out of the neighborhood, Rowan

turned to Billy. "She was free of him until she ended up in the Serenity Center. That may very well be when he found her again."

Billy braked at the intersection and turned to her. "You should check the dates in her journals to see if that time frame coincides with when she started her writing."

Rowan's breath caught. "You're right. Her first entries were just before mine and Raven's fourth birthday. I remember because she was too busy to properly plan the party. Daddy wound up doing most of it."

That had been the beginning of the end.

A gray sedan waited in the parking lot in front of the funeral home when Rowan and Billy arrived.

"Oh hell," he muttered.

"Is that Pryor?"

"That's him."

When Billy shut off the engine, she placed a hand on his arm. "Don't mention anything about Josh yet. If I'm giving either of these men the benefit of the doubt, it's going to be Josh. For now."

Maybe her decision was a mistake, but Rowan had known and worked with Josh for years. No matter how it looked that Anna Addington and her friends were dead after Rowan mentioned going to see her to Josh, she wasn't ready to throw him under the bus.

"For now," Billy agreed.

Pryor was already emerging from his vehicle before Rowan and Billy opened their doors. The clearly agitated agent waited for them at the funeral home entrance doors.

"Did you have something else you wanted to say to me?" Billy asked as they strode toward the man. "An apology, maybe?"

Pryor scoffed. "I'm here to give you a final warning, Brannigan. Stay out of the Addington investigation. Your new deputy chief will be taking your place on the task force and I understand that he'll likely pass along everything he learns to you. I have no problem with that. What I do have a problem with is you—" he turned to Rowan "—and you being involved on any level with the investigation on the ground. Both of you are too personally involved."

"I went to see Anna Addington for personal reasons related to my mother's death," Rowan reminded him. "I've told you that already. I had no idea when I arrived that she had been murdered. I can't possibly interfere with your investigation, Agent Pryor, if I'm not aware I'm walking into part of it."

"If it's related to Addington in any way it's part of my investigation. End of story. Keep that in mind, Dr. DuPont." He pointed a finger at her. "If I find out you're keeping anything from me, I will see—"

"Good night, Agent Pryor." Billy stepped in front of Rowan and stared the man down.

Pryor didn't move for a beat or two, then he walked away. The agent in the passenger seat stared at Rowan and Billy as his boss drove away.

"He knows we're onto him," Rowan said as Billy unlocked the door.

"Makes him nervous." Billy pushed the door open and waited for Rowan to go in first.

The alarm beeped until she disarmed it. Billy turned

on the interior lights. Freud bounded up to them, his tail wagging. Rowan scratched him behind the ears before rearming the security system. At this point she wasn't taking any chances.

Billy was right. The idea that they had Pryor's number did make him nervous.

The question was, did it make him dangerous?

# *Seventeen*

*Saturday, March 14*

Rowan finished the weekly report and filed it with a few clicks of the keyboard. Last night had been a restless one. She'd dreamed of that house in the woods where her mother had grown up. The house had disappeared and the hospital had taken its place. The rest of the dream had sent her fleeing for her life from Julian. But then the woman running wasn't her, it was her mother.

Billy had woken her and pulled her into his arms. No words had been necessary. He had understood that she needed to feel safe. She thought of the ring she had found in his glove box. In truth it still startled her that he wanted to spend the rest of his life with her knowing all that he did about her and the insanity that had followed her since before she was even born.

Beyond the surprise and the happiness, not to mention a hefty dose of giddiness, there was fear. Fear that if she dared to hope that they could actually have a life together that somehow Julian would find a way to tear it apart. The possibility that he would harm Billy terrified her more than anything else.

How did she go on with her life as long as he was out there?

"Ro!"

Billy's voice drifted from the hall. Her heart instantly shifted into a faster rhythm. What had happened now? She closed out of her electronic files and stood. "In here."

He paused in the open doorway of her office. "Lucky Ledbetter is here. He'd like to speak with you."

"You think he discovered something about the ex-wife's cause of death?" Rowan followed him into the corridor toward the lobby. Anna Prentice Addington, her driver and her friend, Cash Barton, had all suffered a single shot to the back of the head. Just like Crash Layton.

Julian was eliminating all the loose ends.

"He found the same sort of Taser marks as on Layton. But his visit isn't about that. He could have called with that info. He needs to speak to you face-to-face."

Anticipation nudged her. "Maybe he found something on the man in the photo. The one who used to work with Burt."

"Could be."

When they reached the lobby, Lucky cradled a foam cup from the local coffee shop. He gave Rowan a nod. "Morning."

"Good morning. Do you have some news for me?"

"I do. I found that fellow in the photo from Burt's house."

Rowan's pulse reacted to the possibility of learning more helpful information. "Is he still alive?"

"He is but he won't talk to you or the chief." Lucky glanced at Billy. "His name is Ernest Vernon. I guess you could make him talk." This, too, he directed at Billy. "But I don't think he knows a whole lot. He said he grew up in the same area as your mother. He recognized her after she moved to Winchester with your daddy," he explained to Rowan, "but she begged him never to tell anyone what he knew. Vernon is the one who gave that photo to Burt after all this business with Addington started. He thought it might mean something."

"You're sure he won't talk to me?" Rowan wanted desperately to hear more about her mother's childhood. Anything he knew could prove useful.

Lucky shook his head. "He said he would disappear before he'd get involved. But he said there was a man your momma visited up on Sewanee mountain. One who knew a lot about the trouble she had. He gave me his name. A Reginald Price. He's a professor at the university up there."

"Thank you so much, Lucky. This explains a lot."

Lucky nodded. "I figure whatever Burt was doing, he was trying to help you."

"I'm certain he was," Rowan agreed.

They spoke a moment about how things were going for Lucky since he'd taken over as the temporary coroner, then Billy walked him to the door, thanking him again for his help.

When he'd closed the door, he turned to her. "I guess we're taking a drive to Sewanee."

"I'll grab my bag and my file."

The road up the mountain was a crooked one. The community of Sewanee was small but thriving. The

University of the South was one of the nation's top private institutions of higher learning. In high school Rowan had been offered a scholarship there but she'd needed to go as far from Winchester as possible. Staying hadn't been an option.

Dr. Reginald Price lived in a midcentury modern home that sat amid the trees in one of the community's most elite neighborhoods. An electric car that a quick call to Clarence had confirmed was registered to Price sat in the driveway, which hopefully meant he was home.

Walking to the front door, Rowan surveyed the neighboring homes. All were immaculately maintained and most had either electric or hybrid cars in the driveway. Any pets were evidently inside since no barking echoed along the block. No cats scurried across the meticulously landscaped yards. The wind was chillier up here than down in Winchester. She wished she had brought her jacket.

Billy rang the bell. The buzz echoed in the house. Then came the yapping of a dog. Not the deep bark of one like Freud, but that of a smaller breed. The door opened and sure enough a tiny white dog danced around the socked feet of the man staring at Rowan and Billy over the rims of his glasses.

"Professor Price?" Billy inquired.

"That's right." He pointed to the sign posted next to his door. "No soliciting."

"I'm Winchester Chief of Police Brannigan," Billy said as he extended his hand.

The man stared at the outstretched hand for a moment before shaking it.

"This is Dr. Rowan DuPont," Billy went on. "We'd like to speak with you, Professor Price."

When the man looked confused, Rowan said, "I apologize for the impromptu visit. But the matter is urgent." She held the folder against her chest. If there was any way this man could shed additional light onto her mother's life, Rowan would be immensely grateful.

"You're the undertaker's daughter. I've been following the case."

"Yes."

"By all means." He stepped back. "Please, come in."

Rowan and Billy followed him inside. The entryway was spacious and spilled right into the living room. Floor-to-ceiling windows revealed a gorgeous view of the valley below. Rowan hadn't realized the houses on this street sat on a bluff.

When they were settled, he turned his hands up. "How may I help you, Chief, Dr. DuPont?"

Billy answered first. "We were told you might be able to help us with some background information on Norah DuPont."

Price blinked. Even behind the glasses it was obvious hearing the name surprised him. "Of course. She was your mother," he said to Rowan. "I don't know why I'm surprised to hear the name after all this time. Actually, I suppose I should have contacted you months ago, but I wasn't sure anything I knew would be useful to the investigation. It was primarily speculation. I'm not one to interject my theories into a situation where they might only confuse and mislead."

"We would love to hear any information, theories, whatever you have," Billy assured him.

"Of course. Why don't you start the conversation

with any questions you have?" Price suggested. "That will get us headed in a helpful direction."

"I was told," Rowan began, "that my mother spoke to you on several occasions."

He smiled and gave a nod. "She did. She asked me many questions for her research—for a novel she was writing."

Disappointment speared Rowan. She didn't want this to be another dead end.

"Do you recall anything about the story she was writing?"

Rowan wanted to high-five Billy for asking the question. She should have thought of going there.

"I do. Yes. The plot revolved around a pair of emotionally damaged protagonists who lured in serial killers and—" he shrugged "—exterminated them, so to speak. She had all sorts of questions about how the main protagonist might go about creating a wall of protection around herself. It was an immensely interesting concept. Ahead of its time. I'm really surprised she was never able to find a publisher for the project. To tell you the truth, I'm surprised it wasn't made into a movie."

"I did an internet search on you," Rowan said. "You teach a class about the survival of mankind through the centuries. Is that correct?"

He nodded. "I do. Murder and those who commit other sorts of atrocities makes up an entire block of my class. It's incredibly interesting, if I do say so myself. Particularly the section on serial killers. Norah was very interested in serial killers who interact with each other, a sort of community of killers."

Rowan was aware of the concept. Actually, it was more than a concept. There was documented evidence of so-called murder clubs and killer coalitions. The item of team killers had been around for some time. Killer couples. There were all sorts.

"I suggested Norah call her team of vigilantes the *killer collective.* I have no idea if she actually used the name, but I was quite pleased that she even considered it."

Rowan asked, "Did she ever show you any photos or discuss any particular characters she intended to use in her novel?"

"The main protagonist had experienced trauma as a child and she was exacting her revenge as an adult with the help of others. These other characters were more like sworn protectors. They would do anything to keep her safe."

A chill rocked through Rowan. "This may seem like an odd question, but did these protectors have any identifying marks? Tattoos? Scars?"

"Why, yes." He laughed. "She asked me about the symbols various cultures used through the years to depict those who served as protectors. It was a very interesting endeavor. I was honored she asked for my help."

Rowan opened up the photo app on her phone and swiped until she reached the series of photos of the tattoos on the bodies of the two men who appeared to have been involved with Norah. She passed the phone to Price.

"Do you recognize any of those symbols?"

"Oh yes." He scrolled through the photos. "You have Celtic symbols, Norse, Wiccan, several tribal symbols. They're broken into pieces for some reason, like a puzzle, but I'm very familiar with them." He passed the phone back to Rowan. "They all have one thing in common—they stand for protection or protector."

Rowan said, "A person who wore these marks would consider him or herself a protector of someone or something."

"That would be the actual intended definition. But there are any number of people who have the symbols inked on their skin simply because they like the design or the romantic idea of what it stands for."

"Did Norah ever discuss any concerns she had with you that felt as if they might be real rather than fiction?"

Price shifted his attention to Billy's question. "I have to say that after I heard about her death, I wondered if perhaps she might have believed the story was real. Perhaps this was her life story or there was an underlying mental illness." He shook his head. "As for the latter, I never once got that impression. She was intense, almost electric. She felt life very deeply. I did not see her as unstable or unwell. Determined, fierce, a little sad, but not ill in any way."

"Sad?" Rowan asked. "How so?"

"She shared with me that the story had taken on a life of its own," Price explained. "She experienced highs and lows with the characters. She spoke with such emotion." He sighed. "As I said, I'm stunned the story was never published."

"She didn't finish the story," Rowan said, her own sadness far too audible in her voice. The statement was true. Her mother hadn't finished any of her stories. Not a single one.

Rowan now understood that it was because they weren't fiction…they were her life.

"Perhaps it was simply too difficult," Price offered. "Some feel more deeply than others."

Rowan bit back the other question she wanted to ask. She got the distinct impression this man had been infatuated with her mother.

"You," he said suddenly, "you've written a book. You should finish her novel." He pursed his lips a moment. "I must say you look so very much like her. I was a bit taken aback when I found you at my door, no matter that I'd seen your photo in the paper and on the news. The similarity is stunning."

"Thank you." She tried to smile, didn't quite make it. "Did she ever speak of any real-life killers?" Rowan asked, steering the conversation back to the reason she was here.

"We discussed a few. Norton Barnard, the Kissing Killer. Alton Cavanaugh, the Perfume Strangler. Oh yes, and Lola Unger, the Movie Murderer. There were others, I'm sure, but those are the ones that come immediately to mind."

Rowan couldn't speak for a moment. The serial killers he had mentioned were among those whose faces and books of skin were found in Antonio Santos's home.

"What about Melvin Mallard or Edgar Young?" Billy asked.

"Yes." Price nodded adamantly. "Now that you mention their names, I recall discussing them as well."

Billy and Rowan exchanged a look. Billy handed the professor one of his cards. "I hope you'll call us if anything Norah said or asked that strikes you as particularly strange comes to mind."

Price accepted the card. "I absolutely will." He shot

to his feet. "Let me find my card." He hurried out of the room.

Rowan turned to Billy. "It's true," she said, her voice low, fragile.

Billy frowned. "What's true?"

"Truth is stranger than fiction."

Price returned with a card for Billy. "I certainly hope you will call me if you ever need any assistance on a case—this one or any other."

Rowan stood. Billy did the same as he offered his hand. "Thank you again for answering our questions."

Rowan shook his hand and thanked him as well. He held on a moment too long, his expression showing all that Rowan had suspected. He had been infatuated with Norah.

Price followed them to the door, chattering on about the classes he taught and how he would have wanted to be a detective if he hadn't gone into teaching. Billy offered to have him ride along on an investigation sometime, if he'd like. This pleased the professor immensely.

Rowan walked away from the professor's home, her heart thumping and her stomach clenching. This was real. All of it. Her mother hadn't been a writer—not in the true sense of the word. She hadn't been mentally unstable either.

She had been terrified of what was out there coming for her. Like Ms. Solomon had said, perhaps she had written the stories to rid herself of the demons.

Rowan just didn't know the whole story of why. But she knew who.

*Julian Addington.*

Ten minutes later they were headed down the mountain once more.

"What're you thinking?"

Rowan blinked, startled out of her disturbing thoughts by Billy's worried voice. "I'm sorry. It's just insane that my mother was somehow involved with all these serial killers. That she grew up with a different name—with different people. Julian may be her brother. It's simply unfathomable and yet it feels like the first truth I've found."

Billy slowed and pulled into the parking lot of a church.

Rowan looked around at the empty lot. "Why are we stopping?"

"Ro, whatever was happening with your mother, it wasn't her fault. She was a victim who tried to run away from her past, but it caught up with her."

"Why didn't she tell him? My father deserved to know what was happening."

"Can you be sure she didn't? If she asked him to keep her secret, then I suppose that's what he did. Maybe for your protection."

She felt ready to burst with all the emotions whirling inside her. Tears burned her eyes, scalded her throat. "But he didn't protect me and neither did she. I walked right into the trap she spent her life trying to escape."

Billy pulled off his seat belt and got out. She swiped away the tears and dropped her head against the seat. She hated when she fell apart like this. Hated that she felt as if the rug had been pulled from under her feet by the two people she should have been able to trust the most.

Billy opened her door. She turned her head to look at him. "I'm sorry."

He reached over her and unfastened her seat belt,

then turned her toward him. "Ro, your mother loved you. I know she did. I saw it every time I was at your house or saw the two of you anywhere. Your father loved you, too. More than life. He would have done anything to protect you. Whatever he did or didn't do, trust me when I say that he thought he was doing the right thing. As a parent, that's all you can do."

She brushed at the fresh wave of tears with the back of her hand and drew in a steadying breath. "You're right. The weirdest part is I think my mother was eyeball-deep in this exterminating of serial killers. Maybe she was the one luring them in and then Santos or Layton did the rest."

At least, she hoped her mother wasn't a killer.

"It's looking that way," Billy agreed.

Rowan closed her eyes and inhaled another cleansing breath, loving that the scent of his aftershave filled her lungs. "Thank you," she said, staring into his eyes and more grateful than ever that he was here, with her.

"There's something I've wanted to talk to you about, Ro. But then Addington happened again."

Rowan searched his face, her heart starting to pound. "Billy, I—"

He pressed a finger to her lips. "Let me finish."

Reluctantly, she nodded.

"I love you, Ro. You know that. I don't want to keep waiting for Addington to be caught or killed or whatever. I want us to get on with our lives. We deserve the chance to move on."

Before she could stop herself, she said, "I love you and you're right. We can't keep allowing him to rule our existence."

He reached into the glove box and dug out that small

velvet box. "This isn't exactly how I expected to do this, but—" He opened the box and withdrew the ring. "Ro, will you marry me?"

The urge to say yes was a powerful force. "Billy, I want to say yes."

His face fell. "Then why don't you?"

She took the gorgeous ring from his fingers and tucked it back into its box and handed it to him. "I want you to take twenty-four hours to think about this." When he would have protested, she touched her fingers to his lips. "Twenty-four hours. If you're still sure you want to do this tomorrow morning, ask me again. I promise I'll give you an answer then."

For a long moment he said nothing, just stared at the box. Then he tucked it back into the glove box and smiled at her. "Tomorrow. This time I'll do it right. On one knee and maybe with a violin playing."

Rowan laughed. "Don't you dare go to extra trouble, Billy Brannigan. The only preparation I want is for you to consider what it is you're about to do and be absolutely certain it's what you really want."

"It's what I want, Ro. I can tell you right now, I won't change my mind."

A smile stretched across her lips as she reached up and touched his handsome face. "You are a good man, Billy. You're the one person in this world I have left who means everything to me. I want you to be a part of my life for the rest of my life. But this is different, this is the sort of commitment that takes all other choices away. I don't want you to make this choice and then be unhappy down the road. I come with a lot of unpleasant baggage."

He turned her around and fastened her seat belt. Then

he kissed her cheek. "Tomorrow, I will ask you again and this time I expect an answer."

She could hardly breathe as he rounded the hood and climbed behind the wheel.

Could she possibly say yes?

# Eighteen

Since there were no viewings or funerals scheduled today, Charlotte had the rare Saturday off. As much as Rowan liked and appreciated her assistant, she was grateful for some time alone. The week had been one bombardment after the other of emotional revelations. Today she needed a few hours of quiet. The nursing home on the bypass had transferred a deceased resident. Rowan hadn't met this ambulance driver before, but then again, she wasn't always here for intakes.

A member of the family was supposed to drop by later this afternoon to go over the arrangements. Rowan placed the paperwork for Tyler Fortenberry on the desk where she had begun the whiteboard list for his preparations. She pulled on gloves and her apron and walked over to the mortuary table.

She surveyed the man stretched out on the table. Fortenberry's gray hair was cropped military short. His face bore the evidence of a hard-lived life. The man was dressed rather oddly to have come from the nursing home. He wore jeans and a button-down, long-sleeved shirt. Generally the intakes from the nursing homes wore pajamas or gowns. Oh well. Perhaps he'd preferred wearing his own clothes rather than the standard uniform of the facility. Or maybe he'd requested to leave the way he'd entered the facility, clothed in his own belongings.

According to his papers, Fortenberry was sixty-three. He had lived in Estill Springs before entering the nursing home and had died of a heart attack. He seemed young to be in a nursing home unless there were other health issues not listed. Apparently whoever filled out his paperwork had been in a hurry to get him off.

"Let's get started, Mr. Fortenberry."

Rowan began with removing his clothes. She unbuttoned his shirt. The shirt would go first, then his shoes and socks and finally his jeans and underwear. Once his body was relieved of those barriers, she would bathe and disinfect his body and prepare for the embalming.

More often than not it was necessary to cut the clothing free of the body. Where had she put the scissors? She pushed his shirt open and froze.

Symbols and images had been tattooed on his chest. Symbols and images she recognized. The same ones she had seen on the bodies of Santos and Layton. Her pulse sped up. His skin felt warm. No lividity.

Frowning, she watched for the rise and fall of his chest. As she waited her right hand moved to her hip pocket and tugged out her cell phone. Still no movement. She reached with her left and felt for a carotid pulse.

The faint movement beneath her fingertips trapped her next breath in her lungs.

This man was not dead.

She muttered a curse and started to enter 911 on her

cell. Billy was upstairs in her office having a conference call with Detective Lincoln. She should go get him but if she left the room—

The man on the table sucked in a big breath.

Her gaze shot to this face just as his eyes opened.

Her thumb poised to hit Call.

His hand snaked out and grabbed her right wrist.

"Drop the phone," he growled.

Rowan tried to jerk away from him, but his grip was far too strong. He sat up, tightened the fingers mana-cling her wrist. "Drop it."

The phone clattered to the floor. "What do you want?" she demanded.

If he was one of them—the so-called protectors who had helped her mother—then he hadn't been sent by Ju-lian. With that idea in mind she tried to relax.

He sat up, swung his legs over the side of the table but didn't hop down. "My name is Robert Johns. There are things I need to tell you. This was the only way to get to you."

His hold on her relaxed and Rowan snatched her hand from his grasp. He let her. "I'm assuming you aren't from the nursing home."

He shook his head. "I needed to get to you without anyone knowing. There are many eyes on you, Rowan. I paid a local ambulance driver to forge some paperwork and drop me off." He shrugged. "Don't blame him. It was necessary."

Rowan picked up her phone and tucked it back into her pocket. As she removed her gloves, she asked, "What is it you went to all this trouble to tell me?"

"All the rest are dead."

"The rest?"

"Santos and Layton. We were the only three who remained."

Rowan untied her apron. "The ones who protected my mother."

"We swore to her that if the need arose we would protect you as well. Time had passed and you were okay. Happy. Doing well in Nashville. We didn't realize Addington had gotten to you until your father was murdered. We were negligent. Complacent. We should have been paying better attention."

Since he'd said as much she decided not to mention how badly that had worked out so far. "I've heard this before—that my mother wanted you to protect me. Exactly what did she ask you to protect me from, besides Julian?"

He glanced at the door.

"It's locked," she said. Even with Billy just upstairs, she had gotten in the habit of locking this door whenever she worked in the mortuary. There was no way to escape if someone trapped her down here in the basement.

Another concept that had sounded good in theory and failed miserably.

"You've been doing some digging," he said as if he were aware of her every move. "You understand that your mother wasn't born in Memphis."

Rowan nodded. "I've been to the house. Her name was Nina Mulligan."

"That's right. Her parents were the epitome of evil. They were serial killers. They celebrated murder like it was Christmas and New Year's all rolled into one. Norah—your mother—said they hosted killing celebrations each year. Each guest would bring a sacrificial lamb."

"Except they weren't lambs, were they?" Rowan had concluded as much after seeing all that wood stained with blood in the barn.

He shook his head. "They buried bodies at that farm. Disguised the celebrations as a pig-slaughtering event. Their neighbors had no idea that during these gatherings there would be a dozen or more serial killers right down the road. But the visiting killers weren't allowed to take anyone from the local community. It was a kind of BYOB thing. Bring your own body."

The idea sent bile climbing up her throat. "Were there other victims throughout the year?"

"Oh yeah. Norah said her father would take trips to other cities. Huntsville, Decatur, even Birmingham, to bring back a victim. Sometimes he used her to lure them in."

Rowan flinched at his words. The load of guilt her mother had carried was no doubt enormous. "These victims would be held in the house or the barn?"

He nodded. "The barn. They made the children feed and water them."

"Children?" Rowan asked this as if she didn't already know the answer. "There was a twin sister, Nora Mulligan, who died?"

"Yeah. Your mother took a variation on her name when she ran away. And there was a brother. His name was Richard but you know him as Julian Addington."

No matter that she had known this to likely be the case, shock still radiated through Rowan. "He killed them? The parents, I mean. The police believed the son was the one who committed the murders."

This man—this stranger—who'd found his way into this room alone with her by playing dead looked at

Rowan with such sympathy that she instinctively knew what he was about to say would change everything. The urge to rush out of the room was nearly overwhelming.

Did she really want to hear any more of this?

The urge to run from it all, to never look back, throttled through her.

"Your mother was only a child, Rowan. She'd seen too much. Survived too much. It was bad enough to live with ruthless killers, being forced to help them, there was also her brother. He was obsessed with her even then. He never abused her physically, but the abuse was emotional. He would tell her that when they grew up the two of them would have a home just like the one they lived in and that other serial killers would envy their life and children. But it wasn't until her parents tried to force her into her first kill that she realized what she had to do. She understood that there was only one way she would ever be free. She killed them. When her brother discovered what she was doing, he tried to stop her. She injured him but he was still able to take the ax away from her. He wiped the handle clean to protect her and then dragged her into the woods. She found an opportunity to escape and she did. She left him injured and dying—at least, she hoped he was dying."

Rowan could only imagine the fear and horror her mother had felt. Like when she had shot Julian, he survived. Came back as if he'd been resurrected. "But he didn't die."

"No. And then, all those years later, he found her again."

"After her bout with depression." Rowan put her hand over her mouth. She felt sick with what her mother had suffered. Their circumstances were so similar. Julian used Rowan's hospitalization to get to her as well.

"Yes. When you and your sister were born, she worried herself sick about your safety. It took a toll on her mental health and she ended up in that damned hospital."

"What happened after Julian found her? Obviously she managed to get back home. Did she talk to my father?"

"She did manage to get back home but she could never tell your father about Julian. He warned her that if she told anyone he would ensure that all she loved would suffer for what she had done. So she never told anyone. But she did make a very important decision."

Rowan dragged off her apron and pitched it onto the foot of the mortuary table just to have something to do with her hands. "To leave us blind and with no idea what we were up against?"

He shook his head. "That was never her intention. She found others who felt the same way she did."

"Like Santos and Layton."

"Yes. There were several others, including myself. We became a collective focused on ridding this earth of his kind."

"The faces and books of skin we found," Rowan guessed.

He nodded. "For the nine years that followed her hospitalization, we cleansed this earth of more than two dozen killers. But we could never get close to the one we really wanted."

"Julian," Rowan guessed.

"He was far too clever. Too careful. When he tired of our attempts he set out to make Norah pay for what she had done to their parents and to him. He had groomed his daughter, Alisha, to kill. Her mother tried to protect her from him, but she failed. She recognized what he was doing too late, I suspect."

Rowan's blood felt cold. "What did he do?"

"He sent Alisha to kill one of you. He didn't care which one. You or Raven, whichever she could take out the easiest. Raven called Norah and told her about Alisha harassing her at that party. The one she went to the day she died."

A heaviness settled on Rowan's chest. Julian had given her half the truth. "My mother went to stop it, didn't she?"

He nodded. "But she was too late. Norah was so distraught that she lashed out without thinking. She killed Alisha. Killing her wasn't the intent. It was a terrible mistake…a gut reaction based on her mothering instincts and her childhood."

The words shook Rowan to the very core of her being.

"Raven's death, what she had done, it devastated Norah. But she still had you to protect. You and Edward."

"Why didn't she tell someone?" Rowan demanded. "The police, my father, someone could have helped her!"

"No one could help her. By then, Julian was untouchable. He had resources Norah couldn't possibly reach beyond. You'll see. He has protectors, too. A few months later, Julian showed up and told her to make a choice. Either she went with him or he would kill you and Edward."

Rowan's hand went to her throat. "Are you telling me this is why she killed herself?"

"The one thing Julian wanted more than anything in this world was her. She was convinced that if she took herself out of the equation that he would stay away."

"Except he didn't."

"I can't say for sure what happened the day she died. I can only tell you her thoughts leading up to that day."

"You don't have to tell me. I know what happened. I found her." Bitterness lashed through Rowan no matter that she understood how her mother could have come to that place.

"We watched after you as she asked. All seemed well until you grew up. You turned into her mirror image and I think, when he saw you, he couldn't resist. He thought he could re-create Norah."

"But then I let him down when he discovered I loved my father more than him."

Johns held her gaze. "I will try and help you, Rowan. But he still has a great many resources. It was imperative that I came to you and told you the real story. You see, I'm the only one left. If I don't survive…" He hesitated a moment. "I needed to ensure you knew the whole story. Norah never wanted you to know the ugly truth, but in that she was wrong."

Rowan steeled herself against the emotions ravaging her inside. "Thank you for telling me."

"I have to go now but I won't be far away."

Rowan watched as he crossed the room, unlocked the door and disappeared. She turned back to the table where he'd lain. He was the last of the protectors who had rallied around her mother. She turned back to the door. And she had just allowed him to walk away.

But at least now she had the whole story.

It wasn't her father, it was her mother who had killed Alisha Addington. She'd killed her own parents.

But she'd had no choice. She had done what she had to do.

Suddenly Rowan knew exactly what she had to do.

She had to end Julian's existence. As long as he was breathing, it would never be over.

Anger tightened in her chest. She owed it to herself. She owed it to her mother.

Billy listened as Lincoln relayed the rest of the briefing from Pryor and the task force. It was no surprise to Billy that they still had nothing. The task force was no closer to finding Addington than they had been a year ago. Dressler was still in the wind. The only real update had been that Laura Brewer was now in stable condition. She was awake and talking.

During her interview she had stated that a man matching Addington's description, along with a second, younger, dark-haired man, had entered the inn and gone upstairs, presumably to his ex-wife's room. A short while later the driver, Garrett, had gone up to the room. Then, perhaps twenty minutes later, Barton had arrived. Brewer thought nothing of this. She had noted these comings and goings before, except for the man matching Addington's description and his friend. She had not seen either of them before. Shortly after Barton's appearance, Brewer had needed to go to the restroom. As she was washing her hands, the door burst open and the dark-haired man shot her. Her only other remark was that he wore dark glasses, like sunglasses, and his hair didn't look real. It had looked like a wig.

Billy was surprised that Addington had actually taken the risk and accompanied the minion who committed these murders. He supposed the man had wanted to look his ex-wife in the eye as she and her friends were murdered. Knowing Addington, he ensured the others were killed first and kept her until last so she could watch her faithful friends make the ultimate sacrifice.

Not for the first time Billy considered how badly he wanted to be the one who put a bullet between the bastard's eyes.

A rap on the open door drew Billy from his troubling thoughts. Rowan stood there watching him. He smiled. "Hey. You ready for lunch?"

She shook her head as she walked in and collapsed into one of the chairs on the other side of her desk. "Not hungry."

"You finished with your new intake already?"

Rowan drew in a deep breath. "He wasn't dead."

"What?" Billy was certain he must have misunderstood her.

"Yeah. He was faking. He wasn't from the nursing home. He was the last of Norah's protectors."

Billy shot to his feet. "Where the hell is he?"

Rowan held up a hand. "Gone."

Billy came around the desk and sat down beside her. "You're telling me that this guy was delivered and got into a room alone with you while I was right here without hearing or knowing a thing?"

She nodded. "You couldn't have known. Even if I had screamed I doubt you would have heard me."

"Why did he go to all that trouble?"

"Since he's the last one, he wanted to be sure I had the whole story. In case he doesn't survive."

"Jesus Christ." Billy gave himself a mental shake, tried to find emotional purchase in all this. "What did he tell you?"

As Rowan recapped the story this Robert Johns had told her, Billy felt himself slumping into the chair. The whole thing was incredible, unbelievable. He had known Norah was a strong woman. He'd also known how much she had loved her daughters.

When Rowan had fallen silent, she stared at him for a long moment. "We could solve several unsolved murders with this information. But it hurts me to consider sharing this with the world."

Billy took her hands in his. "Ro, this man's story—however compelling and logical—is nothing more than hearsay. It's not the kind of evidence we can use to close unsolved cases even if we wanted to. Its value is only in making the people left behind feel better or worse, whatever the case might be."

"I feel better," Rowan said. "At first it was shocking to comprehend that my mother had killed at least three people. But then I realized she did the only thing she could and I'm okay with that."

"I'm going to play shrink here," he offered. "When this all sinks in, you may not feel as calm and accepting as you do now."

She smiled in spite of all that had just occurred. "You're right, and if that happens, I'll suffer through and find my footing again. With your help, Dr. Brannigan."

"Ro, I know you asked me to take twenty-four hours,

but I don't need a cooling-off period. I know what I feel and what I want."

Sadness filled her eyes and that was not at all what he hoped to see. "We don't know how this is going to turn out, Billy. The things Johns told me only reinforce the idea that we won't be okay to move on with our lives until Julian is out of the picture. Now I know how my mother felt. It's terrifying."

"So you're just going to let him keep controlling your life? Our lives?"

"No, that's not what I mean. I promised you an answer and I'm going to give you one. I just need a little more time."

"You're killing me here," he said, his thumbs rubbing her soft palms. "I want us to move on. To live our lives rather than living around him and his actions."

She slipped her hands out of his and cupped his face. "You drive a hard bargain, Billy Brannigan."

His heart bounced. "Does that mean—"

His cell phone rattled on top of her desk. They both looked at it and then back at each other.

"Don't move," he ordered.

Rowan held up her hands. "I'm staying right here."

He leaned across the desk and grabbed his phone. "Brannigan."

It was his mother. She was crying; her voice shook so hard he couldn't understand the words she was saying.

"Slow down, Mom. What's happened?"

"It's your father. They think it's a heart attack. They're loading him into the ambulance now. We're going to the hospital."

His father. Heart attack. Billy's world turned upside down. "Stay calm. We're on our way."

The call ended and he turned to Rowan. "We have to get to the hospital. Dad had a heart attack."

Rowan snatched up her keys from her desk and grabbed his hand. "Let's go!"

# *Nineteen*

Billy's father was in stable condition. Blood tests and the EKG confirmed a heart attack. The doctors were running more tests, monitoring his heart and determining the best next step. Rowan was grateful he had been stabilized for the moment. A heart attack was always terrifying.

Dottie was understandably distraught. Billy had gone back to see his father while Rowan remained in the ICU waiting room with his mother. Only one visitor at a time for now. It was necessary to limit any potential emotional triggers.

"I knew this was coming." Dottie shook her head, a clump of Kleenex clasped in her hand. "I kept telling him he needed to get a physical. He hasn't had one in five years. Men, I swear they won't listen to reason."

"His health appears to be good," Rowan said, in hopes of reassuring the other woman. "He's very active. You said he's never had any blood pressure problems or high cholesterol results. These are factors in his favor."

"But things can change in five years."

This was true. Rowan took Dottie's hand in hers and warmed it. The poor woman's hands were freezing. "For now, we're going to believe the best. We have every reason to expect a good result."

Dottie smiled, the expression faint. "When Billy walked through that door I thought of when he was born. His father was so excited to have a son." Her smile widened, reaching her eyes and chasing away some of the worry. "He was perfect."

Rowan felt her own lips stretch into a smile. Billy was still pretty damned perfect.

"By the time he could walk he was wearing cowboy boots and a hat just like his daddy." Dottie laughed softly. "When he decided to go into law enforcement we were scared to death."

"I can imagine." Rowan couldn't imagine having a child and watching her or him step into the line of fire on a daily basis.

"But he was so certain that was what he wanted to do. His daddy eventually came to terms with the decision so I had to as well."

"It's difficult to watch them grow up," Rowan noted. "They depend on you and you protect them and suddenly they don't want your help or your support. I've listened to more than one mother speak of how difficult it is to accept that transition."

"We're so proud of him." Dottie turned to Rowan then. "You and Billy don't need to waste time. Life is far too short. Things happen." She stared at the door that blocked the view of the corridor that led to the ICU. "Wyatt and I have been together for forty-four years. I can't imagine my life without him."

Rowan put her arm around the older woman's shoulders. "We're going to focus on the positive. He will get through this. He's strong. A Brannigan won't be taken down so easily."

"You're right." Dottie dabbed at her eyes with the wad of Kleenex. "Wyatt is strong. He won't leave me as long as he has any say in the matter."

"I'm certain he won't," Rowan agreed.

Dottie searched Rowan's face a moment. "Billy loves you so much. Truthfully I think he always has. I think that's why he never allowed himself to get serious about anyone else." She laughed softly. "When he was about eleven I think he was in love with your mother." She shook her head. "He thought Norah DuPont was so pretty. His words," she pointed out. "He was fascinated by her."

"She was special," Rowan said, believing it for the first time in her adult life. "I think all the boys thought she was pretty."

"She was," Dottie said. "A bit unique in some ways. But something about her drew people. There was some sort of light inside her that no one could resist."

Rowan watched the animated features of the other woman's face as she spoke. She hadn't realized Billy's mother noticed so much about Norah. Unique was a kind way of saying odd or strange.

"You're like her that way." Dottie met her gaze. "Beautiful and filled with something extra that draws people to you."

Rowan shook her head. "I draw more trouble than I do anything else."

"They need you somehow," Dottie said, her expression turning serious. "You're light, like your mother was, and that light calls to their darkness. To the darkness in all of us."

Dottie spoke so adamantly the sudden spilling of feelings surprised Rowan. Her words had goose bumps rising on her flesh. Perhaps it was her fear for her husband's life making her so giddy and talkative. "Did you ever spend time with her? My mother, I mean?"

Dottie inclined her head and seemed to consider the question. "She came by my house once or twice. She brought tea and seemed to want to chat. I got the impression she wanted to know what I thought about how you were doing. This was after your sister died and I think she was worried about you. She seemed to need reassuring. I told her I thought you would be okay in time. Time heals all things, you know. She was worried about you being alone and I told her she never had to worry about that. Billy and I were always going to be there for you. Wyatt, too."

"And you were," Rowan said, remembering all the times Dottie had played mother to her after Norah was gone. "You took me for my first manicure. Everything I would have needed a mother for, you stepped right in and gave my dad a hand."

Dottie hugged her. "It was the least I could do after what you'd been through. I knew your mother would have wanted me to help."

That Dottie looked away so quickly after saying the words gave Rowan pause. "She wanted you to look after me."

Dottie picked at nonexistent lint on her dark trousers. "Of course. What mother wouldn't?"

It was more than that. "She asked you to."

Dottie's gaze settled on Rowan's. "She said something like, if anything ever happened to her would I help Edward look after you. I said of course I would. All mothers go through that sort of thing after losing someone close to them. It's natural. I didn't think anything of it."

"But this was more." A knowing congealed in Rowan's stomach. "She wanted to ensure you would be there because she had already made up her mind to go."

Dottie pressed her hand to her mouth. A fresh wave of tears brimmed in her eyes. "The idea tortured me for years. I should have realized." She shrugged. "But I didn't. I thought she was speaking about what-ifs. She'd lost Raven. We all go through a sort of life inventory after losing someone we care about."

Rowan hugged her again. "You couldn't have known."

Dottie dabbed at her eyes. "It was hard, after what happened. I felt as if I should have done something more."

"You did exactly what she wanted. You helped me so much, Dottie. I'm not sure if I ever properly thanked you. I think my father would have been totally lost without your help."

"I worried I wasn't doing enough." She sighed. "Wyatt was a big help in my getting past the guilt."

"I'm sorry she made you feel guilty. I'm sure that wasn't her intent." For the first time, Rowan was absolutely certain of her mother's motives. She only wanted to protect Rowan and her father. She had taken steps to try to cover all the bases before she did what she believed she had to do.

Dottie took a big breath and nodded. "Hearing you say that means a lot. We all love you, Ro. We feel like you're part of the family. We couldn't be happier that Billy and you are together."

Billy had told Rowan repeatedly how much his parents adored her. Deep down she had known. His folks were always good to her, had been her whole life.

"Remember what I said about not wasting time," Dottie urged. "You and Billy belong together. Wyatt and I adore watching the two of you. Honestly, you're like a daughter to us. I'm hoping you'll want me to help with picking out a wedding dress when the time comes."

Rowan wondered if Billy had told his mother about the ring and his plans to propose. "When the time comes," Rowan agreed, "I would love your help."

"It's coming," Dottie assured her. "Call it mother's intuition. There's going to be a wedding. The sooner, the better. I'm ready for grandbabies."

*Children.* Rowan was forty. The prospect of having kids was something they needed to approach with caution.

But at this point, she was definitely not opposed.

Another first.

His father was resting now. The sedative had finally kicked in. Billy relaxed marginally. The glass walls of the intensive care cubicle felt like they were closing in. The beep of the monitors, the drip-drip of the IV. The staff rushing about beyond the glass. It was all a stark reminder that his father could have died...still could.

He was stable now, Billy reminded himself. Sleeping. He was incredibly grateful for this reprieve. Things had been touch and go there for a while.

He sat on the chair next to his father's bed, his elbows resting on his knees, his hands clasped together. He'd prayed about a dozen times in the past hour. He was glad his mother had agreed to let him sit with his father for a while. She needed to try to relax, pull herself together a little better. She needed to be strong for herself and for her husband. Billy knew his father well. He took his emotional cues from his wife. Always had. They were that close.

Billy felt his and Rowan's connection was like that.

He was so grateful she was here. Rowan would help take his mother's mind off things.

God Almighty, he wished she would just say yes to marrying him. He knew she wanted to. Addington was the reason she hesitated, the only reason. Outrage swept through him, making his teeth clench. The bastard had been controlling her whole life for more than a year. She couldn't see past the fear of what he might do next. The idea that he could target Billy terrified her.

Somehow he had to convince her not to allow Addington to win.

He hadn't told his parents yet about the ring or him popping the question. Waiting to see what her answer would be had seemed prudent. His mother would be over the moon. He didn't want to build up her hopes in case Rowan said no.

*She wouldn't say no, would she?*

He thought of the way she felt in his arms. Of how

her body reacted to his. The way she looked at him, touched him.

She wouldn't say no.

Putting him off, she might do—out of fear and for no other reason.

Maybe his confidence was inflated but he didn't think so.

They hadn't talked about kids, but he'd seen the way she looked at little ones. She wanted children. He was certain of it. Just something else her fear wouldn't allow her to wish for.

Damn Julian Addington.

The nurse appeared at the door to his father's room. Billy glanced at him to ensure he was still sleeping before pushing to his feet. He slipped out of the cubicle, the door swooshing shut behind him.

"You have more test results back?" His gut clenched at the idea that this could be bad news.

"The doctor will be in to speak with you shortly, but I wanted to give you a heads-up for your mother. They're going to transfer your father to Huntsville Hospital. He'll likely be there a couple of days depending on the procedure they decide to do. She may want to run home and get a few things. They won't allow her to ride in the ambulance, so she'll need someone to drive her."

"I'll be going with her. About how long do you think we have before the transfer?"

"Perhaps an hour," she said. "As soon as the doctor can he'll go over all the details with you and Mrs. Brannigan."

"Thank you. I'll step out to the lobby and let them know."

The nurse gave him a reassuring smile. "Don't worry. We'll keep an extra close watch on your father until you're back in the room."

Billy thanked her and exited the intensive care unit. He strode directly to the small waiting room. His mother and Rowan stood the instant they saw him, fear claiming both their faces.

"He's still stable," he quickly assured her. "No change. He's resting."

His mother released an audible sigh. "Thank God."

"Any updates from the doctor?" Rowan asked.

He nodded. "That's why I came out." He took his mother's hand. "They're going to transfer him to Huntsville. The nurse said you should go home and get a few things since he might be staying a couple of days. I'll drive you to Huntsville so don't bother getting your car."

His mother looked uncertain.

"I'll take you home to get some things, Dottie," Rowan offered. "We'll make it fast."

"Good idea," Billy agreed.

"Okay." Dottie looked from him to Rowan and back. "We'll be back quick."

Billy hugged her and then Rowan. "Drive safe."

"Don't worry about us," Rowan promised. "We'll be fine."

He watched them go and worry gnawed at him despite Rowan's reassurance. Pryor still had an agent following her around, but Billy wasn't so sure that was a good thing. For once he agreed with Dressler: he didn't trust Pryor. For that matter, he didn't trust either one of them.

He pulled out his cell and put through a call to Lincoln. "Can you send someone to my parents' house to make sure Ro and my mom get back to the hospital safely?"

He'd brought Lincoln up to speed on the situation as soon as his father was stabilized.

Lincoln put his hand over the phone and shouted something; Billy couldn't make out the muffled words. Then he said, "Done. Is your father still doing okay?"

"He's hanging in there." Billy headed back to the ICU, not wanting to be away from him any longer than necessary. "They're going to transfer him to Huntsville. Rowan and I will be taking Mom, so I'll be out of pocket for a while."

"You do what you have to do," Lincoln said. "Everyone here will have you and your family in our prayers."

Billy sighed as he stood outside the glass entry doors. "I'm scared, Clarence. Scared to death."

"I know you are, man. It's going to be all right. We've got everything under control here. Your dad is in good hands."

A loudspeaker announcement on Lincoln's end of the line had Billy frowning. "What's going on there?"

"Some kind of power outage. We've been without electricity for about half an hour now. Duck River folks are working on it. Somebody said something about a transformer blew and the backup generator didn't kick in."

"Damn. Sounds like you've got your hands full, so I'll let you go."

"Godspeed, Billy."

"Thanks." He ended the call and tucked the phone

into his pocket, then pressed the button to get back into the ICU.

The lock clicked and the door opened. He walked straight to his father's room, went inside and stood at the foot of the bed. Wyatt Brannigan looked so frail. So pale and fragile with all those monitors, the oxygen mask and the IV attached to him.

Billy closed his eyes and said another prayer. For his dad and for Rowan.

Rowan pulled into the driveway of the Brannigan home and a Winchester PD cruiser pulled in behind her.

"What's wrong?" Dottie followed Rowan's gaze and looked behind them. "Has something happened?"

The pitch of her voice rose in tandem with her obvious panic.

"I'm sure it's just a security detail Billy sent."

As the officer approached her window, Rowan powered it down. Before she could speak, he said, "I'm Officer Radisson, ma'am. Chief Brannigan asked that I provide security for you ladies."

Rowan nodded. "Thank you, Officer Radisson. We'll be inside for a few minutes, then we'll be returning to the hospital."

"Yes, ma'am. I'll be right here." He started back toward his cruiser.

Rowan opened her door and got out. Dottie did the same, moving quickly toward the porch.

"The sun feels good today," Rowan said to make conversation while the older woman fiddled with her keys. "Your tulips are beautiful."

Dottie's porch was surrounded by colorful tulips.

She flashed a faint smile. "Thank you. Wyatt helps me plant new bulbs every fall."

The keys fell to the floor and Rowan picked them up. "Why don't you let me do this?"

Dottie nodded. "I'm a mess. I'm sure they're planning some sort of surgery."

Rowan pushed the key into the lock. "Probably. The good news is—" she opened the door and waited for Dottie to go in before her "—these cardiologists get better all the time and Huntsville has an outstanding reputation in the field. He'll be in excellent hands."

"Hope so."

Rowan closed the door and followed Dottie to her and her husband's bedroom. "Do you have an overnight bag?"

"There's a black one in the closet."

"You start gathering what you need," Rowan suggested, "and I'll locate the bag."

The closet was larger than Rowan had expected. She surveyed the overhead shelves and then the floor beneath the hanging clothes.

"There you are." She grabbed the bag and headed back into the bedroom.

Dottie sat on the foot of the bed holding her husband's pajama top. Probably the one he'd slept in last. Rowan sat down beside her.

"We're going to see that he gets the best care possible." Rowan squeezed her hand. "Let's get you packed so we can make that happen."

Dottie swiped at the tears on her cheek, then hugged Rowan hard. "Thank you."

"You need a couple of really comfortable changes of clothes," Rowan suggested.

They packed a pair of worn soft jeans, Dottie's favorites, and a pair of cotton slacks. Two sweaters since it would likely be cold in the hospital. Underthings and toiletries. She packed a change of clothes for Wyatt, then exchanged her house shoes for her most comfortable shoes.

Rowan considered the bag as they were about to close it. "Let's grab some snacks and a couple of bottles of water."

"Good idea," Dottie agreed.

Some breakfast bars and peanut snacks along with the water went into the bag and they were ready to go. Rowan carried the bag out of the house. Officer Radisson rushed over and grabbed it. He loaded the bag into the back of Rowan's SUV.

Rowan turned to Billy's mother. "You have your and Wyatt's driver's licenses? Insurance cards?"

Dottie nodded. "And I have a little cash and my credit card."

"Sounds like you have everything you need." Rowan turned to Radisson. "We're heading back to the hospital."

"Yes, ma'am. I'll be right behind you."

Dottie appeared calmer as they made the return trip to the hospital. Rowan glanced in the rearview mirror and noted Radisson behind her. She checked the mirror again. Where was Pryor's agent? She hadn't noticed one on the way to Dottie's house. No one had parked on the street or in the driveway as Radisson had.

Maybe Pryor had pulled his detail.

Rowan's cell vibrated on the console. Worry seared through her. She hoped Billy's father hadn't taken a turn for the worse. She reached for the cell.

"Is it Billy?" Dottie's terrified gaze collided with Rowan's.

Rowan checked the screen. "No. It's Lucky Ledbetter."

Relief rushed through her, making her feel shaky. She imagined Dottie experienced the same. "Hey, Lucky."

"Rowan, I'm at Evan Harrison's house. His wife passed and he wants me to bring her to you. I heard Billy's daddy was taken to the hospital and I didn't know if you could take him today. Is Charlotte at the funeral home?"

Rowan remembered Mr. Harrison. He'd run the hardware store in town when she was a kid. His wife had always been there helping him. She kept lollipops under the counter for the kids who came in. "Let me call Charlotte. One of us will be there. Give me half an hour."

"That'll work. I'm a few minutes from finishing up here."

"Okay. Thanks, Lucky."

Rowan ended the call and put one through to Charlotte. Three rings and the call went to voice mail. "Charlotte, call me back if you can. Thanks."

Frustration gaining a foothold, she turned into the hospital parking lot.

"Don't you worry about going to Huntsville with us, Ro," Dottie insisted. "You and Billy go on and do what you have to do."

"We're not letting you do this alone, Dottie."

Officer Radisson parked and insisted on carrying the bag into the hospital with them. When they reached the ICU, Billy was already coming out the door.

"Perfect timing." He looked to his mother. "You should go in and give Dad a hug before they load him up. We'll head out when you're back."

Dottie hurried to the double glass doors and hit the call button.

Rowan tried Charlotte again. Still no answer. "Damn it," she muttered.

"What's wrong?"

Billy looked emotionally exhausted and she did not want to bother him with this. But she had no choice. "Lucky called. Evan Harrison's wife died. He asked Lucky to bring her to DuPont's and I can't get Charlotte." She closed her eyes and shook her head. "I need another mortuary assistant."

"Why don't you stay here and do what you have to do," Billy suggested. "Officer Radisson will stay with you. As soon as Mom and Dad are settled, I'll be back."

"I want to be there with you." Rowan rubbed at her forehead. "I can get him checked in and head that way."

"No." Billy shook his head. "I don't want you coming alone. Stay here. I'll call in backup for Radisson."

"I don't need two cops, Billy."

"I do," he argued.

"Fine. Whatever makes you feel more comfortable." She handed him her fob. "Be careful and keep me posted. Do not rush back, do you hear me, Billy Brannigan? Stay as long as you need to."

He pulled her against him and kissed her long and meaningfully on the mouth. "I will stay as long as I need to. And you stay home. No secret rendezvous or taking any chances. You got that?"

"Don't worry. I won't have time for secret rendezvous. I'll be plenty busy."

Rowan waved goodbye to him and headed to the elevator. Officer Radisson fell into step with her.

She suddenly thought of all the little things she wished she had said to Billy. Like how much she loved him and, most important, *yes*, she would marry him.

# *Twenty*

Winnifred Harrison was seventy-nine years old but until the day she died she never left the bedroom without her hair styled, her makeup properly applied and her outfit for the day just so. Her gray hair was cut in a neat bob and her dentures were white enough for a toothpaste commercial.

Rowan had donned her gloves and apron. No need for the face shield just now. She'd prepared the bathing concoction. Her father had preferred using his own personal recipe for the cleansing process. A good antiseptic but also a cleansing solution with a pleasant scent. The lady had nice skin; no matter that she was older and the ravages of age had taken their toll, the texture and elasticity were surprising youthful. Muscle tone was very good, and her figure was trim.

"Your friends will all be jealous at how good you're going to look in your casket, Mrs. Harrison." Rowan smiled and shook her head. How many times had she heard elderly ladies chatting about how so-and-so had looked in his or her casket? As time marched on, she supposed even the finality of death became a social event.

Growing up her father had taught her many things about the business of death. There were those in each community who felt it an obligation to show up for a viewing if for nothing more than to sign the guest registry. No matter that he or she might not have seen the deceased in half a lifetime, the act of making an appearance and signing that registry was a self-imposed social requirement.

Rowan recalled well watching the ladies huddle in groups at the visitations when she was a child. It was the perfect time to catch up on the latest gossip and to pass along thoughts and suspicions about neighbors. The men, however, passed the time discussing hunting season or some aspect of the latest harvest, politics or new businesses coming to the area. Children were always brought along, no matter how young. It was expected that every member of a family would make an appearance. Each and every one dressed to impress.

When Rowan had finished the cleaning and massaging of the body, she moved on to the next steps, setting the face, sealing and packing wherever necessary. She made the essential incisions and began the embalming process. While the pump did its work, Rowan made the usual notations on her whiteboard and in Mrs. Harrison's file. Once the embalming was done, she would drape Mrs. Harrison and place her in the refrigeration unit until tomorrow. Her husband had requested to have the visitation tomorrow evening and the funeral on Monday. He had brought his wife's preselected burial clothes. She'd chosen the dress at her favorite department store for just this occasion. A lovely rose-colored suit with a double-breasted jacket along with her favorite pearls. He and his wife had made prearrangements years ago with Rowan's father, so the casket selection and the dozens of other little decisions had already been made. The step having been taken beforehand provided a good deal of relief during this painful time.

Mr. Harrison had been waiting patiently at the funeral home when Rowan arrived from the hospital. The two of them had gone over his wife's wishes no matter that all were documented in her file and then he'd asked a question never posed to Rowan before.

*May I come by before I go to bed and kiss my wife good night?*

What could she say? Yes, of course.

When the embalming was complete. Rowan closed the incisions she'd made for the hoses and put the finishing touches on Mrs. Harrison. When she'd clothed her in the provided underthings to include a full slip, she draped the lady in a sheet and moved her to the refrigeration unit. She would add the dress and pearls tomorrow.

It wasn't quite six yet; she didn't expect Mr. Harrison would drop by before nine.

Rowan cleaned up the mortuary room and scrubbed her arms despite having worn gloves and an apron for her work. She climbed the stairs up to the first floor rather than take the elevator. Officer Radisson had made himself at home in the lobby reading a magazine. Rowan noticed the soft drink can and snack wrapper on the table next to his chair. She was glad he'd taken her advice and checked out the lounge. Freud was curled up at his feet. He raised his head, spotting Rowan before the officer.

Radisson shoved the magazine aside and stood. "You finished up for the evening, Dr. DuPont?"

"I am. Mr. Harrison may be coming by later but until then I'm going upstairs to find something to eat. Would you like to join me?"

"Thank you, ma'am, but my orders are that once you've retired to the living quarters to continually patrol the first floor."

"How about I bring you a sandwich?"

He couldn't hide the smile her offer prompted. "If you insist."

Rowan returned the smile. "I do." She glanced at Freud. "Come on, boy."

She climbed the stairs, the German shepherd on her heels. Tired didn't begin to describe how she felt. She checked her phone again, hoping to have heard from Billy about his father. Nothing since the last text letting her know that they had arrived, and his father was being further evaluated.

On autopilot, Rowan went through the motions of making peanut butter sandwiches. She rounded up a paper bag and added one sandwich, an apple and a bottle of water as well as a napkin.

"If only I could tie this to your back and send you downstairs with it," she said to Freud.

He cocked his head and studied her.

"Come on. Let's take the officer his dinner."

Officer Radisson thanked her, insisting peanut butter was his favorite sandwich. She decided not to mention that the old reliable had been hers and Billy's lunch or dinner more often than she preferred to admit. She was relatively certain she hadn't eaten so much peanut butter in one year since she was ten or so.

When she was back in her living room, her cell rang. *Billy.*

"Hey." She collapsed onto the sofa and held her breath in anticipation of the news.

"He's still stable but they want to go ahead and do the surgery tonight. They've discovered three major blockages and waiting is too risky."

Rowan rubbed at her forehead and the throb that had started there from the day's endless tension. She couldn't just sit here. "I'm going to shower and drive down there."

"There's nothing you can do. Mom and I are stuck in this waiting room for the next several hours. I'll call you as soon as he's out of surgery. When he's settled in for the night, I'm taking Mom to the hotel on Gallatin and then I'm coming home. You and I will come back together tomorrow."

She didn't like being more than an hour away. "I don't know, Billy. I feel like I should be there."

"Ro, I've got Radisson in the lobby and Pace in the parking lot. I'll feel better if you stay put. Pryor's guy is probably around there somewhere."

Rowan went to the window and surveyed the parking lot and the street. "I don't know. I think he's called off his surveillance. I haven't seen anyone since the cemetery."

"I swear," Billy growled, "the man is a whack-job."

She chuckled. Billy was right. "Just keep me posted,

please. I don't care what time it is. I want to know what's happening. Give Dottie my love."

"As soon as I know anything, you will, too. Love you, Ro."

"I love you, Billy." Should she just tell him? No, no. She wanted to give him his answer in person. "See you tomorrow."

The call ended and she suddenly felt intensely lonely.

Maybe she'd have a glass of wine and take a long hot bath. The sooner this day was over, the happier she would be.

Her cell sounded off again and she dragged it from her pocket, her pulse already speeding up at the idea that something may have gone wrong with Billy's dad in the blink of an eye.

*Charlotte.*

Rowan relaxed. She was probably returning her call from earlier. She frowned, but that had been hours ago. Two or three, she couldn't say for sure.

"Hey, Charlotte."

"Ro, I need your help."

Rowan stilled. Her pulse accelerating once more at the fear in her friend's voice. "What's wrong?"

Charlotte laughed nervously. "You know my husband is never home when I need him. He's always out of town at the worst possible times."

The high tension in the other woman's tone had ice forming in Rowan's veins. "What's happened, Charlotte?"

"When I came home this evening, Penelope needed me to help her with a school project. Stupidly I climbed up on a chair and then on the counter to get something in that very top shelf above the refrigerator and I fell. I can't call my momma. She's got the flu."

"How badly are you injured?" Rowan was already moving toward the table where she'd dropped her purse.

"I… I'm not sure. My ankle might be broken. I can't walk on it and I need to go to the ER. I thought about calling an ambulance but—"

"Don't do that. I'll be right there," Rowan said as she grabbed her purse and the fob for Billy's truck. "Should I call—"

The connection dropped off.

Charlotte probably hadn't realized Rowan was still talking or maybe she hit the end call button before she intended to. It happened.

Rowan gave Freud a pat on the head. "Stay, boy."

She locked up and hurried down the stairs.

Radisson was on his feet before she reached the final step. "My assistant, Charlotte Kinsley, needs me to take her to the ER. Should I drive, and you follow, or do I ride with you?"

Rowan didn't really see any reason for them to take both vehicles, but she wasn't familiar with all the rules uniformed officers were required to follow.

"How about I ride with you," he offered. "You'll be more comfortable in your private vehicle."

"All right."

In the parking lot Radisson explained the situation and instructed the other officer, Rose Pace, the one Billy had sent as backup to Radisson, to keep an eye on the funeral home and that he and Rowan would be back soon. Until then they would likely be at the ER with Charlotte Kinsley. He promised to keep the officer posted.

As Rowan pulled out of the parking lot she surveyed the street in both directions. Pryor had definitely pulled his detail. Fine by her. She was sick to death of his self-indulgent tactics. The man was so damned arrogant. She hoped Josh was able to pull together the necessary evidence to take the guy down if he was in fact the leak. The possibility that she might be giving Josh the benefit of the doubt and then some crossed her mind. She had known him a long time, but she'd known Julian a long time as well.

Right or wrong, Josh had himself in a precarious situation. Even if Pryor was guilty of what Josh alleged—and Rowan didn't doubt it, but she also couldn't confirm the allegation—things could still go badly for him.

Darkness had settled in for the night by the time they reached Charlotte's home. The colonial-style two-story was showing some age, but it was a lovely house. The home was surrounded by ten acres complete with a beautiful old barn. Somewhere out there in the dark goats and chickens roamed. It was a really nice place to raise children. Rowan had been here a couple of times. Charlotte and her husband had done most of the renovation work themselves. Rowan had a tremendous amount of respect for anyone who could conquer those sorts of DIY projects.

Rowan pulled into the driveway, the truck's headlights reflected off the taillights of Charlotte's minivan. As Charlotte had said, her husband wasn't home. His new promotion was keeping him away from home more often these days. Unfortunately, according to Charlotte, it was the only way to move up in the company. With two kids, he had needed that promotion. Rowan hoped that Charlotte's promotion at the funeral home would boost their income and simultaneously their quality of life as well.

Radisson followed her up the sidewalk and to the front door. Rowan pushed the button and the doorbell chimed inside. Charlotte's daughter, Penelope, opened the door. She was eight. Her brown eyes were big and round as if she'd expected the bogeyman at the door.

Rowan gave her a smile. "Hi, Penelope. Your mommy called and said she needed my help."

Penelope drew open the door, clinging to it as if it were a buoy in rough waters. She didn't say a word, much less smile. The child was truly afraid. Rowan walked in, Radisson right behind her.

"Where is your mommy?" Rowan asked, surveying the living room.

The child burst into tears as an arm snaked around her neck. The muzzle of a handgun bored into her skull.

Julian kicked the door closed, revealing his presence.

All the emotions—shock, hatred, disgust—that had been simmering inside her for a year burst from Rowan. "You son of a bitch. Release that child!"

"Put the gun down, sir." Radisson stepped forward, one hand extended outward, the other resting on the butt of his service revolver.

Julian stared at him. Didn't say a word.

Rowan repeated her demand. "Let her—"

An explosion rent the air. Rowan witnessed the flash from the barrel of Julian's weapon. Felt the spray of blood spew from the man next to her.

The bullet seared into Radisson's skull, shearing off a good portion of the right side of his head.

He dropped to the floor, his weapon still holstered.

Rowan's heart stumbled and the ability to breathe fled.

"It's time for you and me to go, Rowan."

Rowan shifted her attention to the man who had spoken. The man she had admired, respected and for whom she had felt such deep affection.

The man who murdered her father and countless others. The one holding a small child as protection. Bastard.

An ache twisted even as anger detonated.

"I am going to kill you," she said, the words as cold and hard as she felt at that moment. What she would give to watch the life drain from his body!

"I would love to hear you explain how you intend to manage such a feat considering you are unarmed, and your protector is—" he glanced at the officer lying on the floor "—out of commission."

"Where is Charlotte?"

"She's quite well, I assure you."

Rowan moved her head side to side. "I'm not going anywhere until I see her and her son." Charlotte had two children. Where was the boy?

"As you wish." He motioned with the gun. "They're in the dining room."

Rowan swung her attention to the child. "Don't worry, sweetie. Everything is going to be fine. This evil man will not hurt you." She glared at Julian and then turned her back on the bastard. She hurried to the dining room.

Bound and gagged on the floor, Charlotte flopped like a fish who'd washed up onto the shore. The frantic grunting sounds tore at Rowan's heart. Her son, ten-year-old Parker, was bound and gagged and curled up next to his mother. Her smashed cell phone had been slung across the floor.

Rowan dropped to her knees and reached for the tape wrapped around her friend's mouth and head.

"Do not touch her," Julian ordered. "Restrain the child as I've restrained the others and we'll be on our way."

Rowan glared at him. "I swear if you hurt them, I—"

"I won't hurt them as long as you do exactly as I say."

A hundred possibilities to overtake him went through her mind but none of them were feasible at the moment. Her only choice was to do as he demanded and hope they walked out of here without anyone else dying. She had to make that happen for Charlotte's sake.

Julian pushed the little girl toward Rowan.

"I'm so sorry to do this, sweetie." She picked up the duct tape and tore off a strip to cover her mouth, muffling her pitiful sobs. She secured her hands behind her back just as Julian instructed and then she bound her ankles. Rowan exchanged a look with Charlotte. She tried to relay with her eyes how deeply she regretted this nightmare invading her friend's home, touching her children.

Rowan stood. "What now?"

"Bring the tape with you."

She reached down and picked up the roll from where she'd left it on the floor.

"We're going out the back door. My car is parked near the barn."

Rowan glanced back at her friend once more, then did as she was told. Julian locked the door as they left. It wasn't until then that she noticed he had Charlotte's handgun tucked into his waistband.

"Down the steps." Julian motioned to the steps on the other side of the porch.

Rowan crossed the porch and descended the four steps.

"Pick up the gasoline can."

She whipped around and stared at him. "What?"

He motioned with his weapon at the large red plastic container sitting on the grass next to the steps.

"Pick it up and start dashing it onto the house."

Fear coiled around her heart like a snake. "No."

"Do it or I will secure you in the car and then do it myself."

"We either leave them alive or I'm not going."

He waved the gun. "I think you will go just as you restrained that helpless little girl. Your options are limited, dear Rowan."

She shook her head. "I'll run and you can shoot me or not, but I won't do this."

For a moment Julian simply stood there as if he couldn't decide whether she would actually dare defy him.

Then he took a step toward her. "Very well, let's go. We have quite a drive ahead of us."

Rowan started toward the barn. A lone light between the house and the barn provided just enough illumination for her to find the gravel drive and follow it toward her destination. A black sedan waited. Her heart pounded harder and harder as they approached the car. She wondered if Julian had his friend waiting in the car—the one Laura Brewer had seen with him at the inn when his ex-wife was murdered.

There was no one in the car.

Her body sagged with relief.

Julian opened the trunk. "Get in."

Again, she didn't bother arguing. Instead, she climbed in and lay down on her side.

"Secure your ankles with the tape. Do it right," he cautioned. "I'd hate to have to go back and use that gasoline."

Rowan bound her ankles together, not as tight as she could have but tight enough.

"Now put a strip over your mouth."

Her glower fixed on him, she pulled a length of tape free from the roll and then plastered it across her mouth.

"Turn on your side with your hands behind your back."

She did as he asked, and he secured her hands. Tight.

"Enjoy the ride, Rowan."

He closed the trunk.

Darkness swallowed her.


The surgeon entered the waiting room.

Billy pushed to his feet, his heart swelling into his throat. His mother stood beside him.

"Mrs. Brannigan, your husband came through the procedure like a champ. We'll be keeping him a couple of days, but at this time all looks optimistic."

"Thank you, Doctor," his mom said.

Billy echoed the sentiment.

"When can we see him?" she wanted to know.

"It'll be a little while, but the nurse will come and let you know soon. For now, relax. We're out of the woods."

After the surgeon walked away, Billy hugged his mother. Tears burned his eyes and he barely held them back. She wept against his chest.

When they settled back into their chairs, he said, "I should call Ro."

His mom nodded. "Please do. She'll be worried."

"I'll be right back." Billy squeezed his mother's hand and stepped out into the corridor.

He pulled his phone from his pocket and it vibrated in his hand. He'd shut off the ringer once they settled in the waiting room. The number was one of the department's cell phones. Worry twisted his gut.

"Brannigan."

"Chief, this is Officer Pace. We may have a problem."

The backup he'd sent for Radisson. "What sort of problem, Pace?"

"Officer Radisson and Dr. DuPont left more than an hour ago and they haven't returned. I've tried to call Radisson a couple of times and he's not answering."

"Where were they going and why didn't you go with them?" His worry morphed into frustration and no small amount of fury.

"Radisson told me to stay and keep an eye on the funeral home. They were going to a Charlotte Kinsley's house to take her to the ER. He said he'd keep me up to speed, but I haven't heard from him again. I've just arrived at Mrs. Kinsley's home and your truck is here and so is Kinsley's minivan, but no one is answering the door. I just tried Radisson's cell again and I can hear it ringing inside."

"Call for backup, Pace, and get in there, now! I want to hear back from you in two minutes."

Billy ended the call and rushed back into the waiting room. He crouched down in front of his mother. "Something has come up and I need to get back to Winchester. I want you to call me if there's any change in Dad's condition. I'll be back as soon as I can."

Her eyes widened as if she'd just realized the most likely possibilities. "Is Ro all right? What's happened?"

He shook his head. "I don't know but I'm going to find out."

She hugged him hard and told him to go.

Billy's phone rang again before he reached the bank of elevators. He hit the button to call an elevator as he answered his cell. "Tell me something good, Pace."

A moment of silence passed that felt like an eternity. "Radisson is dead, sir."

Outright fear punched him in the chest. "Rowan?"

"She's not here. Charlotte Kinsley and her children were restrained and gagged in the dining room but they're okay."

"Let me speak to Charlotte. I want you to get Lincoln over there." The elevator doors opened, and Billy stepped in, hit the button for the lobby.

"Chief—" Charlotte's voice was wobbly "—it was him. Addington. He took Rowan with him."

The breath left Billy's chest and for a moment he couldn't speak or even think. Then he said, "I'm on my way."

# Twenty-One

The car braked to a stop.

Rowan stilled, listened for sound. The engine continued running but the car wasn't moving anymore.

Her wrists were raw from trying to twist her hands free of the tape. Her ankles, too. The effort was likely futile, but she had to try. While she'd tugged and twisted, she'd also worked hard to focus on the amount of time that passed since Julian had forced her into this trunk. An hour at least. Maybe more.

They could be in Huntsville or Nashville or anywhere in between.

The door opened and a shift in the vehicle warned that Julian had gotten out. Was he stopping for gas? Or maybe to pick up someone else? His friend? The dark-haired man who had helped him murder his wife and her associates?

Rowan squeezed her eyes shut and fought to slow her respiration. Whatever Julian intended to do—whatever happened once the trunk lid opened—her chances of survival were far better if she did not panic. It was essential that she remain calm and keep her head clear of the distress lingering just beneath the surface of her composure. She was well aware how he thrived on the fear and panic of his victims. She refused to allow him the satisfaction of seeing her mounting apprehension.

Though she was admittedly apprehensive, she was not afraid of him. Death was not something to which she looked forward. The idea of never seeing Billy again and causing him pain scared her more than the concept of dying. These were things she did not want to happen. He had been so kind to her, always, she didn't want to be the reason he suffered. But *this* would be difficult for him.

At the same time these worrisome thoughts nagged at her, she was also grateful for the possibility that in all likelihood this nightmare was about to be over— one way or another.

She supposed there was a silver lining to the darkest clouds.

The vehicle shifted again as, presumably, Julian slid behind the steering wheel once more, then they were moving forward again. Slowly this time. Half a minute later the car stopped a second time. Once more he exited, the shifting of the vehicle confirming his movement.

Rowan strained to hear. There was no traffic noise. No sound at all.

Gravel crunching had her holding her breath. The slide of a key into the lock, the twist and then the lock popping preceded the trunk lid opening.

Rowan's gaze shot upward. She blinked repeatedly at the trunk light blaring in her face.

Julian stared down at her. "I'm going to cut you loose

and I expect you to do exactly as I ask. You have the power to make this as difficult or as easy as you like."

Psych 101. Allow the patient to believe the power belonged to her.

He removed a knife from his pocket and cut her ankles free, then her hands. She rubbed her wrists, peeled the tape from her mouth with a grimace, then the remains stuck to the skin around her wrists. When he'd pocketed the knife, he offered his hand. As much as she wanted to slap it away, it would be foolish not to accept his assistance getting out of this damned trunk.

Besides, she wanted him to believe that she intended to be completely cooperative. Also Psych 101.

When she was on her feet. He said, "Bring the tape. We'll need it later."

She reached into the truck and picked up the tape, then backed away a step, putting a small space between them. She didn't want to smell the scent of him, to feel his warm breath against the chill of the night. "Where are we?"

He closed the trunk; she blinked again to adjust to the sudden darkness. Slowly the moonlight and stars allowed her to get some sense of place. Woods surrounded their position.

"I thought you would recognize the place, Rowan."

She turned around to see beyond the car, beyond the narrow drive. An old white house sat just ahead in the sparse moonlight like a ghostly apparition against the darkness.

Not just any house...*the* house. The house where her mother had lived as a child.

"Why are we here?"

"We're here because this is home, Rowan. I thought

you might want to hear the whole story. The *truth*. Isn't that what you've wanted all along?"

A new outrage roiled inside her. How she hated this man. Even as the sheer hatred seethed under her skin, pulsed against her breastbone, he was right. She wanted the whole story. The *truth*. Or at least his version of it.

"Are you capable of spewing anything other than lies, Julian? You've lied to me since the first time we met. Every single thing about you is a lie."

"Shall we go inside? This wind is chilly."

He didn't wait for her answer; he grabbed her by the arm and ushered her forward. She didn't resist. For now, she would hear him out. Her curiosity wouldn't allow her to do otherwise, no matter that whatever he told her would as likely be a lie as the truth. They climbed the few steps and crossed the porch.

He slid a key into the lock and opened the door.

"How did you get the key?" Images of the real estate agent lying on the floor of her office with her throat slashed whipped through Rowan's mind. She winced. Another murder because of his obsession with her.

"I've always had a key."

He prompted her across the threshold, flipped a switch that filled the room with dim light.

Bile churned in her belly. "You bought the place."

"I did. Decades ago. The house had been sitting empty like a tomb without a single corpse for all that time. Of course, I couldn't walk into the attorney's office and announce that I was the long-lost heir and wanted to take possession of what was rightfully mine. I purchased this abandoned property by paying the back taxes. It was all quite simple."

Rowan turned on him. "Nothing about any of this is

simple. I know what these people were. What they did.
I also know what *you* did."

He laughed, those blue eyes of his twinkling with
the sort of condescension that came naturally to a man
as arrogant as Julian Addington. "You have no idea."

She struggled to slow down the fury escalating in her
blood. She couldn't lose control. Her future depended
on her ability to outwit her mentor. To outmaneuver
him intellectually and emotionally.

And then to run like hell.

"I wish you could have seen the barn in those days."
He smiled, obviously remembering. "It was a work of
art. Our father—oh, wait." He searched her face, his
smile slipping into a frown. "I'm sure you know by now
that your mother was my sister."

"Yes." She hated to acknowledge the idea, but it was
part of that truth for which she'd searched so long and
hard. She couldn't pick and choose the parts she accepted. It was all or nothing. "But since my mother
didn't claim you, I don't think I will either so don't expect me to call you uncle."

He chuckled, the sound a mere rumble. "We were
inseparable as children. I was her protector. Her only
friend." He sighed. "You see, Rowan, this was something you and your mother had in common. Neither of
you were ever very good at making friends. Sad, but
true. Quiet, withdrawn. The classic wallflower."

"Why would my mother bother making friends?"
Rowan ripped the tape from the hem of her jeans, first
one leg and then the other. "It wasn't like she could
bring anyone home. They might end up planted in the
garden or on the dinner menu."

He laughed outright then. "I can honestly say we

never once consumed a human victim. Human cannibalism was not a part of our profile, as your friends at the Bureau would say."

Rowan tossed the wad of tape across the room. "I am curious about one thing, Julian. Did you go into psychiatry in hopes of learning what made your mother and father want to kill? What makes you want to kill? Was it some blind attempt to understand and heal yourself?"

The sheer delight in his eyes made her want to tear into him with her bare hands.

"You would never know that I didn't attend university or medical school, would you? My ability to pull off the charade was utterly brilliant. The real Julian Addington, however, did graduate at the top of his class. A list of honors followed his name. I found this quite pleasing."

"You stole his identity." She should have realized. The Bureau should have found this trail. How had he gotten away with all this and no one noticed one damned thing?

"Come, let's sit down." He clamped a hand around her arm once more and ushered her toward the worn sofa. He took the roll of tape from her and placed it on the table next to the sofa. "Addington was hardly the only blond-haired, blue-eyed candidate I considered. But he had no surviving family and his brilliance intrigued me. He had a great deal of money, which was a nice perk, and that lovely old Victorian his grandmother had left him. It all worked out remarkably well, don't you think?"

This was one aspect she had not considered. Of all people, she knew how intelligent Julian was. Still, how had he fooled her and everyone around him so thoroughly?

Rowan shook her head. "What made you decide to murder your biological parents? Perhaps you blamed them for making you the monster you are." She considered the idea. "No," she amended. "I think you wanted all the glory for yourself. Or maybe you just wanted my mother all to yourself?"

Despite the anger and hatred and disgust she felt, some small part of her needed to know why he had done this to her...to her mother. Mainly she wanted to know if what she had been told was the truth. Had her mother murdered her parents or had it been Julian, as the police had suspected? She needed to understand how and why.

"Very well," he said. "Just remember, you asked. It was your mother who took the ax to our parents. She turned into a regular Lizzie Borden when she hit puberty. I tried to stop her, and she almost killed me, too. And then she disappeared. Left me for dead." Fury tightened his face, flashed in his eyes. "It took me forever to find her once more. And then I made sure she paid dearly for what she had done."

Every ounce of willpower Rowan possessed was required to prevent the outrage from exploding out of her. "You and your parents ruined her. Devastated her. Turned her into what you were, and she didn't want to be anything like you."

The fury on his face told her she'd gotten it right.

"She was a coward. Not worthy of being one of us. She had no idea the sheer beauty of taking a life. The extraordinary gift of feeling that life drain away and yet feeling your own surge to greater heights."

"If she wasn't worthy, why bother with her? Why not just leave her alone? Why destroy her life?"

"She didn't deserve to live after what she did," he argued. "I wanted her to suffer as I had. I wanted to watch her squirm and wallow in the fear of what might occur next."

"I see," Rowan goaded. "You couldn't stand that she had a normal life with a normal family. You didn't have that. Your wife hated your guts and your daughter was a killer just like you. Every part of your life was fake, a lie. You were envious."

"Touché." He laughed. "Perhaps I was jealous of what she had with Edward. After all, she was mine. We were meant to be, and she took that away from me. So I took something from her. Your sister. If not for your mother's interference, my daughter would have taken you as well, but in the end, I was grateful she did not, or the past twenty years would have been immensely lonely for me."

Rowan struggled to even out her respiration, to slow the spiral toward losing control of her emotions. "You insisted my father killed Alisha. How can I trust anything you say under the circumstances? My mother isn't here to defend herself so it's easy for you to lay all the blame on her."

"But you believed all of it, didn't you, Rowan? Every story, every lie—you accepted it all without hesitation. You wanted to believe what was easiest, what was safest. Edward suffered the same plight. He didn't want to see the truth."

Rowan swallowed back the bitter taste his words evoked. The bastard was right. She had accepted the easy way out. Not now. Never again. "You're the reason she's dead. You—" she flung the accusatory words at him "—made her feel as if she had no other choice and she ended her life. You took her from me. And then you took my father. Give yourself a pat on the back, Julian. You've succeeded in making me feel the pain, making me want it to end."

"Dear, dear Rowan." He shook his head as if she were a distraught child. "You are so naive. Do you really believe that your mother would have purposely left you for any reason? Oh, I'm sure she considered it, thinking that the move would be in your best interest. But no, she would never have left you willingly."

Dread and uncertainty abruptly swallowed all her anger, leaving her vulnerable. "I know what she did. I found her." A blast of renewed anger had her adding, "You know the story well, you bastard." How many times had they discussed that painful event?

"You did find her," he agreed. "That was the plan. That was the beginning of you and me, Rowan. The first time I reached into your life and touched you."

The blood roaring through her body suddenly quietened. "What are you saying?"

"You mother was dead before she ended up hanging from the end of that rope." He held out his hands, turned them up. "I squeezed the life out of her miserable existence with these very hands, but first I promised her that in time I would have you for myself. I taunted her with how devastated you would be that she had taken her life and left you behind. It was the perfect revenge."

"You killed her." The words were barely audible. *I couldn't stay.* The dreams of her mother saying those words to her were nothing more than what her mind wanted to believe. The truth was something entirely different.

Her mother hadn't killed herself. She hadn't left Rowan.

"I did," Julian agreed, "and it was the most exhilarating moment of my life. Nothing has ever come close to that moment. Believe me, I've attempted to re-create that incredible high."

Rowan drew back her hand to slap him, but he grabbed her wrist before her palm impacted his jaw. "I hate you," she spat.

"You see, Rowan, I've watched you grow. Watched you mature into the woman you are. But, like your mother, you disappointed me. Now I'm going to watch you die. I only hope that taking your life will be as incredible as taking hers was."

"Then do it, you son of a bitch, and let's end this now."

She would fight to her last breath to kill him first.

"Not just yet," he said in that cunning, scheming tone that told her this was far from over. "If I had only wanted to end your life, I could have done that months ago. But I waited for the perfect moment and it finally came. Now, you must wait. Because before I take your life, there's something I want you to watch."

Billy pulled over into the grass in front of Charlotte Kinsley's home.

Every minute of the past hour had felt like an eon. An ambulance, the crime scene van and four WPD cruisers were already scattered around the yard. No sign of the coroner, which meant they hadn't discovered any bodies since Billy last spoke with Lincoln. Two unmarked sedans sat in the mix. Most likely Pryor and some of his people.

If the man was smart, he wouldn't get in Billy's way. Not right now.

He strode across the yard, the two officers guarding the perimeter waving him on past. He pushed through the front door and stopped to assess the scene. Charlotte and her two kids were huddled on the sofa. Lincoln sat in a ladder-back chair directly in front of them. Pryor and his agent hovered behind him. Cops and forensic techs were combing through the place.

"Chief Brannigan—" Pryor strode toward him "—you cannot be here. You are no longer a part of this task force. You need to exit the premises ASAP."

Outrage—so hot, so fierce—shot through him, and Billy could hardly restrain the urge to pound the guy right there in front of half a dozen or so witnesses. Instead, he leaned close to the man and said for his ears only, "Back the fuck off or I will rip your head off right here."

Being reasonably smart in addition to incredibly arrogant, Pryor turned on his heel and marched back over to his pal. The two immediately started to confer quietly behind Lincoln's back.

Billy walked straight to the sofa and crouched down near Charlotte. "You okay?" he asked. He gave a nod to Lincoln and his deputy chief stood.

"I need to return a call. I'll be in the kitchen for a moment, Chief."

"I keep telling myself," Charlotte said, her voice shaking, "that I should have done something different. I should have looked before I opened the door. I should have found a way to knock him out." She shook her head. "This is my fault."

Billy gave her hand a squeeze. "First, this is not your fault. Addington wasn't going to stop until he got what he wanted. If he hadn't done it today, it would have been tomorrow or the day after. Second, you did exactly what you should have done by cooperating with him. You know as well as I do what he would have done if you had refused." He didn't want to spell it out with the kids sitting right there.

Charlotte managed a slight nod. Her face was red from crying. The devastation in her eyes was the worst.

Billy braced against the fear that wanted to sprout inside him. "Did he say anything while he was here—to you or to Rowan—that might give us some idea where they were going when they left?"

She shook her head. "Nothing like that. He mostly just told her what he would do if she didn't do exactly what he said."

Billy gave her hand another squeeze. "Have you called your husband?"

She nodded. "He's on his way home."

"When you've finished your statement with Detective Lincoln, why don't you let us take you to your momma's house. We'll need to do a little more forensic work around here. You all can stay at your momma's until tomorrow, if that's okay."

She nodded. "I don't want to be here until I know Rowan is okay."

Billy's gut clenched. "I understand. I'll have Detective Lincoln get this wrapped up and take you now."

"Thank you." She hugged her kids to her shoulders.

"I just need to get them someplace they'll feel safe. It'll be a while before we feel that way again here."

Billy gave her a nod and went into the kitchen to catch up with Lincoln. "How close are you from being finished with questioning her?"

"She's told us all she knows." Lincoln shrugged. "I don't see any reason to keep her and the kids any longer."

"Get them on over to her momma's. They've been through enough tonight."

"I knew this was coming." Pryor's voice preceded him into the room.

He and his fellow agent strolled right up to Lincoln and Billy.

Every muscle in Billy's body tensed with the need to kick the shit out of the guy. Instead, he ignored him and asked Lincoln, "Have you spoken to the neighbors to see if anyone saw anything?"

Neighbors were few and far between out here, but there was always the chance someone looked out a window at just the right time.

"We're working on that now," Lincoln said. "Nothing to report yet and I'm doubtful we'll find anyone who'll say anything."

Billy figured as much. Somehow they had to find Rowan. Fast. "Charlotte didn't see the color or the make of the vehicle he was driving?"

Lincoln shook his head. "We've got nothing, Billy. Not one damned thing."

"This is what she wanted," Pryor said, daring to break into the conversation again.

"Get Charlotte and the kids out of here," Billy said to

Lincoln, then he turned around, glowered at the special agent in charge. "What the hell does that mean, Pryor?"

"I'm saying," he dared to gloat, "that Rowan intended to find a way to disappear with Addington. She has her own agenda. I've suspected it all along. She and Dressler have been plotting this together. We've traced at least one call from him to her in the past week."

The man had obviously lost his damned mind. Just when Billy would have told him as much, his phone vibrated. He snatched it from his pocket. Didn't recognize the number.

"Excuse me." He turned his back on Pryor and walked away. "Brannigan."

He prayed the voice on the other end of the line would be Rowan's or Addington's. At this point he would love to hear from the son of a bitch.

"It's Dressler."

Billy's hopes flattened. "I'm listening."

"I was following Rowan when she drove your truck to her assistant's house."

Renewed hope gushed through Billy. "Are they going to run more tests?"

Dressler hesitated before saying, "Pryor is there?"

"Yeah. That sounds good."

"Got it. I saw Addington put her in the trunk of a car. I followed him when he left."

Billy held his breath.

"We've ended up at this house in the middle of nowhere just across the state line in Alabama. The GPS says it's a place called Lick Fork, near Princeton."

Billy fought to keep his tone even. "I'm familiar with that one."

"I think you need to come now."

"Okay. Glad you called. Keep me posted."

Billy put his phone away and turned back to the two agents loitering nearby, no doubt to eavesdrop. "My father's in the hospital. Heart attack."

Pryor nodded, though his expression remained indifferent. "I heard."

Lincoln walked in and Billy was grateful. He had to get out of here without Pryor having him followed.

"Charlotte and her kids are on the way to her mother's," Lincoln confirmed.

"Good." Now all Billy needed was a legitimate excuse to get the hell out of here himself.

"Detective Lincoln," Pryor interrupted, "what are your people doing to get this situation under control? Have you issued an APB for DuPont? If you don't consider her a suspect in this mess, you'd better reconsider your profession."

Billy gave the man a shove and got in his face. "I don't know who you think you are, you little son of a—"

"Did you see that?" Pryor demanded of Lincoln. "He assaulted me!"

Lincoln grabbed Billy and pulled him away. "Listen to me, man." He ushered Billy across the room, out of earshot from the two agents.

"Get me out of here," Billy murmured to his old friend. "I've got a heads-up from Dressler. I'll text you the details."

Lincoln searched his eyes for a moment. "Just don't do anything we'll all regret."

"If you don't get this guy out of here," Billy shouted, sending a glance at Pryor over his shoulder, "I'm going to—"

"Go back to the hospital, Chief. Stay close to your

Dad. We've got this under control," Lincoln urged calmly. "We'll keep you up to speed."

"Arrest him!" Pryor insisted. "I want him charged."

"Get out of here, Brannigan," Lincoln ordered.

Billy headed for the door.

Behind him, Lincoln said, "Back off, Pryor. You pushed him first. I saw it with my own eyes."

Both agents protested the accusation.

Billy didn't look back and didn't hesitate. He was out the door and rushing across the yard before the two federal agents stopped complaining.

He slid behind the wheel of Rowan's SUV and drove away. He was a good hour away from the house where Addington had taken her.

Getting there before it was too late was all that mattered.

# Twenty-Two

"It's time I showed you something."

For an hour or close to it Rowan had listened as Julian told her story after story about his family's exploits. He had no accurate count of how many people had been slaughtered on this farm. He had named off several known serial killers from past decades. None as prolific as him, or his family apparently. But Rowan had recognized several of the names.

Her mind felt numb with the notion that these people were her grandparents. Her mother had grown up in this hellhole.

Julian motioned for her to stand, using the weapon he'd not once laid aside. "Come."

She stood. He guided her into the kitchen. Opening a drawer in the cabinet nearest the back door, he reached inside and withdrew a flashlight. Clearly he'd been here and made certain preparations. Her throat constricted at the possibilities that might await anyone who attempted to rescue her.

He ushered her out the back door and into the night. The flashlight came on, its beam bobbing with their movements. He seemed to know the path, though it was long overgrown. As Rowan's eyes adjusted to the night, she decided their destination was the dilapidated barn.

When they reached the entrance, he paused. "I've waited a long time to share this with you, Rowan."

She stared at him; the faint glow from the flashlight illuminated his face. "Why does it matter? You're going to kill me anyway."

His smile was at once sinister and indulgent. "Because I want you to know your heritage before you take your last breath."

They moved through the interior of the barn. There were places where the loft had already fallen in, creating a maze of timbers. Julian pointed out the dust-covered chains in each stall that had been used for holding cells. The rough-hewn wood enclosures were stained with the same dark red as were parts of the wooden walls.

The image of people, naked and terrified, chained in those stalls flashed through her mind. In the middle of nowhere surrounded by the woods and fields, no one would hear their screams.

All this time she had yearned to know the whole truth, now she wasn't so sure she wanted to learn more than she already had.

Julian stopped at a stack of old hay bales. "I'll need you to move these aside."

While he watched, his weapon trained on her, she moved the heavy bales aside. The odor of mold, decay and dust filled her nostrils. Years of absorbing the humidity had made the bales heavier. She struggled with the weight, the twine holding the bales together cutting into her palms. Sweat beaded on her skin. Oddly it didn't bother her. Instead, it reminded her that, for now, she was still alive.

When she had moved the ten bales, she dusted off her hands and turned back to the man in charge of this macabre quest.

"Feel around on the ground, push the loose hay aside. You'll find a handle and a lock." He turned the beam of the light more directly on the area where the bales had been stacked.

She dropped to her knees and pushed aside the dust and hay until her hand bumped into something metal. An old iron handle with a padlock.

He tossed a key onto the ground next to her. She used it to release the padlock. When she had removed it from the handle, she handed both the lock and the key to him. He tossed them aside as if they no longer mattered. Then he grabbed Charlotte's gun and tossed it across the barn.

His gaze collided with hers. "Don't think I didn't notice you looking at it. Now, open the door."

Hatred expanding inside her, Rowan wrapped her fingers around the handle and pulled. The trapdoor was wood, old heavy wood. The patina of the wood matched the dusty ground and the hay that had sat atop it. When she pulled the door away from the opening, she propped it against the barn wall.

The beam of the flashlight poured into the opening, revealing a ladder. She couldn't see much beyond the ladder itself. It appeared to go down at least eight or ten feet.

"You go down first," he instructed. "When you reach the bottom, sit down on the ground with your back against the wall opposite the ladder. I'll be right behind you."

Rowan did as he asked. The beam of light remained aimed downward, providing enough illumination for her to see each rung as she descended downward. When she reached the bottom, she took the few steps to the far wall and sat down. Didn't feel like dirt beneath her, more like brick. She really hoped there were no rats or spiders.

He descended the ladder and turned to face her. With the flashlight between them, she could see that the floor was brick. The walls, too. Overhead was more timbers like the ones inside the barn. The space wasn't exactly a basement; it was only seven or eight feet wide but continued on for a distance she couldn't estimate since pitch-black lay beyond the beam of the flashlight.

"This way." He gestured with the light for her to move on into the tunnel.

She got to her feet and moved in the direction he had indicated. The corridor-like tunnel went on for a dozen or so yards, then it opened into a larger room.

Rowan's breath fled her lungs as her gaze moved over the walls, following the beam of light as if she had no choice in the matter. She had to look.

"Oh my God." The words seeped out of her.

She could have been standing in the catacombs beneath Paris. Skulls and bones lined the walls, reaching the ceiling.

"This," Julian said, "is your birthright. Death is who you are, Rowan."

Billy pulled over on the main road, right behind the car that Dressler had parked there. The agent emerged from his car and Billy did the same. He had called Lincoln and given him the location. Backup was maybe thirty minutes out.

There was time for Billy to find Addington and do what he needed to do before backup arrived.

"They went to the barn and they haven't come out unless they have since I came out here to meet you."

Dressler looked like hell. His clothes were rumpled. Just jeans and a sweatshirt. Not the usual suit and perfectly polished shoes. This case had taken him down. Billy thought of all the homicides attributed to Addington and it was no wonder.

No one involved had escaped being touched by the evil that was Julian Addington.

"Lead the way," Billy offered.

Dressler headed up the long drive with no light. Billy had tucked his flashlight into his back pocket. He had his service weapon in his waistband at the small of his back and a backup piece Lincoln had given him in his jacket pocket.

"How much do you know about this place?" Dressler asked, keeping his voice low.

"More than I want to," Billy admitted. "Evidently the Mulligan family held killing celebrations."

"You know Rowan's mother was his sister."

"Yeah." That part sickened Billy just a little. But Norah couldn't help being born into the family. What set her apart was what she did as soon as she was old enough to comprehend what they were.

"I imagine Rowan is upset considering what she's learned?"

"Who wouldn't be?" Billy felt sick for her.

"How'd you manage to give Pryor the slip?"

Billy glanced at him, couldn't really make out his expression in the scant moonlight. "I started a fight with him. Got kicked out of the crime scene."

"I wish you'd kicked his ass."

"Trust me," Billy said, "I wanted to."

They fell silent as they approached the house. Billy drew his weapon, his instincts going on point. Dressler drew his weapon as well. Slowly, soundlessly, they moved into the house, and then from room to room. The place was empty.

"They're still in the barn," Dressler said.

"The barn is ready to fall in on itself," Billy pointed out. "Seems unlikely they would hang around out there for long."

Something wasn't right. Billy's instincts were screaming at him.

"We should go on out there and check it out," Billy suggested when Dressler seemed to stay lost in his own thoughts.

Still the man said nothing, so Billy turned away and started for the back door.

"I wouldn't do that if I were you, Chief."

Billy turned around to face the man. Dressler had a bead on him, center chest.

"What's going on, Dressler?" Not that the question was actually necessary.

"He made me an offer I couldn't refuse," Dressler said with a shrug. "I keep the Bureau off his trail and he would give me what I needed to close the tough cases." Dressler laughed. "He made me a legend. I owe him everything. Rowan is his coup de grâce. Everything about this moment has to be perfect."

"Is Pryor in on this, too?" Billy decided to keep him talking as long as possible.

Dressler laughed. "That tight ass? You must be joking. He was just a way to throw you and Rowan off my scent. She trusts me, you know. I think she had a thing for me there for a while."

Billy nodded. "Yeah, I know. She mentioned that she had hoped the two of you would get together one day." The lie tasted as bitter as the red sumac berries he'd eaten as a kid. "Too bad you screwed that up, Dressler."

The agent laughed so hard he lost his breath. "Now that's rich, Brannigan." He waved his weapon cavalierly. "You, of all people should—"

Billy snaked out his right hand and grabbed the other man's weapon by the barrel, turning it away from him. Dressler tried to get an aim back on him, but Billy twisted hard and yanked the weapon free of his grasp.

Dressler went for his throat with both hands.

They hit the floor. The wind whooshed out of Billy's lungs.

Billy gored the muzzle of his service revolver into the guy's skull. "Get off me," he growled, his voice squeaking out despite the pressure on his throat.

Dressler stilled. He stared Billy in the eyes. "I can't let you screw this up."

His fingers locked hard around Billy's throat once more.

Billy pulled the trigger.

The bullet plowed through Dressler's skull, sending blood spraying across Billy's face. He shoved the bastard off him and scrambled up, wiping his face with his forearm.

If Addington was anywhere near the house or barn,

he was bound to have heard the shot. Billy clicked off the living room light, pitching the house back into total darkness. He moved back to the front door and slipped out. Stepping carefully to cut down on the noise, he moved around the end of the house and started for the barn he and Rowan had seen when they were here before.

He found his way to the barn without breaking his neck. His heart was thundering. That he hadn't heard a sound, or encountered anyone, worried him. Where was Rowan? Where the hell was Addington?

Inside the barn was dark as hell. He squinted, peering into the darkness. On the far side was a glimmer of light. His weapon leading the way, he eased in that direction, careful to check the path with one boot before moving.

The light was coming from a hole in the floor. No, he decided, not a hole.

An access door that led down to a basement or cellar. He peeked down into the hole. There was a ladder and at the bottom a flashlight lay on the ground. The flashlight was in the on position as if someone had accidentally dropped it there.

He readied to start down the ladder.

"No! Billy!"

*Rowan.*

He whirled around. Addington rushed at him, a knife raised high above his head.

Billy pulled the trigger.

The knife sliced across his arm.

His weapon hit the ground.

Billy grabbed for Addington with his left arm, pulled him into a bear hug and twisted.

Addington growled like an animal and raised the knife again. Billy shoved him away.

The knife swished through the air, glancing off Billy's shoulder.

He winced at the burn of the blade slicing through his jacket and the skin beneath.

Addington screamed and scrambled for purchase.

His body had slipped into the hole in the floor. Billy moved closer. The bastard's fingers were bracketed on the edge of the opening, his legs dangling beneath him searching for the ladder. The flashlight backlit his struggle. His eyes were wide with terror.

In the background Rowan was asking if he was okay.

Billy got down on his hands and knees and put his face close to the bastard's. "Backup will be here any minute. Your source in the FBI is dead. It's over, Addington. You're going away for the rest of your life."

More than anything else in this world he wanted this bastard to die. He wanted to be the one to end his life. But he had sworn long ago to uphold the law and that duty included him, not just the people under his watch.

Billy extended his hand. "Take my hand and I'll pull you up."

Addington stopped wiggling his legs to find the ladder. He stilled completely. A smile stretched across his face.

"Son of a bitch." Billy grabbed for the man's arm.

He let go of the ledge, almost pulling Billy down with him before he slipped out of his grasp.

Addington hit the floor some ten feet below.

Billy watched a moment to make sure he didn't move. Then he felt around for his weapon and scooted away from the hole. He stood and hurried to find Rowan, following the sound of her voice in the darkness. She was shackled inside one of the stalls.

"You okay?" He shoved his weapon into his waistband and cupped her face, felt her damp cheeks.

"I'm okay."

"You're not injured?"

She shook her head. He felt the movement and relief roared through him.

"Do you know where the key is?"

"He has it." She shuddered. "Oh my God, you're bleeding." Her hand had found the place on his forearm that Addington had sliced into.

"Don't worry. Help will be here any second. I need to go down into that hole and make sure Addington is dead and get the key."

"Please be careful."

Billy kissed her and hurried back to what he now understood was a trapdoor, not a hole. He peered down to the place where Addington had landed.

He was gone.

Fury coursing through his veins, Billy climbed onto the ladder and hurried down into the cellar or basement or whatever the hell it was.

He grabbed the flashlight and looked around. No sign of Addington in the small room, he pointed the flashlight into the tunnel that split off from the small room. Nothing there either. His weapon readied to fire, he moved down the narrow corridor. The corridor ended in a larger room. Addington lay on the floor in the middle of the room. He'd dragged himself that far but didn't appear able to move any farther.

The sound of voices echoed overhead. Billy recognized Lincoln's.

Help was here.

His attention moved back to Addington. The bastard was still alive.

Billy stepped forward and the beam of light landed on a skull.

He stalled. "What the hell?"

He roved the beam over the walls, turning all the way around.

Bones and skulls lined the walls.

Addington grunted something like a laugh.

Billy snapped his attention back to the bastard on the floor. He walked to where he lay and crouched down.

"You see now what you're getting into, Chief Brannigan?" Addington coughed, the sound gurgling.

Billy had heard that sound before. He'd helped rescue a couple of cavers. One had serious internal injuries with bleeding. He'd suffered that same gurgling cough.

"Julian Addington, you're under arrest," he said, wanting the bastard to know he had lost before he took his last breath. He listed off a litany of charges.

The old man tried to speak again, the sound more of that nasty gurgling. Then he stopped trying to speak or move.

"Brannigan!"

*Lincoln.* "Down here," Billy called back. He checked for a pulse. Nothing.

The bastard was dead.

Footsteps echoed in the tunnel. Lincoln burst in followed by Pryor.

"Is he dead?" Lincoln asked.

Billy stood. "He's dead."

"What happened with Dressler?" Pryor demanded.

Billy checked Addington's pocket, found the key

he needed. "He was the leak. He'd been working with Addington his whole career. He said the bastard made him a legend."

Pryor tossed out another question, but Billy was through talking for now.

He pushed to his feet and walked past the man.

Pryor shouted after him, but Billy ignored him.

Four of Billy's officers were moving through the barn. A paramedic and Officer Pace were with Rowan. Billy moved between them and freed her from the shackles.

She hugged him hard and he did the same. The tears burning his eyes could not be fully contained and he didn't give a damn.

Rowan drew back. "Is it over?"

He nodded. "It's over."

The paramedic was urging Billy to let him have a look at his injuries, but Billy wasn't listening. All he could do was hold Rowan against him.

It was finally, really over.

# *Epilogue*

*Six months later...*

Rowan held the paint chips against the wall. She couldn't decide between the rosemary mint green and the pastel sweet pink.

She smoothed a hand over her protruding belly. "How could there be this many decisions to make for one tiny baby?"

For the first time since she was a child Rowan was completely happy. Julian Addington was gone forever by his own hand. He had made the decision to ignore Billy's offer of help and to let go of that ledge. Two weeks after that awful night she had realized she hadn't had a period in a while. She'd taken a pregnancy test and it was positive.

Two months later she and Billy were married. They made the decision that she would move into his home. She liked that it was out of town and had lots of acres of peace and quiet around them. Charlotte was now running the day-to-day operations of the funeral home. Two new assistants had been hired. DuPonts had operated the funeral home for a century and a half but Rowan didn't want this baby growing up as the undertaker's daughter.

This little girl was not going to grow up surrounded by death.

Rowan surveyed the progress on the nursery. The furniture was here. The bedding…everything had been decided except the wall paint color.

She had narrowed it down to two colors. Billy would just have to make the final decision. Leaving the paint chips on the white dresser, she headed outside to find her husband. She paused in the kitchen and watched Billy from the window over the sink. He told her every day how happy he was. How grateful he was that she was his wife and that they were having a baby. He also loved that the baby was a girl. His parents were over the moon.

The investigation into Julian Addington was now closed. The FBI had discovered undeniable evidence that Josh Dressler had worked with Julian since his career began. The brown wig had been found in the car Josh had been driving that night. He had helped Julian murder his ex-wife and her friends. There was no way to know how many other murders he had been involved with. In Josh's home they had discovered evidence that suggested he was Addington's biological son. Since Josh's parents were dead, there was no way to know how that came about, but DNA confirmed it was true.

Rowan never wanted to think of the case again. Last month she'd had a bit of a scare. She'd been in Tullahoma shopping and she'd run into Robert Johns, the last of her mother's protectors.

They hadn't spoken. The length of a storefront window had stood between them. For a long moment they simply stood there and stared at each other. Finally, he smiled, gave her a nod and walked away.

Rowan wasn't looking back anymore except to admire photos of her parents and to cherish the good memories.

She was looking only to the future and it looked amazing so far.

\* \* \* \* \*

*Look for the next book in Debra Webb's*
*Winchester, Tennessee Thrillers series coming*
*in December wherever Harlequin Intrigue*
*books are sold!*

*Halle Lane's best friend disappeared twenty-five years ago, but when Liam Hart arrives in Winchester, Halle's certain he's the boy she once knew. As the pair investigates Liam's mysterious past, can they uncover the truth before a killer buries all evidence of the boy Halle once loved?*

*Read on for a preview of*
Before He Vanished
*by* USA TODAY *bestselling author*
*Debra Webb.*

# *One*

*Friday, March 6*
*Winchester, Tennessee*

Halle Lane listened as her fellow newspaper reporter droned on and on about the upcoming community events in Winchester that he planned to cover, which was basically everything on the calendar for the next month.

She couldn't really complain. Halle was new. Hardly ninety days on the job, but she knew Winchester every bit as well as Mr. Roger Hawkins. She couldn't bring herself to call him Rog. The man was seventy if he was a day and he'd covered the social events of Winchester for about fifty of those years.

How could she—a fading-star investigative journalist from Nashville—expect to get first dibs on anything in Winchester? Hawkins had the social events, including obituaries. Her boss and the owner of the newspaper, Audrey Anderson-Tanner, generally took care of the big stories. The only potential for a break in the monotony of covering barroom brawls and petty break-ins was the fact that Audrey was pregnant. At nearly thirty-eight, she was expecting her first child.

Halle had wanted to jump for joy when she heard the news last month. She was, of course, very happy for Audrey and her husband, Sheriff Colt Tanner, but mostly she was thrilled at the idea that she might actually get her hands on a real story sometime this decade.

So far that had not happened. Audrey had covered the big federal trial of Harrison Armone last month. His son's widow, the sole witness against him, had been hiding out in Winchester for months. Surprisingly for such a small town, Winchester had more than its share of big news happenings. This time last year a body had been discovered in the basement of this very newspaper building. Halle's gaze shifted to the head of the conference table, where her boss listened with seemingly rapt interest as Hawkins went on and on.

It seemed Winchester also had more than its share of family secrets. A man posing as a Mennonite had turned out to be a former member of a Chicago mob. Not a month later, Sasha Lenoir-Holloway had uncovered the truth about the deaths of her parents. Cece Winters had come home from prison a few months back and blown open the truth about her family and the cult-like extremists living in a remote area of Franklin County.

Nashville had nothing on Winchester, it seemed.

"This all sounds good, Rog," Audrey said, her voice pulling Halle back to the here and now.

The boss's gaze shifted to her and Halle realized her mistake. She had been silently bemoaning all the stories she'd missed and now it was her turn to share with those gathered what she was working on for this week's Sunday edition.

"Halle, what do you have planned?" Audrey asked.

For five endless seconds she racked her brain for something, anything to say.

Then her gaze landed on the date written in black across the whiteboard.

March 6.

Memories whispered through her mind. Voices and images from her childhood flooded her senses. Blond hair, blue eyes…

"The lost boy," Halle said in a rush. The words had her heart pounding.

Of course. Why hadn't she thought of that last month or the month before?

Audrey frowned for a moment, then made an "aha" face. "Excellent idea. We've just passed what? Twenty-four years?"

"Twenty-five," Halle confirmed. "Andy Clark was my neighbor. We played together all the time as kids."

Brian Peterson, the editor of the *Winchester Gazette*, chimed in next. "What makes you think Nancy Clark will allow an interview? She hasn't in all these years."

Audrey made a frustrated face. "That is true. You tried to interview her for both the ten-year and the twenty-year anniversaries, didn't you?"

Brian nodded. "I did. She refused to talk about it. Since her husband passed away year before last, she's practically a shut-in. She stopped attending church. Has whatever she needs delivered." He shrugged, shifted his attention to Halle. "Good luck with that one."

Halle's anticipation deflated. Hawkins looked at her as if she were something to be pitied.

"Still," Audrey said, "if you could get the story, it would be huge. Maybe since you and the boy, Andy, played together as children before he vanished, she might just talk to you."

Halle's hopes lifted once more. "I'm certain she will."

The conference room started to buzz with excitement. Titles were tossed about. Potential placement on the front page above the fold.

All Halle had to do was make it happen.

Halle cruised along the street on the east side of the courthouse, braking at a crosswalk for a mother pushing a stroller. That little ache that pricked each time she saw a baby did so now. Passing thirty had flipped some switch that had her yearning for a child of her own.

Now that she was back home, her chances of finding a partner, much less having a child, had dropped to something less than zero.

Winchester was a very small town compared to Nashville. With a population of around ten thousand, if you counted Decherd in the mix, it truly was the sort of place where everyone knew everyone else.

There were times when this could be a very good thing. Like when Andy Clark went missing twenty-five years ago. Halle had been just a little kid, but she remembered well how citizens from all over this county as well as those surrounding it had rushed to help look for Andy. Headlines about "the lost boy" scrolled across every newspaper in the state. His face was all over the news. Detectives and FBI agents were in and out of the Clark home for months.

But Andy had vanished without a trace.

Halle turned onto South High Street. The Clark home was on the corner of South High and Sixth Avenue. The historic Victorian was among the town's oldest homes. A meticulously manicured lawn and sprawling front porch greeted visitors. She pulled to the curb in front of the house and shut off the engine. The ancient maple on the Sixth Avenue side of the lawn had been Andy's and her favorite climbing tree.

Next door was Halle's childhood home. Her parents, Judith and Howard, had been thrilled when she'd announced last Christmas that she would be moving back to Winchester. They had, of course, insisted that she move back into her old room. As much as she appreciated the offer and adored her parents, that was not happening. Eventually the two had talked her into taking the apartment over the detached garage where her aunt Daisy, the old maid everyone always whispered about, had once lived, God rest her soul.

Considering she would have her own parking spot and a separate entrance, Halle decided it wasn't such a bad idea. She would have her privacy and her parents would have their only daughter—only child, actually—living at home again.

A win-win for all involved. As long as she didn't dwell on the fact that she had turned thirty-two at the end of last month and that her one and only marriage had ended in divorce two years ago or that her ex-husband had since remarried and had a child—no matter that he had said they were too young for children when she had wanted one.

Not.

Maybe the garage apartment was fitting considering her mother's peers all now whispered about her unmarried status. *Bless her heart, she's like poor Daisy.*

Halle heaved a weary sigh.

The divorce had turned her world upside down, shaken her as nothing ever had. She'd lost her footing, and the upheaval had shown in her work. Just as she'd begun to pull her professional self together again, she'd been let go. Cutbacks, they had said. But she'd known the truth. Her work had sucked for two years.

It was a flat-out miracle they had allowed her to keep working as long as they had.

Luckily for Halle, Audrey was open to second chances. She had understood how one's life could go completely awry. Though the *Winchester Gazette* was only a small biweekly newspaper, it was a reasonable starting place to rebuild Halle's career.

She climbed out of the car, draped her leather bag over her shoulder and closed the door. The midmorning air was crisp but Halle much preferred it to what would come between June and September. The melting heat and suffocating humidity. The not-so-pleasant part of Southern living.

Stepping up onto the porch, she heard the swing chains squeak as the breeze nudged this wooden mainstay of every Southern porch gently back and forth. On the other end of the sprawling outdoor space stood a metal glider, still sporting its original green paint, offering a restful place to sit and watch the street. But Mrs. Clark never sat on her porch anymore. Halle's mother had said the lady rarely stepped out the door, just as Brian had also mentioned. But Mrs. Clark did come to the door as long as she could identify the person knocking or ringing her bell. Whether she opened the door was another story.

Halle hadn't attempted to visit her in years. She was relatively certain she hadn't seen the woman since her husband's funeral two years ago. The one thing Halle never had to worry about was being recognized. With her fiery mass of unruly red curls, the impossible-to-camouflage freckles and the mossy-green eyes, folks rarely forgot her face. The other kids in school had been ruthless with the ginger and carrottop jokes but Andy had always defended her...at least until he was gone.

God, she had missed her best friend. Even at seven, losing your best friend was incredibly traumatic.

Halle stepped to the door and lifted her fist and knocked.

"What do you want?"

The voice behind the closed door was a little rusty, as if it wasn't used often, but it was reasonably strong.

"Mrs. Clark, you might not remember me—"

"Of course I remember you. What do you want?"

It was a starting place.

"Ma'am, may I come inside and speak with you?" She bit her bottom lip and searched for a good reason. "It's a little chilly here on the porch." Not exactly true, but not entirely a lie.

A latch clicked. Anticipation caught her breath. Another click and the knob turned. The door drew inward a couple of feet. Nancy Clark stood in the shadows beyond the reach of daylight. Her hair looked as unruly as Halle's and it was as white as cotton. She was shorter than Halle remembered.

"Come in."

The door drew inward a little more and Halle crossed the threshold. Her heart was really pumping now. She reminded herself that just because she was inside didn't mean she would manage an interview.

*One step at a time, Hal.*

The elderly lady closed the door and locked it. So maybe she anticipated Halle staying awhile. Another good sign.

"I was having tea in the kitchen," that rusty voice said.

When she turned and headed deeper into the gloom of the house, Halle followed. She knew this house as well as she knew her own. Until she was seven years old it had been her second home. More of those childhood memories whispered through her, even ones her mother had told her about before Halle was old enough to retain the images herself.

Her mother had laughed and recounted to her the many times she'd had tea with Nancy while the babies toddled around the kitchen floor. The Clarks had not always lived in Winchester, Halle's mother had told her. They had bought the house when their little boy was two years old just before Easter. Judith Lane had been thrilled to have a neighbor with a child around the same age as her own. Halle had been twenty months old. Even the fathers, Howard and Andrew, had become fast friends.

It was perfect for five years.

Then Andy disappeared.

The shriek of the kettle yanked Halle's attention back to the present.

"You want cream?"

"That would be nice." She forced a smile into place

as she stood in the kitchen watching Mrs. Clark fix the tea.

Nancy prepared their tea in classic bone china patterned with clusters of pink flowers ringing the cups. She placed the cups in their saucers and then onto a tray. She added the matching cream pitcher and sugar bowl.

Halle held her breath as the elderly woman with her tiny birdlike arms carried the tray to the dining table. To be back in this home, after so many years, to be talking with this woman who'd occupied a special place in her heart because of her relationship to Andy was enough to make Halle feel light-headed.

"Get the cookies," Nancy called over her shoulder.

Halle turned back to the counter and picked up the small plate, then followed the same path the lady had taken. They sat, added sugar to their tea and then tested the taste and heat level. Mrs. Clark offered the plate of cookies and Halle took a small one and nibbled.

Rather than rush the conversation, she reacquainted herself with the paintings and photographs on the wall. Beyond the wide doorway, she could see the stunning painting over the fireplace in the main parlor. Andy had been five at the time. His hair had been so blond, his eyes so blue. Such a sweet and handsome boy. She hadn't a clue about what handsome even was or any of that stuff back then; she had only known that she loved him like another part of her family...of herself. They had been inseparable.

"Twenty-five years."

Halle's attention swung to the woman who sat at the other end of the table. She looked so frail, so small. The many wrinkles on her face spoke of more than age. They spoke of immense pain, harrowing devastation.

Worrying for twenty-five long years if her child was alive. If he had been tortured and murdered.

If she would ever see him again.

"Yes, ma'am," Halle agreed.

Nancy Clark set her teacup down and placed her hands palms flat on the table. "You want to write an article about him, don't you?"

Halle dared to nod, her heart pounding. This was the moment of truth. Would she be able to persuade Mrs. Clark to open up to her, to give her the answers she needed as much for the story as for her own peace of mind? "It would mean a great deal to me."

"If you've done your homework, you're aware I've never given an interview. Nor did my Andrew."

"I am and I understand why."

Her head angled ever so slightly as she stared down the table at Halle. "Really? What is it you think you understand?"

Halle nodded. "How can you adequately articulate that kind of loss? That sort of pain? You loved him more than anything in this world and someone took him from you. How could you possibly find the right words?"

Mrs. Clark's gaze fell first, then her head bowed.

Halle held her breath. Whether the lady believed her or agreed with her, Halle did understand. She had loved Andy, too, and she had missed him so very badly.

Deep down she still did. A part of her was missing. There was a hole that no one else could possibly fill. The bond between them had been strong.

When Mrs. Clark lifted her head once more, she stared directly at Halle for so long she feared she had said the wrong thing. She was making a decision, Halle knew, but what would it be?

"Very well," she said slowly but firmly. "I will tell you the story and *you* can find the right words. It's time."

Halle's lips spread into a smile and she nodded. "I would love to."

Silence filled the room for a long minute.

"I was almost forty before the good Lord blessed me with a child."

Halle reached into her bag for her notepad and a pen. "Do you mind if I take notes?"

A glint of bravado flashed in Nancy's gray eyes. "I'd mind if you didn't."

A nervous laugh bubbled up in Halle's throat, and she relaxed. She placed her notepad on the table and flipped to a clean page, then readied her pen.

"Andrew and I were so happy when Andy came into our lives," Nancy said, her voice soft, her gaze lost to some faraway time and place. "We wanted to raise our boy somewhere safe, with good schools. We did a great deal of research before selecting Winchester." She sighed. "It was perfect when we found this house right next door to a couple who had a child almost the same age." She stared at Halle for a moment. "Andy adored you."

"I adored him."

Distance filled her gaze once more. "We were happier than we'd ever believed it was possible to be."

"What do you remember about that day, Mrs. Clark?"

It wasn't necessary for Halle to be more specific. The other woman understood what she meant.

"March 1. Wednesday. I walked to school with you and Andy that day. It was chilly, like today." Her lips— lips that hung in a perpetual frown—lifted slightly with a faint smile. "He was wearing that worn-out orange hoodie. He loved that thing but it was so old and shabby. I feared the other children would make fun of him."

"I remember that hoodie. I begged my mother to get me one just like it but, you know my parents, they're hard-core Alabama football fans. No orange allowed. And don't worry, no one ever made fun of Andy. All the other kids liked him."

Mrs. Clark dabbed at her eyes with her napkin. "Thank you for saying so."

"My dad picked me up early that afternoon," Halle said. "He'd had to take Mother to the hospital."

Nancy nodded. "I remember."

What Halle's mother had thought was a lingering cold turned out to be pneumonia. She'd almost waited too long before admitting that she needed to see a doctor. They'd hospitalized her immediately. Halle had stayed with her aunt Daisy for a solid week in that garage apartment where she lived now.

But that day, March 1 twenty-five years ago, the police had arrived before supper. Within twenty-four hours reporters from all over the state were camped out on the street.

Andy Clark had vanished.

"I was late," Nancy confessed, pain twisting her face. "Andrew was at work in Tullahoma and I had a flat tire. With your parents at the hospital, there was nothing to do but call someone to repair my tire. By the time I was backing out of the driveway, school had been out for only fifteen minutes but that was fifteen minutes too long."

"According to the police report," Halle said, "witnesses stated that Andy waited about ten minutes and then started to walk home."

She nodded. "There were witnesses who saw him less than a block from home."

Whoever took him had snatched him only a few hundred yards from his own front door.

"There was never a ransom demand," Halle said. "No contact at all from the kidnapper."

"Nothing." A heavy breath shook the woman's frail shoulders. "It was as if he disappeared into thin air."

"You and your husband hired private investigators." Halle's parents had said as much.

"The police and our community searched for weeks. But there was nothing. Not the hoodie. Not his backpack. Nothing. No other witnesses ever came forward."

These were all details Halle already knew. But perhaps there would be others she didn't. Something that no one knew. There was one thing she would very much like to know. She hoped the question wouldn't put Mrs. Clark off.

"I would like to ask you one question before we go any further."

The lady held her gaze, a surprising courage in her expression. "I'm listening."

"What made you decide to grant an interview now? To me?"

The courage vanished and that dark hollowness was back.

Halle immediately regretted having asked the question. When she was about to open her mouth to apologize, Mrs. Clark spoke.

"I'm dying. I have perhaps two or three months. It's time the world knew the whole story. If anyone tells it, it should be you."

A chill rushed over Halle's skin. "I will do all within my power to tell the story the way you want it told."

"I'm counting on you, Halle. I want the *whole* story told the right way."

Halle nodded slowly, though she wasn't entirely clear what the older woman meant by the *whole* story. But she fully intended to find out.

Whatever had happened to Andy, the world needed to know.

Halle needed to know.

### THEN

*Wednesday, March 1*
*Twenty-five years ago...*

Halle hated her pink jacket.

Pink was for scaredy-cat girls. She was a girl but she was no scaredy-cat.

She was a brave, strong kid like Andy.

She wanted an orange hoodie like the one he wore.

"Wear this jacket today," her mom said with a big sigh, "and I will get you an orange one."

Halle made a face. She might only be seven but she wasn't sure if her mommy was telling her the truth or if she was just too tired to argue.

"Promise?"

Judith smiled and offered her little finger. "Pinkie promise."

Halle curled her pinkie around her mommy's. "Okay."

"Come along," Mommy urged. "Andy and his mom are waiting."

At the door her mommy gave her a kiss and waved as Halle skipped out to the sidewalk where Andy and his mom stood.

He had on that orange hoodie and Halle hoped her mommy was really going to get her one.

"Hey," Halle said.

Andy tipped his head back the tiniest bit. "Hey."

He had the bluest eyes of any kid in school. Halle wondered how it was possible to have eyes that blue. Bluer than the sky even.

"How are you this morning, Halle?" Mrs. Clark asked.

"I'm good but my mommy's still a little sick." Halle didn't like when her mommy or daddy was sick. It made her tummy ache.

"I'm sure she'll be better soon," Mrs. Clark assured her. "That pink jacket looks awfully pretty with your red hair."

Halle grimaced. "Thank you but I don't like it very much." She gazed longingly at Andy's orange hoodie.

He took her hand. "Come on. We're gonna be late."

Halle smiled. He was the best friend ever. They were going to be friends forever and ever.

They walked along, swinging their clasped hands and singing that silly song they'd made up during winter break.

*We're gonna sail on a ship...*

*We're gonna fly on a plane...*
*We're gonna take that train...*
*We're taking a trip...*
But Andy wasn't supposed to go without her.

*Don't miss* Before He Vanished
*by Debra Webb, available now wherever*
*Harlequin® books and ebooks are sold.*
*www.Harlequin.com*

She wiped up stray crumbs, then tried to smile at him. "Coffee?"

"I've intruded too much."

She put a hand on her hip. "I might have thought so earlier, but I'm not feeling that way now. This is important. I give a damn about Larry, and now I give a damn about you. You might not want it, but I care. So quiet down. Coffee? Or something else?"

"A beer if you have another."

As it happened, she did. "I buy this so rarely that you're in luck."

"Then why did you buy it?"

"Larry," she answered simply.

For the first time, they shared a look of real understanding. The sense of connection warmed her.

She hadn't expected to feel this way, not when it came to Duke. Maybe it helped to realize he wasn't just a monolith of anger and unswaying determination.

As Cat returned to her seat, she said, "You put me off initially."

Another half smile from him. "I never would have guessed."

A laugh escaped her, brief but genuine. "I'm usually better at concealing my reactions to people. But there you were, looking like a battering ram. You sure looked hard and angry. Nothing about you made me want to get into a tussle."

He looked at the beer bottle he held. "Most people don't want to tangle with me. I can understand your reaction. I came through that door loaded for bear. Too much time to think on the way here, maybe."

"You looked like walking death," she told him frankly. "An icy-cold fury. Worse, in my opinion, than a heated rage. Scary."

"Comes with the territory," he said after a moment, then took a swig of his beer.

She could probably wonder until the cows came home exactly what he meant by that. Maybe it was better not to know.

*Don't miss*
Conard County Justice *by Rachel Lee,*
*available May 2020 wherever*
*Harlequin Intrigue books and ebooks are sold.*

Harlequin.com

HIEXP0420